SIMON & SCHUSTER
presents

The Search For WondLa

by

TONY DITERLIZZI

with illustrations
by the author

SIMON & SCHUSTER
BOOKS FOR YOUNG READERS
NEW YORK LONDON TORONTO SYDNEY

SIMON & SCHUSTER BOOKS FOR YOUNG READERS
An imprint of Simon & Schuster Children's Publishing Division
1230 Avenue of the Americas, New York, New York 10020

SIMON & SCHUSTER BOOKS FOR YOUNG READERS is a
trademark of Simon & Schuster, Inc.
For information about special discounts for bulk purchases,
please contact Simon & Schuster Special Sales at 1-866-506-1949
or business@simonandschuster.com.
The Simon & Schuster Speakers Bureau can bring authors
to your live event. For more information or to book an event,
contact the Simon & Schuster Speakers Bureau at 1-866-248-3049
or visit our website at www.simonspeakers.com.
Book design by Tony DiTerlizzi and Lizzy Bromley
Logo design by Thomas Kennedy
The text for this book is set in Adobe Garamond and Lomba.
The illustrations for this book were rendered with Staedtler Pigment Liner
pens on vellum paper and were colored digitally.
Manufactured in the United States of America
0810 QUT
2 4 6 8 10 9 7 5 3 1
Library of Congress Cataloging-in-Publication Data
DiTerlizzi, Tony.
The search for WondLa / Tony DiTerlizzi. — 1st ed.
p. cm.
Summary: Living in isolation with a robot on what appears to be an alien world
populated with bizarre life forms, a twelve-year-old human girl called Eva Nine sets
out on a journey to find others like her. Features "augmented reality" pages, in which
readers with a webcam can access additional information about Eva Nine's world.
ISBN 978-1-4169-8310-1 (hardcover)
[1. Science fiction. 2. Human-alien encounters—Fiction. 3. Identity—Fiction.] I. Title.
PZ7.D629Sd 2010
[Fic]—dc22
2010001326
ISBN 978-1-4424-1303-0 (eBook)

FIRST
EDITION

Within

the pages of this book you will find a hidden feature: a
three-dimensional interactive map allowing you to follow
the sights and sounds of Eva Nine's journey, brought to life
through the wonders of *Wondla-Vision* (also known
as Augmented Reality).

The illustrations on pages 123, 277, and 433 are the keys
to unlock this hidden feature. Just visit WondLa.com for
directions. You'll need a computer with Internet access
and a webcam to get started.

If you do not have access to a webcam, you
can see noninteractive maps and a video at

WondLa.com

Contents

PART I

PART II

PART III

PART IV

*If you want your children
to be intelligent,*
READ THEM FAIRY TALES.
*If you want them to be
more intelligent,*
READ THEM MORE FAIRY TALES.

—Albert Einstein

PART I

CHAPTER 1: ALONE

Eva Nine

was dying. The tiny scarlet dots on her hand mirrored the glowering eyes of the snake that had just bitten her.

Sitting down on the prickly ground of dead brown pine needles and small cones, she felt the curdled coil of nausea wind its way up her throat from her stomach.

She dropped the sweaty handful of moss that she had scooped up from the forest floor.

"Kindling," her Omnipod had instructed her earlier in its chirpy voice. "Find a flammable substance such as dry twigs or moss to begin your fire." The large gathering of boulders Eva had found had seemed like the perfect place to make a shelter for the night, and the surrounding area was blanketed in ashen puff-patches of reindeer moss. As she had knelt down to gather a clump, Eva had realized there was a rust-colored, mottled snake just next to her, sunning itself in the fading light. She'd realized too late, though, to avoid its bite.

Now, with trembling hands, she fumbled through her dingy satchel to retrieve her Omnipod. The handheld metallic device was flat, like a magnifying glass, with a small circular hole in the middle of it that resembled an eye. Eva's heart pounded, as if trying to escape her chest. She swallowed, interrupting the hectic meter of her breathing. The shoulder patch on her tunic blinked off and on in warning.

"This is Eva Nine," she whispered into the Omnipod. "Initiate I-M . . . um, I-M . . ."

Eva closed her eyes and concentrated. She put the device to her forehead, as if the Omnipod would whisper to her brain the command she needed.

"Greetings, Eva Nine. How can I be of service?" the device chirped.

"I . . . um . . ." Her hands shook. "I need you to initiate Independent Medical—"

"Do you mean Individual Medical Assistance? IMA for short?" the Omnipod corrected her.

"Yes," she answered, licking her dry lips and trying to hold her insides in.

"Is this an emergency?"

"Yes! I need help right away!" Eva yelled at the Omnipod.

"What is the nature of your emergency?"

"S-snake bite," Eva said with a gulp. The nausea lurked just under her tongue, ready to leap out.

"Hold, please. Initiating Identicapture." Eva watched as three tiny lights on the Omnipod flickered in a rhythm around its central eye. "Begin Identicapture of said snake. We need to determine if it is a poisonous species or not."

Through glassy eyes Eva scanned her immediate area; she could no longer focus on the terrain around her, let alone find a snake disguised as the forest floor. Her eyes rolled up into her head. Her breathing slowed. She let the Omnipod slip from her fingers.

Eva fell back, like a slain giant collapsing in a

miniature forest of moss. She looked up at the fading light of the cobalt blue sky. Her Omnipod lay alongside her as it repeated, "Please begin Identicapture."

All Eva could whisper was, "Dead. I'm totally dead."

A voice from the heavens echoed through the landscape. It was a kind and graceful voice, like the sort she'd heard coming from a beautiful woman in an old movie.

"Eva. Eva, dear, please get up," the voice said. Just like in an old moving picture, Eva could also hear the slightest bit of static hidden in the dulcet intonation.

The pine trees seemed to whisper the girl's name as the cool of evening blew in. Somewhere in the distance a whip-poor-will beckoned the night. Eva cracked open her pale green eyes into little slits.

"Eva Nine," urged the voice, "get up."

The girl rolled onto her side. Lying on the forest floor, she examined the tuft of moss in her hand. She saw that the delicate network of stalks really did make it look like a shrunken tree, albeit a washed-out lifeless one. *How does such an insignificant plant survive in a big world?* she wondered. *What is its purpose? What is my purpose?*

"Eva, please—"

"I'm dead," Eva announced to the sky. "Or couldn't you tell? I'm gone. Deceased. No more. Deeeaaaaad!"

She turned her attention back to the little moss tree and pouted. "It's not like you have to worry about that," she muttered.

The clump of moss in her hands vanished, dissipating into a cloud of light motes. Eva curled up into a ball, shutting her eyes as the world around her also evaporated into nothingness. Emptiness.

The voice was right next to her now. "Eva, what happened?"

"Leave me alone," the ball replied.

"You were not paying attention," the voice said with a sigh. "You had a ninety-eight percent chance of discovering the snake, had you done a simple LifeScan sweep. It was right there in plain view."

Still curled in a ball, Eva said nothing.

"Of course, I have to mark you as a failure on this particular survival skill test. We shall try it again tomorrow. All right?" said the voice.

A warm hand brushed Eva's half-braided dirty-blond hair. At last Eva stood up.

Two dark orbs, emitting an amber glow from deep within, reflected Eva's own face in a distorted fashion, like a fish in a fishbowl. Large automated eyelids clicked open and closed in a lifelike manner. Several other eyes, small and unblinking, studied the girl, recording endless data and sending it to a computerized brain. A brain that was contained in two metallic canisters mounted on the back of a head—the front of which displayed a mechanized silicone-rubber face.

"What is going on with you, Eva?" the automated lips mimed. "This test should have been effortless for you to pass. Is everything all right?"

One of the robot's telescoping arms extended from a carousel of several additional arms folded up around the cylindrical torso. Four wiry fingers, also tipped in silicone rubber, rubbed Eva's shoulders in a reassuring fashion.

"How is your concentration?" the robot asked. "I noted that you did not rest a full ten hours last night, which indicates that you may not have achieved enough REM sleep. That can have quite an effect on your performance."

"Not now, Muthr." Eva shrugged the robot off. "I need to be alone."

She crossed the wide squarish white room and headed for the low doorway. Buff-colored rubbery floor tiles absorbed the sound of her plodding footsteps. Though the chamber was only dimly lit, there was still enough light coming from the holo-projectors mounted around the ceiling to show that the room itself was empty of anything . . . except for the human girl and the pale blue robot.

Eva sulked as she shuffled into the main hub of her living quarters. When the large doors to the holography chamber slid shut behind her, a pastoral scene was projected onto them in vivid detail. Cottony clouds drifted aimlessly across a brilliant azure sky over distant lavender mountains. This gave the effect that the entire hub was like a grand outdoor gazebo, displaying a magnificent vista in the round—though one projection was not working properly and flickered into a corresponding nighttime scene, ruining the illusion.

"Welcome back, Eva Nine." The intercom spoke in a relaxed tone. Its words reverberated throughout the octagonal chamber. "How may I help you?" Water trickled in a distant stream, and songbirds sang, filling the vestibule with ambient sounds coinciding with the scenery.

"Hi. Please open bedroom doors, Sanctuary," Eva said, stomping across the hub toward the far window. Projected on it was a spectacular view of a misty waterfall cascading down from a colossal mountaintop. The cast image crackled when the girl passed through it, as through a holographic curtain, into the open doors of her dimly lit bedroom.

"Close doors, please." Eva flung her jackvest onto her medi-seat. She sat down on the edge of her foam bed and kicked off her sneakboots. As she flopped back onto the oval mattress, Eva stared up at the myriad of pipes and exhaust shafts that wound through her white ceiling. There were water stains on the corner ceiling tiles of the small room, like large ochre flowers blooming from the pipes. One of the overhead lights flickered in an annoying, erratic tempo.

With her hands behind her head, Eva rubbed the raised round mole on the nape of her neck. The warmth of her electric bed permeated through her tunic in a comfy sort of way. Her eyelids drooped, and she had begun to doze off when her bedroom doors slid back open.

"Eva, you forgot your equipment satchel and Omni-pod back in the holo-chamber," Muthr said, rolling into her room balanced on a single tread-worn wheel. "Honestly, dear, how can you expect to pass your training if you do not take care of your things?"

"Muthr!" Eva continued staring up at the stained ceiling, refusing to look Muthr in the eye. "Just leave it. I'll put it away later."

The robot picked Eva's dingy jackvest up from the chair. The discarded garment had been perfectly hidden among the stuffed toys, dirty clothes, and electra-papers that were strewn about the room. "Put it away as you have done with the rest of your belongings? I sometimes wonder—"

"Please, Muthr, I just want to be alone for a while," Eva barked at the ceiling.

Muthr hung the jackvest on the empty row of coat hooks lining the wall. "Dinner is at eighteen hundred hours. Please be timely, Eva," Muthr said. After Muthr rolled out of the room, the doors slid shut behind her. Eva reached under her head and grabbed her pillow. As she squeezed it over her face, she screamed.

I am making

spinach and strawberry salad," sang Muthr as Eva walked into the kitchen and flopped down at the booth.

The eggshell-and-cream colors of the kitchen walls and numerous stacked cabinets did little to make the compact room appear cozy. A scratched, scuffed oven dominated the far wall, with a large exhaust vent growing out and up through the ceiling. Mounted next to it was a sink that had a variety of faucets and taps dangling over it like metallic-ringed tentacles. Eva picked at a dried bit of food on the steel tabletop.

"I am so glad that we were able to fix the irrigation system in the greenhouse last week. Our crop production is already up seventy-six percent," Muthr said, setting a bowl full of strawberries in front of Eva. "Here, you can cut these up."

Eva picked up a strawberry the size of her fist and grabbed a knife from the knife block.

"That is a filet knife," Muthr pointed out, gingerly taking the utensil from the girl. Another wire-veined hand handed Eva a small chef's knife. "This should work fine."

Eva placed the immense strawberry on its side, ready to slice.

"Are you not forgetting something? Are your hands washed?" Muthr asked, still facing the sink, where she was now washing spinach leaves. Eva rolled her eyes and joined her.

At the sink Muthr prepared the food in her usual efficient manner. One hand passed a clean wide, wavy spinach leaf to another, which then placed the leaf on a cutting board. There, a third hand cut the spinach up into perfect squares. "I have been thinking," the robot said, "we need to back up and review some of the basic procedures before we continue with our outdoor training."

Eva dried her hands on her tunic, leaving damp

splotches along the hem. "R-review?" she sputtered. "How long is that going to take?"

"If we start tomorrow, several more weeks—or twenty-four more days, to be exact," Muthr answered, scraping the chopped spinach into a steel salad bowl.

"Twenty-four days?" Eva said, shocked. "Why don't we just go out and do some of these exercises for real? I'm sure I'd do a lot better." She lopped the green star-shaped top off a strawberry and sliced the fruit.

"You know good and well that you are not yet ready," Muthr replied, opening a large cabinet door. The cabinet was stocked full of marked containers of different sizes meticulously arranged as in a giant spice rack.

"I am ready," Eva said. "I know more than you think." She slid the quartered strawberry next to the bowl and grabbed another, even larger than the first. "And besides, maybe if we explore, we'll find . . . you know . . . others."

"'Others'?" repeated Muthr. She paused and rotated her head. With her large eyes, the robot looked like a mechanized owl observing Eva. "What others are you speaking of?"

"You know . . . others. Humans, like me," Eva

said, keeping her gaze focused on cutting the ripe red fruit.

"Eva Nine, we have been over this numerous times before." Muthr grabbed a hanging pot above her. When she placed it under one of the faucets, water automatically began to fill it up. "And, as I have told you before, there are no indications of others down here like you. That is what makes you so special."

Eva mouthed the last line in perfect unison while she lopped the top off another strawberry. "But I think that's why we need to leave. To explore and find out for sure," she countered.

"You failed the simplest of tasks today—a LifeScan sweep. You are not yet ready." Muthr returned her attention to her cooking. "Stove top, burner one, heat level six, please."

"But I am so cooped up in here," Eva said in a despondent tone. "Can't we go out for just a little bit?"

Muthr replied, "You will in time, my dear. Now—"

"I don't think you understand, Muthr. I—"

"I do understand. Now please pay attention. Focus on what you're doing." Muthr's tone was stern.

"How can you understand?" Eva slapped the knife down onto the tabletop with a loud clang.

"You're not me! You can't get bitten by a snake! You . . . you're not even human!"

The kitchen was silent except for the clicking of Muthr's blinking eyes. She studied Eva with her deep dark orbs. The pot on the stove began to burble softly. Somewhere high above, an exhaust fan hummed as it sucked the heat up and out of the room.

Eva sneered at the robot, waiting for a reaction. She wondered what Muthr was thinking with all of those zeroes and ones coursing through her electrical nervous system. It was then that Eva realized that she was bleeding.

"Eva!" gasped Muthr, wheeling toward her.

"I just nicked myself with the blade. That's all," Eva said, putting her thumb into her mouth. As she lapped the tiny wound with her tongue, she could taste her blood. She could feel the pulse of her own heart.

"Now, that is not the way to address a minor cut, Eva." Muthr rolled closer, extending a rodlike arm. "Let me see it."

Eva pulled out her thumb and allowed Muthr to study it. At the same time, dinner preparations resumed, as Muthr dropped several pills from the cabinet into the simmering pot of water. The small kitchen began to fill with the scent of roasted chicken.

"This is exactly what I am talking about," Muthr said. "Now, what you need to do is sterilize the site. Then place a small medical sticker on it so that it may heal without infection and with minimum scarring."

"I'll be fine, Muthr. It's just a tiny cut." Eva yanked her hand back. "I'll live."

"Eva, please just—"

"Fine!" Eva yelled. She stormed out of the kitchen, muttering under her breath, "It's not like you'll ever die."

She walked out to the hub, manually activating an adjacent door, which led to the supply room. As the door slid shut behind her, Eva walked past the labyrinth of shelves containing all manner of household items: electro-gaskets, holo-bulbs, lumen-packs, various cleaning products, and hydration kits.

"Hello, Eva Nine. May I help you find something?" asked the calm tone of the Sanctuary over the intercom.

"I'm okay, Sanctuary," Eva replied, stopping in front of a rack holding medicinal supplies. "I'm just looking for a small medi-sticker."

"Medical sticky bandages with SpeedHeal ointment are located on the bottommost shelf," the Sanctuary said.

"Thanks," Eva said, pulling open a metallic bin. She grabbed two, pocketing one of the medi-stickers in her tunic. She ripped open the plastic packet with her teeth and placed the medicated sticker over the congealed blood spot on her thumb. Pausing in the shadowy aisle of shelves, Eva listened. Through the ply-steel walls she could hear Muthr humming as the robot set the table. Eva walked to the very back of the storage room and stared at the faint outline of a sealed doorway.

A doorway she wasn't supposed to know about.

"Eva, dear?" Muthr's harmonious voice came in over the intercom. "Did you find the medi-stickers?"

"I did," Eva replied, though she knew the question was pointless. Muthr and the Sanctuary were linked. "I just want to grab some other things, um . . . electra-paper . . . to write notes for tomorrow's class."

"Good thinking," Muthr said. "Dinner is ready!"

Later that evening Eva relaxed in her cozy electric bed, watching her favorite holo-show, *Beeboo and Company*. Muthr entered her faintly lit room and moved through the clutter on the floor. "I thought I asked you to pick this up," she said as she approached Eva.

"Come in," Eva said sarcastically while she watched brilliantly colored cartoon characters cavort about her bedroom. A blue raccoon was trying to help an orange octopus build a home using sticks and rocks, but the house kept collapsing. A cat wearing a silver suit emblazoned with a logo for the Dynastes Corporation giggled, announcing, "You two need building blocks!"

"Pause program, please," commanded Muthr in that cheery tone of hers. "I made some notes of my own and thought you might want this," she said, handing Eva an electra-paper.

As Eva studied the semitransparent sheet, faint lines of text scrolled up to meet her roving gaze. "This is just a list of the six basic survival skills," she said. Eva looked up at Muthr, causing the text to stop scrolling. "We've gone over this before."

"Well, we need to go over it again until you get it right," Muthr replied.

"What?" Eva said, aghast.

The robot put a hand on her shoulder. "I am going to quiz you on what each of these skills means tomorrow," Muthr said. "Pass this quiz with a perfect score, and we can continue with the fire-starting exercise right where we left off today. All right?"

Eva looked back at the list. "We won't have to start all over again?"

"We will not have to start all over again *if* you pass tomorrow's quiz," Muthr said. "You have a ninety-nine percent chance of doing this, so I expect you to perform exceptionally." Muthr turned away, rolling out of the room. "Good night, dear."

As the bedroom door slid shut, Eva could hear Muthr command the Sanctuary to power down for the night. She looked at the list, the words faintly glowing on the electra-paper:

SIX BASIC SURVIVAL SKILLS FOR HUMANS

1. Trust Technology
2. Signal Others
3. Find Shelter
4. Create Fire
5. Procure Food and Water
6. Know First Aid

Eva slid out of bed and threw a blanket over the life monitor peering down from above. She pulled on her sneakboots, then grabbed her satchel from the nightstand. As she did so, her Omnipod was knocked onto the floor. Jostled, it projected a life-size hologram of a girl in workout attire. Her face bore an uncanny resemblance to Eva's.

"No, no, no!" gasped Eva, reaching down for the device.

"Who's ready to warm up with some jumping jacks?" the hologram girl asked in a far too cheerful tone. Eva whispered to the Omnipod, "Deactivate Gym Buddy!"

"Deactivating," the device whispered back. The hologram evaporated, leaving a whitish glow illuminating Eva's face. "Is there anything else I can assist you with, Eva Nine?" it asked.

"Just a sec," Eva replied, slipping her bony hand through the Omnipod's wrist strap. Watching her door, Eva waited to see if the noisy outburst had attracted Muthr. Finally, she told the Omnipod, "Please command the Sanctuary to discontinue tracking my location and reporting to Muthr until instructed otherwise."

"Tracking of Multi-Utility Task Help Robot zero-six discontinued."

Eva opened her bedroom door and stepped out into the main hub. From under the soles of her sneakboots, she could hear the squish of disinfectant seeping up from the floor tiles as the Sanctuary began its nightly cleaning. The stinging scent of cleaner hung in the air, causing Eva's eyes to water and the inside of her nose to burn.

She snuck along the perimeter of the hub on a path farthest from Muthr's quarters, the control room, in hopes that the ever-vigilant robot would not hear her.

Thankfully, the door to the supply room was malfunctioning and could no longer be voice acti-vated. Eva tapped a glowing green button, and the doors slid open with a low hiss. Eva froze, wait-ing for the doors of Muthr's quarters to slide open in response. What would she tell her if she were caught? Medi-sticker, she thought. The old one fell off in the shower tonight.

Eva slipped into the supply room, her body heat activating the overhead lights. Watching the door slide shut, she brought the Omnipod close to her mouth.

"Omnipod, please instruct the Sanctuary to open the back hatch in the supply room," she whispered into the device.

"Doorway opening."

The door in the back of the room slid open with a hiss. Eva's silhouette stretched out into the dank, murky darkness. Eva whispered, "I'm on my way."

Eva pressed

a glowing red button, causing the door to slide shut behind her. She ran her fingers over a logo, an emblem stamped into the ply-steel composed of the letters *HRP*.

The Omnipod entered lumen mode, and the device created a strong beam of light from its central eye. As Eva made her way down the long, winding corridor,

she thought back to her first discovery of the secret hallway. . . .

She'd been five years old, playing hide-and-seek with Muthr.

Eva's favorite place to hide had been the empty cabinet under the kitchen sink, but she had grown some and could no longer fit under there.

Instead, Eva had found her way into the very back of the labyrinthine supply room and had hidden behind the last shelf full of nutriment capsules. Giggling, she had leaned against the back wall, sliding into the shadows and awaiting the sound of Muthr's playful voice. On the cold surface of that wall, Eva had felt the unmistakable seam of a doorway.

Muthr had found her moments later trying to get the Sanctuary to open it. The robot had told her it was a malfunctioning door that had been sealed off long before Eva Nine had been born.

Eva had soon forgotten about the mysterious door, until the day she'd made the other discovery.

Putting a pair of rolled-up woolen socks away in her dresser, an eight-year-old Eva had found something scratched into the metal on the *inside* of the top drawer. Printed in blocky lettering was: "CP01: OMNISCIENT: FLOOR PLAN."

Eva had puzzled over this cryptic code for days. She'd wondered if she should go and ask Muthr about its meaning. She'd pondered this idea, but had hesitated, for it was also at that time that Eva had started to realize that she and Muthr were truly not the same. This observation had led to a notion that had itched at the back of her mind: She wasn't being told everything.

There were other humans depicted in the holo-shows and programs that she watched—but none living in the Sanctuary. Where could they be? When she had asked Muthr, Eva had received the same response: "There are no others like you. That is what makes you so very special."

Eva had returned to her dresser and stared at the words written inside the drawer.

That was when she'd asked her Omnipod what a "floor plan" was.

The device had prattled out a lengthy defini-tion, projecting lavish holograms of various archi-tectural layouts, then had asked if she wanted to know more. She had not.

Eva had then asked what "omniscient" was. The Omnipod had answered that "omniscient" was an adjective derived from a seventeenth-century word meaning "to know everything."

Finally, Eva had asked what "CP01" was. Here, the Omnipod had had no answer. It had replied that the letters and numbers could be some sort of code, perhaps even for another computer or device.

Still puzzled, Eva had looked at that cryptic message day after day, trying to determine its true meaning. In time, she'd forgotten about it. A year later, she'd been removing her old clothing, which no longer fit, from her dresser drawers.

Once again, she'd spied the secret words.

"Show me the Sanctuary's floor plan," she had instructed the Omnipod when she was nine years old. Once again, a dazzling hologram had floated up, expounding in great detail about the different chambers of the girl's home. Immediately, Eva had realized that there were holes in this hypnotic display—pieces of the Sanctuary that were missing. The Omnipod hadn't been showing her everything.

Eva had asked to see the Sanctuary's *entire* floor plan.

The Omnipod had asked for a username and a password.

Eva had replied, "CP01. Omniscient." . . .

She now approached the halfway point of the long hallway. The humidity had increased as she'd trekked farther down the winding corridor. Moisture clung to the walls, and small fungi dotted the ceiling in places.

"Almost there," whispered Eva, her voice echoing through the darkness. When Eva had first wandered into this new, uncharted area, she'd been thrilled and terrified all at once. Now she moved without hesitation. Her destination was just ahead. . . .

She remembered a time when she had realized there was more to the world than just her life in the Sanctuary. When she'd been six, she had asked Muthr about it as she'd sat down to breakfast. "Why aren't there trees in our house?"

"Because trees cannot grow here," Muthr had replied, dropping a pill into a cup of water. It had fizzed as it had plunged to bottom of the cup, disintegrating.

"But we have plants in our greenhouse. And my programs show trees. Big, enormous oak trees, growing in large forests," Eva had said as she'd slurped up her drink. Muthr had told her the taste was like freshly picked oranges.

The robot had put an arm around her, "Well, Eva, there are trees. But they cannot grow here, where we live. They grow . . . above us."

"Can we go and see them?" Eva had been excited at the idea of exploring a big forest towering right above them. "We could play hide-and-seek and have a picnic."

"All in due time," Muthr had replied, setting a bowl of oatmeal-flavored mush in front of her. *All in due time. . . .*

Eva finally arrived at the end of the hall. Another door, identical to the one she had opened in the supply room, stood shut in front of her, its manual control panel darkened from water damage. She knelt down, adjusting the light on the Omnipod from a solid beam to a soft, luminous glow.

The area surrounding the door was lined with a collection of odd and unusual objects that had been placed carefully in little organized rows leading to the door. The items ranged from clothing—shoes and crisply folded tunics—to toys and games, such as an animated rattle and a giggling ball. All had one thing in common: They were items that belonged to Eva that she was not yet ready to discard. She sat down facing a group of dingy stuffed animals at the head of this arrangement and opened her satchel.

"Hi, everybody!" Eva addressed the toys and objects huddled at the shadowy door. "Sorry it's been a while. I've been so busy with my exercises and stuff. How are you?"

The toys did not reply.

"Good. Good," Eva replied. "Oh, me? I'm all right . . . I suppose."

She showed her bandaged thumb to the toys. "I got cut—see? Yeah, I'm okay. Thanks for asking. It happened while I was prepping dinner. No, no, don't worry, I'll be fine." She rubbed her bandaged thumb against her forefinger. "But I totally flunked my fire-starting test today. I got bit by a snake and died. Can you believe it?"

The silent collection stared back at her.

Eva winced. "I know, I know. I think Muthr wanted me to fail and put it there on purpose—so I just dropped dead. I thought she was going to blow a gasket!" Eva chuckled. The hollow laugh echoed on the damp walls surrounding her.

She sighed, slumping into the shadow outside of the Omnipod's glow. Her eyes downcast, Eva spoke in a melancholy tone, "What am I going to do, guys? It's not that I want to fail these exercises. I want to pass them. I mean, the sooner I pass them, the sooner I can get out of here. . . . I'm sorry. You're right—the sooner *we* can get out of here." Eva stared at the glowing faces of her old toys, illuminated by the Omnipod. "I just . . . I just want to have friends. Not that you guys aren't great friends and all. But, you know." Eva picked at a loose string of climatefiber hanging from her sock. "I want to meet people . . . like me."

A muffled banging sound reverberated down the hall from the direction of the Sanctuary. She stopped talking and listened . . . but now all was silent.

She addressed the toys again. "What's that? No. Now I have to take a quiz tomorrow to see if I still remember my basic skills. My basic skills! It's like Muthr doesn't want me to leave at all. It's not fair." She pulled the electra-paper out of her satchel. Its pale glowing lines flickered in the darkness as Eva rolled up the sheet. She slid it carefully inside a small sneakboot standing loyally with its mate next to the stuffed animals. "Guess what? Here's what the quiz is on. I wanted to make sure you all had the list too."

Eva's eyes rested on a small, thin item hiding in the organized hoard. She plucked it up carefully and examined it closer. It was a blackened, crumbling, flat piece of material—different from anything else she'd ever held before.

When she'd first discovered this item more than a year before, Eva had tried to identify it with her Omnipod, but the device had concluded that, "There is insufficient data. Not enough information to make an identification." Eva had determined that it was likely a small piece of tile or even paneling, possibly a sign of sorts, as it was square shaped. On it was an image (a broken one, since it no longer moved) of a little girl holding hands with a robot and an adult.

The only item in Eva's secret collection not given to her by Muthr.

The only item in her secret collection not identifiable by her Omnipod.

An item another human had left for her, here, by this sealed door.

Proof.

She couldn't make out who exactly the adult in the image was. The scorched damage obscured the face in soot. However, she could see two letters on this worn piece of paneling: *L* and *a*. There was a second, smaller piece to this puzzle, which she had discovered as well. Eva had glued this missing fragment to the top of the panel. It, too, had fancy letters printed on it: "Wond."

"WondLa," Eva had dubbed it. She studied the picture in her hands. The girl was smiling. The robot was smiling. Eva was certain the adult was likely smiling too as they all walked together in unison through a field of flowers. Moving as one. As friends. Exploring the forests above.

But Eva's robot would not allow her to explore. She wouldn't even let her leave the Sanctuary.

A Sanctuary that had been connected to another Sanctuary.

A Sanctuary that had been connected to *many* other Sanctuaries.

Eva had seen the omniscient floor plan.

However, like the door before her that led to the adjoining Sanctuary, they were now all closed off to her.

"I don't know why Muthr doesn't want me to have other friends," Eva said as she returned the WondLa back to its place. "But she'll never find out about the WondLa, or us . . . until it's too late."

Lifting the Omnipod up from the floor, Eva scanned the collection of unmoving toys. The soft light illuminated their blank faces. She paused on one, a grungy Beeboo doll.

"I brought you a medi-sticker too," Eva said as she ripped open the little packet with her teeth. Eva placed the sticker on the doll's soiled paw. "I don't want you to get an infection when we escape from here."

As she stood to leave, a tremendous shock wave rattled the entire Sanctuary, raining dust and debris from the corridor ceiling down onto Eva Nine.

The Omnipod

light danced wildly about the secret passageway as Eva rushed back toward the Sanctuary. She activated the door controls as another loud reverberation rocked the walls, causing her to stumble through the open doorway and back into the supply room. The shelves inside vibrated with each rumble, and several containers of disinfectant fell to the floor. Holding on to the shelves, Eva snaked her way to the front of the room just as the door hissed open. Standing in the entrance was Muthr.

"There you are!" exclaimed Muthr. She thrust Eva's jackvest and a large food container into the girl's hands. "I have been looking everywhere for you. Do you have your Omnipod?"

"Yes," replied Eva, holding up her right hand, the device hanging from her wrist.

"May I have it, please?" Muthr asked.

Eva handed the Omnipod to her. Immediately its tiny lights began flickering in rhythm to a tiny light on Muthr's torso. "What is that?" Eva shouted over another tremendous bang. The sound was coming from above them. All the lights in the Sanctuary flickered.

"Is this another exercise? Or a drill? Because—" A shrieking siren cut her off, a noise Eva Nine had never heard before. With large eyes—frightened eyes—she watched the robot. Muthr was silent and stoic, but lights blinked in rapid succession all over her head.

"Muthr, what's happening? What is the Sanctuary telling you?" Eva asked. She huddled close to the robot as another shock wave boomed overhead.

Muthr blinked out of her trance and addressed Eva. "An intruder has breached the Sanctuary's doors and is now descending to the main entrance. Come now. We have only minutes to get you to safety." With that, the robot spun around and wheeled out into the main hub. Eva hopped along behind her, slipping her jackvest on over her beige tunic. The Sanctuary shook again.

"Kitchen doors, open, please," Muthr commanded, and she barreled through the adjacent door.

"Wait—the kitchen?" Eva stopped in the doorway, confused. "Why are we going into the kitchen? Shouldn't we head to the control room?"

"Not now, Eva, dear." Muthr grabbed Eva by the wrist and yanked her inside. The robot slid open a small hidden panel near the doorway and began typing a sequence of numbers into a security keypad. The kitchen doors slid shut and locked. Over the sound of the alarm, Eva could hear the other doors in the Sanctuary lock as well. Next, the ambient sounds of the central living hub, along with every appliance within the Sanctuary, powered on with the volume at maximum level.

"This noisy diversion will not buy us much time, so we must be quick," Muthr said. She looked directly at Eva and placed two hands on her shoulders. "Now, listen very carefully to me, Eva. You must *leave* the Sanctuary and head up to the surface for safety. This intruder is clearly not benevolent, and I will not have any harm befall you."

Eva gasped. "Leave? Now? I mean, I want to, but—"

Muthr's voice remained calm while explosions tore apart the Sanctuary outside the kitchen door. "Do not worry, my child," she said. "I will be all right. I know we were not finished with your exercises. However, you—"

"Room two fire sensor has detected smoke,"

announced the Sanctuary over the intercom speaker. "Please seal off the room and begin extinguishing sequence."

Muthr wheeled Eva over to the cooking exhaust vent, and began removing the corner screws from the intake grill at once with all four of her arms. "Eva, inside here is a ladder that will take you directly to the surface."

Eva blinked, dumbfounded. *There was an escape hatch right here in the kitchen all this time?* The floor plan on the Omnipod had shown only one way out, and that was through the robot's quarters.

A loud sonic vibration, just outside in the central hub, rattled the walls of the Sanctuary. A mighty explosion erupted, as if a door were being blown to pieces.

Eva backed away from the kitchen doorway a bit, and bumped into Muthr, who had now removed the grate. She set the grate down and continued with her instructions. "I have been closely monitoring the nearby terrain. If the reports are correct, we are concealed in a densely wooded area near a river. Once you reach the ground level outside, you need to run from here as fast as you can and find a place to hide among the trees." Muthr supported Eva as she climbed up onto the stove top and stepped inside the exhaust shaft. It smelled smoky, like burnt toast. "Stay put until daylight," Muthr said, "and above all, do not let this intruder spot you."

Kneeling down in the exhaust shaft, Eva looked at Muthr. Her heart was pounding in tempo with her rapid breathing.

This is not an exercise.

"Rooms three and five are also detecting smoke," the Sanctuary's intercom spoke in its eerie, calm tone. Another explosion interrupted its report, "—begin extinguishing sequence."

Room 5. That's my room.

My life is in there. My clothes . . . my bed . . . my entire holo-show collection.

Room 5 was where Eva had dreamed up countless plans of how she was going to find others, just like her, and bring them back safely to her home. Friends and family would live with her and Muthr in the Sanctuary, just like the picture depicted on the WondLa.

Another explosion rocked the kitchen.

"Eva, I need you focused and alert," Muthr said, handing her the Omnipod. "Remember what we have studied and all that you have learned." The robot lifted up the grate and began screwing the bolts back in. "Trust technology, and *do not* return unless you hear word from me. Understand?"

Eva nodded as it dawned on her what was happening. Her eyes started to sting. This scenario wasn't on any list. Sure, she had wanted to explore the surface, but not this way.

Not alone.

"Room six fire sensor has detected smoke," reported the Sanctuary. It might as well have been greeting Eva, its tone of voice was so calm. "Please seal off the room and begin extinguishing sequence." Static fuzzed over part of the announcement. Despite the growing heat from the fire outside, Eva's entire body trembled as if she were chilled.

"Muthr! You . . . you have to come with me!" yelled Eva. The smell of smoke now drifted into the kitchen. "Please!" She panicked. "There's room for you in here! I can help you up! Don't leave me!"

Muthr put her hand on the grill. "Eva, listen. Listen very carefully to me." Eva curled her fingertips around Muthr's, gripping so tightly that the blood rushed out of them. The robot continued, "I have shut the exhaust fan off, but it is on a timer. It will restart soon, so you have to hurry. When you get to the top of the vent, there will be a wheel. Turn it counterclockwise to open the hatch and climb out."

Smoke wormed its way into the kitchen from

under the door, carrying a nauseating stench of smoldering metal and melted plastic. Outside, Eva could hear a loud hum followed by a piercing sonic vibration. The kitchen door buckled from the explosion, but did not open. Muthr spoke in that slightly distorted melodious voice. "Eva, I love you very much, and I hope that I will see you again," she said, "but you must go, NOW!"

Muthr moved away from the grate. Eva pounded on it, screaming, "No! No! No!"

A metal covering slid down, sealing the exhaust vent shut. Eva could hear a tremendous explosion and the kitchen door blow open. Frightened, she sat frozen at the bottom of the vent for the longest minute of her life. She listened to the rummaging and pilfering going on beyond the grate covering in what had once been her kitchen—what had once been her home.

Eva thought of Muthr. She thought of her old friends hiding in the secret corridor.

She started climbing her way up toward a distant flickering light at the top of the shaft. It seemed like miles away, and the light above turned into a tiny star shape every time tears streamed out of her eyes.

Panting, Eva was approaching the nonmoving exhaust fan. As she neared the large unit, she could hear it chirp in a steady electronic beat. From below, Eva studied the fan's wide greasy blades, encrusted with gray clumps of filth, as the chirping sped up in tempo.

The fan is on a timer—Eva recalled Muthr's instructions—*you have to hurry.* She grabbed hold of the fan's central motor and pulled herself up past the flattened blades. The chirping sped up yet again. Sitting atop the large cylindrical motor, Eva caught her breath. The chirping became a rapid beep. Eva stood on top of the unit and could see a wheel-shaped handle above her lit by a single utility light. Grasping the wheel, she tried to turn it.

It did not budge.

"Turn, turn, turn," pleaded Eva.

The chirping stopped and the fan's motor started up again. The vibration jolted Eva so much that she almost lost her footing. The toe of her sneak-boot thrummed as the blades whacked at it.

Another sonic shock wave echoed its way up the shaft, and Eva shrieked. The wave was followed by a rending sound at the bottom of the shaft, and metal clanging. The grill covering had been removed, and smoke now began to wind its way up the exhaust vent.

Sensing the additional heat, the fan spun even faster. The entire unit vibrated, groaning under the additional weight of Eva on top of it. Through the fumes burning her vision, Eva risked looking down. Below, she could make out the glow of fire coming in from the kitchen grill, growing like an angry orange-red snake up toward her.

Vertigo tried to topple Eva. She refocused on the wheel, pulling on it with every bit of strength that she possessed until it finally let out a low squeak and moved ever so slightly. The smoke was now so dense that Eva could no longer see her own hands in front of her. She coughed as noxious vapors filled her lungs. Mucus ran from her nose into her gritted teeth.

"Come on!" she yelled as she blindly pried the wheel loose from its frozen position. At last the wheel spun freely just as the old, rusted bolts holding the fan unit below her gave out, one at a time. With each turn the top vent of the shaft opened a little more, sucking up the fire and its smoky breath. The fan came loose from the shaft walls, plummeting down to the flames below. Hanging from the wheel, Eva pulled herself up and grasped the edge of the vent opening. She squeezed her lithe body through the vent, and then tumbled down to the ground below.

A ground Eva Nine had never set a foot upon in all twelve years of her life.

CHAPTER 5: ABOVEGROUND

Wiping ash and grit out of her burning eyes, Eva Nine stumbled away from the Sanctuary's underground exhaust vent and into the surrounding wood. She knelt down next to the thick trunk of the nearest tree to catch her breath.

"C-cold," she stuttered. "I c-can see my breath." Eva wriggled her fingers through the mist coming from her mouth and watched it dissipate as it drifted away above her. She fell backward and looked up through the boughs of the trees and saw stars, millions of them, speckling between the patches of thick clouds in the night sky. The soft glow of the moon permeated through the cloud cover as Eva absorbed the utter enormity of the evening sky stretched over her. She was witnessing it all for the first time.

"It's so big!" She gaped in astonishment. "And brighter than I thought it would be."

The crisp night air smelled moist and mysterious. Eva felt the climatefibers in her clothing tighten to warm her body as her tunic announced the outdoor temperature and her body temperature. She ignored the report and peered into the woods that surrounded her.

Huge wide, squat trees—almost as big as her Sanctuary—grew in broad clusters. Their cup-shaped branches swayed and creaked in rhythm with sounds of odd chortles and burbles coming from deep within the dense undergrowth. Spindly bulb-tipped plants had sprung up in the spaces in between the trees and were swaying gently in unison as if moved by a midnight breeze.

A familiar booming sound rocked the forest, causing the unseen residents to squawk and croak in fright. The shadowy creatures rustled about all around the girl. Eva crawled behind the trunk of the tree and hid. She jumped when she heard the muffled chirp of her Omnipod. With jittery hands she rummaged through her satchel and pulled the device out. Risking a peek around the trunk of the tree, Eva whispered into the Omnipod, "This is Eva Nine. Proceed."

The device whispered back, "Greetings, Eva Nine. You have one unplayed message from Multi-Utility Task Help Robot zero-six. Sent twelve minutes ago. Shall I play recorded message?"

"Yes." Eva felt loneliness creep into her being.

A three-dimensional image of Muthr projected over the device. "Eva, dear," the hologram said, "this message was recorded on the chance that you have successfully escaped the Sanctuary. I know you have yet to explore the surface, but you need to listen very carefully: Get as far away from the Sanctuary as possible and hide for the night. Once you find shelter, begin signaling to the nearest settlement, HRP underground facility fifty-one. I need you to remain hidden and wait for either a live message from me or a return message from those coordinates. Remember, your Omnipod will help you in the interim. Eva, stay strong."

"End of message," finished the Omnipod.

"I'm not waiting." Eva sent the distress signal, returned the device to her satchel, and peered back around the tree trunk. A thin ribbon of smoke drifted up from the exhaust vent into the night sky. In it were the burnt, atomized remnants of her Sanctuary. Perhaps even of Muthr.

"Stupid robot." Eva wiped her eyes with the back of her sleeve. "I knew we should have explored the surface sooner."

Another large tremor rippled up from the shaft, followed by the emergence of a dark, burly figure from another opening in the ground, farther in the distance. "The main entryway," Eva whispered, remembering the floor plan that the Omnipod had showed her.

The large, shadowy figure remained still at the entryway as it surveyed the forest. Eva couldn't make out many details from her vantage point, but whatever this intruder was, it was big and had many legs and arms. It lifted its large head and snorted loudly, then abruptly stopped. Turning, the intruder raised a long rodlike apparatus right in Eva's direction. She could hear a distinct electronic hum rising in pitch, followed by a *woom* sound of intense sonic vibration. The tree trunk Eva was hiding behind exploded, throwing her backward.

The concentrated sound wave had blasted a hole, the size of Muthr, through the thick trunk. Digging herself out of the debris that had dropped down onto her, Eva heard the groan of the weakened trunk as the tree began to topple. She scrambled out of the way, and the sprawling treetop crashed into the ground behind her, sending leaves and branches flying in all directions.

She got up and took off, running through the dense woods. Soon Eva could hear only her footsteps padding across the soft forest floor.

Is he gone? Did I outrun him? she thought.

Just to the right of her another tree was reduced to splinters by a sonic explosion. She was being followed.

She ran for some time, zigzagging through the undergrowth. Her lungs burned from the crisp, chilly night air. As she dashed around the enormous trunk of a tree, Eva tried to locate her attacker. She leaned against a low branch and caught her breath, wondering where she was.

Eva looked up through the wide leaves above her. In the shadowy forest there wasn't enough moonlight for her to take in her surroundings and find a safe place to hide.

Perhaps if I get to a higher vantage point, I can

see more. She grabbed on to the branch. Like she had done many times on the monkey bars in the Sanctuary's gymnasium, Eva lifted herself onto the branch and tested her weight on the platform of hardened leaves: They held her.

Eva hopped from leafy platform to platform. In moments she found herself on the moonlit top of the irregular tree. Peering over the edge of the topmost bough, Eva could see the swift-moving tapered shape of her assailant below.

Once again the intruder stopped and sniffed the air. It circled the neighboring tree trunks. Though her tunic and jackvest kept her warm from the cool of the night, Eva shivered from fear and slid back onto the leafy platform to hide.

I have to lead him away from me, she thought. *But how?*

She peered back down below her. In the wan light she could see that the intruder was still in the area, poking around in the bush with his bulb-tipped weapon. Some ways away a covey of birds, silhouetted in the night sky, fluttered up. The intruder froze and listened. Hunting.

A distraction, Eva thought. *But with what?*

She opened her satchel, and discovered that there wasn't much inside: the Omnipod, lip balm,

Glitterglow nail polish, a hydration kit, a drinking container, a few electra-notes . . . and the package of foodstuffs Muthr had given her. Curious, Eva opened the package. It was a pouch full of food: SustiBars, Pow-R-drink packs, water purification tablets, and nutriment pellets.

Nutriment pellets. Perfect, she thought, picking up one of the large brown pills.

Eva glanced back down, spying the intruder still circling below. Moving ever so quietly, she sat up and threw the pellet. It pinged as it banged off a distant tree. The dark intruder bolted through the undergrowth toward the disturbance.

Eva waited a beat.

One more, she thought. *This time throw it as far as you can.*

She stood up and hurled another pellet out into the darkness, but she heard nothing and sat back down. As she waited, Eva looked down at the surrounding ground for signs of the intruder. Hours passed. Inkblot shadows of the canopy swayed and rolled on the forest floor in the cloudy light, almost as if the ground itself were moving. The swaying movement began to have a hypnotic effect on the tired girl. Eva curled up in the wide cupped leaves of the tree and waited for morning.

Eva was

summoned from her sleep by a chorus of soft, low hoots.

She jolted upright, startled. "Where am I?"

Though it was still fairly dark, most of the stars had faded into the early morning predawn, and Eva could see that thick clouds still hung above her. The cool, misty breeze that wafted over her face smelled sweet, like flower-scented soap.

As she took in the dimly lit world around her, Eva spied the source of the hooting. Three distinctly marked birds were roosting on a leafy platform right next to her. Eva leaned over for a closer view in the dusky light—each was nearly as large as she was. One of the creatures flapped its finlike wings and warbled a warning, but did not fly off.

"Wow, birds. Actual living birds. Right here. Right next to me," whispered Eva. As she watched them preen themselves, Eva pulled out her Omnipod. She whispered to it, "This is Eva Nine. Initiate Identicapture, please."

The device glowed as it responded, "Identicapture enabled. Proceed."

Eva aimed the Omnipod in the birds' direction and the device emitted an electronic ping. Seconds later, a perfect three-dimensional hologram of the bird, with its three pairs of wings, floated like a model over the Omnipod's central eye. Underneath the hologram, charts and menus fluttered as the Omnipod attempted to identify the creature. At last the device reported, "Kingdom, phylum, and species: unknown."

"That's weird," Eva said. She examined the Omnipod for damage. "I thought you could identify anything." As she flipped the device over, a glimmer of bright light reflected from its lacquered metallic finish, spooking the roosting birds. Eva watched as the flock chattered loudly and flew off toward the horizon. She then discovered the source of the reflected light. Beneath heavy, hazy clouds a colossal ball of brilliant white appeared in the sky. Beams of light erupted from its fiery core, skewering the purple-blue sky as they illuminated it.

"Oh, no!" cried Eva. She cowered into a ball on the leafy platform. "It's too big! It's too big!" Eva covered her eyes with her hands. "It's much brighter than the holos. It's going to burn me!"

A warmth radiated into her body, and cracks of orange light leaked in between her pale bony fingers. After she dared a peek through them, Eva drew in her breath and sat up. The sun rose in the moody morning sky, unveiling the surrounding landscape as it did so.

Far to the east, just below the rising sun, a jagged horizon of mountains poked their enormous pointed backs up toward the hazy atmosphere. As far as Eva could see, a forest thick with interlocking trees stretched to the north and to the south. From the forest edge, gravel and stones peppered the plain, which surrounded Eva's tree in all directions. Behind her, to the west, more thickset irregular trees—like the one she was perched in—were clustered together. Their entire mass was a rich olive green, and as Eva studied them closely, she realized that they were . . . moving.

Moving?

She scooted to the edge of her leafy platform and gaped down at the ground below. Lichen-plastered rocks and loose gravel scrolled underneath at a steady pace as the tree ambled on hundreds of small rootlike legs. It reminded Eva of the holograms she had seen of millipedes crawling over the ground.

"Walking trees? I don't remember studying

those," Eva said, perplexed, her brow furrowed.

Her tunic chirped, "Your hydration level is low, Eva Nine. Please hydrate immediately. Thank you."

Eva sat up and tapped the patch on the shoulder of her tunic to confirm that she had received the message. The animated shoulder patch showed a graphic of Eva with statistics, such as height, weight, body temperature, and the time.

She scanned several of the cup formations that made up the tree's leaves. The birds' roost had a small puddle of water at the bottom of it—like a sink. Eva hopped over to the wide leafy platform and dipped her hand into the puddle. She lifted the chilled water to her nose and sniffed it as it ran through her fingers, but smelled nothing. After pulling out her drinking cup, she scooped up the water and stuck her tongue into it. A faint taste of cabbage was present; otherwise, the water was unremarkable. She dropped in a water purification tablet and drank.

Eva paused, wondering if she'd waited long enough for the water to become purified. *Is this water poisonous? Am I going to get sick?* She tried not to focus on the water, or the expanse of the illuminated dawn sky above her, and pulled out her Omnipod. "Check for messages, please."

"You have no new messages—voice or otherwise."

"Can . . . can you send a message to Muthr?"

"Attempting voice connection to Multi-Utility Task Help Robot zero-six . . . ," said the Omnipod as the little lights began to flicker around its central eye.

"Come on." Eva picked at the medi-sticker on her thumb. "Be there, please."

"I am sorry, Eva Nine. I am not receiving a reply," the Omnipod said. "Would you like to leave a message?"

"No, thanks." Eva stood up and scanned the forest. She squinted through the wandering trees and flocks of flying creatures.

Where am I? she wondered. *I was in the woods last night, but not anymore. How long have we been traveling?*

In the far distance she saw it.

To the southeast, a small wisp of smoke curled and evaporated just above the treetops—the smoke from the Sanctuary's exhaust vent.

Muthr.

Eva scrambled down the wandering tree and hopped onto the pebbled ground. As the tree lumbered on, she stepped out from its shadow and onto the winding open plain that lay between her and what remained of her underground home.

Eva inspected

the round, smooth stone cradled in her hands, half-expecting it to disappear in a cloud of light motes—but it did not. She turned it over and over in her hands. For one thing, the brown and blue striped stone was heavy, much heavier than Eva had imagined it would be when she'd picked it up from the ground. This was contrary to everything she'd ever held in the holography chamber. There, everything was as light as the filtered air that filled the Sanctuary.

This is real, she thought as she held the stone out in front of her, *all of this.*

Sand and gravel crunched under Eva's sneakboots as she marched across the winding plain. The odometer on the shoe's heel clicked as it counted out the distance. She stopped and checked her progress.

"I've gone almost two kilometers. That's the farthest I've ever walked."

Eva looked back over the plain. The tree she had been traveling on had now joined the others and was indistinguishable from the rest. They were like a holographic herd of green elephants. Looking up at the sun's rays, which were trying to force their way through the overcast sky, Eva felt a wave of cold numbness overtake her. She felt vulnerable and frightened—she had never been in an open space this vast.

Ever.

Her sweaty grip loosened, and Eva dropped the stone. She stood, frozen in place.

I need to run, she thought. *Run as fast as I can back home.*

"But I can't do that," Eva said aloud. "I need to be strong."

I wish I could fly. Then I could explore the whole world from the safety of the clouds.

"I wish I was safe back in my room." Eva swallowed. "I could be watching *Beeboo and Company* right now."

But now I am free. No one can tell me what to do.

"No one? There is no one here! Where is everybody?" Eva shouted.

I must search for them. I must find them.

"I'm tired. I don't know if I can do this." She looked down at her rock and moped.

I need to prove to Muthr that I was right and she was wrong.

The numbness passed. Eva wiped her damp palms on her tunic. She turned toward the distant smoky column and began walking again, thinking of the robot as she trudged forward. "Muthr was right. I'm a failure. I don't think I am ready for surface exploration," Eva said, pulling out her Omnipod.

"Eva Nine," the device greeted her. "How may I be of service?"

"Begin transmission signal," she commanded. "Coordinates are at HRP facility . . . number . . . um . . . Hold on. Can you replay Muthr's message from last night?"

"Of course," chirped the Omnipod.

"Eva, dear," Muthr's recording said as the projection of her head reappeared, "this message was recorded on the chance that you have successfully escaped the Sanctuary. I know—"

The Omnipod shut off abruptly as Eva stumbled over a rough inconspicuous rock lying on the ground in front of her. The rock began chattering as it scuttled out from under Eva on its numerous legs.

Its stony exoskeleton opened up, revealing a pair of brightly colored membranous wings. It buzzed as it flew away, and then it landed near a large hole some ways off. Eva watched it settle, changing its color to match the cluster of ivory-colored stones and sticks that surrounded the hole. "The rocks walk too?" Eva asked. "Maybe I do have a lot more training to do." She rechecked her position and hiked toward the forest where her Sanctuary was nestled.

Eva studied the odd-shaped congregation of plant life up ahead, and then her gaze drifted up to several birds circling a weeping tree adorned in long, droopy branches. At the center of the topmost bough was a bright object, which Eva concluded was some sort of fruit. She restarted Identicapture, in hopes of getting a better holo-scan of the birds, but then one of the birds alighted on the fruit. As fast as whips, all the dangling branches on the tree snapped up, muffling the bird's cries as they smothered the animal.

"Agh!" Eva stepped back, horrified. "What is that?" She aimed the Omnipod at the tree and waited for the device to capture an image. A hologram model was rendered in vivid detail, rotating over the Omnipod's central eye. Once again the device replied, "Kingdom, phylum, and species: unknown."

"Unknown?" Eva asked, astounded. "How can that be? It's clearly some sort of tree." Her eyes were wide as she witnessed the tree devouring the bird.

"Its size, form, and coloration do not match any of my records," the Omnipod reported in its chirpy tone. "If anything, its basic form and actions are similar to that of an animal from the genus *Hydra*—"

"So that's what *this* is, then?" Eva stared at the hologram of a hydra floating over the Omnipod. Its thin wispy tentacles waved about in a free-flowing fashion over its tubelike body.

"However," continued the Omnipod, "all species of this genus are miniscule. Most are microscopic."

"That," Eva said, pointing to the tree, "is hardly microscopic." The tree relaxed its branches back to their original position. The bird was gone.

"Agreed," the Omnipod said, "which is why I concluded it was unidentifiable."

"But you said it looks like that hydra thingy," Eva said. "So it must be an animal." She watched more birds circle the fruit. She realized that the weeping bird-catchers were everywhere in the forest.

"Its coloration and texture are similar to a large group of plants called algae, but I cannot make a definite conclusion," the device added. It now displayed various types of algae with arrows pointing to various ponds, lakes, and seas where the plants could be found. Another bird squawked in the distance as another tree ate.

What is going on? Eva wondered. *Why didn't I learn about these? They are more dangerous than the stupid holographic snake that bit me.* She felt another wave of numbness chill her down to her legs. "I've got to get back to the Sanctuary."

The Omnipod replied to Eva's statement, "There is a Sanctuary entryway approximately five hundred and sixty-eight meters straight ahead and slightly to the south. I can synchronize the distance with your sneakboots if you like."

"No, thanks," Eva said as she surveyed the forest edge. In the morning shade of the bird-catchers, she saw what appeared to be a large boulder, angled at one side and half submerged in the earth—the ground-level entrance to a Sanctuary.

But it was not *her* Sanctuary.

Eva ran across the gravelly plain toward the entryway. Like the holograms she'd seen of underground subway entrances, the open doorway led down into the earth at a gradual angle. Its outside walls were splotched with large lichens. Enormous pale mushrooms grew from the entryway's pitted roof. The door itself was nowhere to be found. Eva concluded from the entryway's eroded appearance that the Sanctuary had been vacant for a long time.

She pulled a strand of brown-blond hair out of her eyes and peered down into the descending entrance. The darkness below revealed nothing.

Perhaps there is someone in here who can help, she thought, *someone like me. Maybe their transmitter is broken just like ours was, and they've been trying to reach Muthr and me all these years.*

Eva called down the shaft, "Hellloooo!" The sound echoed as it bounced down into the dark depths.

A high-pitched squeak answered from below, and out burst a swarm of ugly tiny flying crab-things. Eva shrieked, holding her hands up to cover her face. The twittering critters fluttered up into the morning sky above her. Next, a deep, low bellow sang out over the entire landscape. A gigantic shadow darkened the entryway from above.

What appeared to Eva as an enormous flying whale drifted high up over the open plain. With its massive maw the air-whale consumed the entire swarm of flying crabs. It then continued on its way, buoyed by a pair of mighty air sacs. Stunned at the sheer size of the whale, Eva cowered. She didn't raise her Omnipod until the air-whale had disappeared over the treetops on the far side of the plain.

Eva caught her breath and leaned back against the side of the pitted entryway. She said to the device, "This is Eva Nine. Initiate LifeScan. Please sweep the area for any other detectable life-forms."

"Initiating LifeScan." A radar image floated over the Omnipod's central eye. Eva bit at the medisticker on her thumb and watched a blueprint of the Sanctuary entrance rotate in front of her. She saw several tiny dots appear scattered about—and one large dot, glowing brightly. The Omnipod reported, "There are several small life-forms of no serious consequence. However, there is a larger, active life form that is making its way toward the entryway stairs from below."

Eva's throat clenched. "Is it human or robot?"

"Unknown."

Standing tall, Eva scanned the immediate area. Though the entryway was near the forest edge, she was still a ways from the line of trees.

"Life-form almost to the surface." Eva detested how the Omnipod maintained its cheerful tone.

This might be the intruder from last night, she thought. *What do I do? What do I do?* She scanned her surroundings. "I can't run for it. I'm too far away," Eva whispered through fast breath. She looked back at the glowing dot on the Omnipod. *Whatever this is will make it to the surface before I get to the woods.*

"Heart rate BPM acceleration detected, Eva Nine," her tunic announced. "Please—"

Eva tapped the shoulder patch, silencing its report. She ran to the sloping back of the Sanctuary entrance, throwing her Omnipod into her satchel. After grabbing hold of the stalk of a large mushroom, she pulled herself up the back of the entryway and scrambled onto the tiny angled roof.

The footsteps became louder as whoever—or whatever—it was approached the surface. Eva held her breath and curled up tightly in a ball. The hairs on the back of her neck stood up. She could *feel* the thing near her.

Maybe it won't see me. Maybe it will leave.

Time stopped as she waited, her body curled with her hands over her head. Her neck began to hurt. There was no sound to be heard at all except the far-off chortling of the birds.

Has it gone back down?

"Ovanda say tateel?" a voice barked.

Eva slowly unfroze from her position, and dared a peek over the edge of the roof.

There her eyes met the gaze of a being she knew her Omnipod would also not be able to identify.

CHAPTER 8: STUCK

Eva looked at the creature's catfish-whiskered mouth as it spoke. Its lanky figure was much smaller than last night's intruder's. Its cerulean blue body was partially covered by the baggy faded brown jacket that it wore.

"Ovanda say tateel?" the bipedal creature repeated. Eva assumed the words were a question by the way the being spoke, and she assumed it was a male by its gruff voice, but she couldn't be too sure. She scooted far from him to the back of the entryway roof.

"O-van-daa . . . saay . . . taa-teel?" He gestured with large hands. In one, he held a cylindrical bottle half-full of a milky liquid. "Say tateel? Dat?"

"Who are you?" asked Eva in a shrill tone. "How did you get in there?"

Did you kill whoever lived inside and steal their jacket?

The creature turned its narrow head and blinked, birdlike, as he regarded Eva with his indigo eyes. "Bluh. Shassa avanda say tateel," he mumbled as he walked back down the steps into his Sanctuary.

Eva sat, perplexed, on the rooftop and waited.

In the distance, she could hear the air-whale call across the heavens.

Nothing else happened.

"I KNOW this isn't on the stupid survival list!" She slid down the back side of the entryway and tiptoed back to the opening. Peering inside, she spied no sign of the creature in the darkness.

She cleared her throat. "Hel-lo . . . in . . . there,"

she said in a succinct manner. "My . . . name . . . is . . . Eh-va . . . Nine. Do . . . you . . . live . . . here?"

A deep belch resonated up from the room below.

"If you can just tell me where the people are that lived here, it would really—"

"Saaga na SASHA!" yelled the creature, stomping up the stairs. He emerged from the shadows of the entryway, waving his arms wildly.

Eva fell back onto the ground with a shriek. Belly up, she scrambled on her hands and feet like an insect, scurrying away from the angry creature.

"Zaata! Zaata!" He shooed her away.

"Don't hurt me!" Eva cried. "I am just trying to get back home." As she sat up, the Omnipod slipped out of her satchel. It caught the creature's brooding eyes. In seconds he dashed on his backward-bending legs to Eva. He scooped up the Omnipod before she could grab it.

Eva jumped up. "Give that back! It doesn't belong to you!" She pointed at the device.

"Bluh," burped the creature, and pocketed the Omnipod.

Eva scrunched her nose at the sour stench that reeked from its mouth. "Oh, you're disgusting!" She fanned her face with her hands. "What are you drinking?"

"Bluh, napana." The creature turned and walked away from her, taking a last swig. He threw the empty bottle onto the ground before reentering his Sanctuary.

"Wait! I need my Omnipod! That's mine!" cried Eva. Without turning to acknowledge her pleas, the creature slipped back down the stairs into the gloom.

"How am I supposed to make a fire?" she yelled. Fuming, Eva paced around the entryway. "I am not going down there!"

He'll kill me, she thought. *He'll eat me and take my jackvest.*

"Ugh! What am I going to do?" She moaned. "I can't find my way back to my Sanctuary without the Omnipod."

I could wait until he's sleeping, then steal it back.

"No, that won't work. Who knows *when* he sleeps? Who knows *what* he even is? It's not like anyone is here to tell me!"

From the forest the whip-crack of another weeping bird-catcher could be heard as it caught breakfast.

Eva stopped, scanning the line of trees. Far off, she could still make out the faint wisp of smoke streaming up into the late morning haze. She looked back at the corroded old Sanctuary entrance. "Dumb Omnipod," she muttered, and stormed off toward her home.

"I wonder what Muthr will think when she finally calls me and that thing answers," she mused. "She'll say, 'Hi, Eva, dear. Are you still alive?' and she'll get, 'Blaaga, blaaga, blaaga!' on the other end. It serves her right for not bringing me up here sooner." Eva crossed her arms as she approached the edge of the forest. Here the moss grew in wide mats covering the forest floor and over the trunks of the nonmoving trees. Broken beams of sunlight greeted all sorts of unusual growths rising out of the ground.

As she looked up at the dangling branches of a bird-catcher, Eva skirted the base of the vicious tree. Above, she could hear the call of the birds, but could not see them through the swaying jigsaw canopy. A neighboring tree snapped its thick tendrils up, capturing its prey. Startled, Eva stumbled into a large rounded pink shrub covered in thin dew-tipped stalks.

"Eww, what is this?" She tried to pull her hand free from the plant's sticky grip, but her arm became entrapped. Gluey globs adhered to her legs and feet. Eva kicked at the numerous stalks, but soon became a gummy mass on the shrub. She looked over her shoulder. Next to her were the remains of another hapless trapped creature. Its skin was now transparent, revealing the skeleton within. All of its other organs were gone.

"Ovanda!" She yelled the words that the mysterious creature had said to her. "Ovanda tateel! Help me, please!"

The forest remained silent. Panic overtook Eva and she began thrashing about, trying to wriggle free. "Tateel! Ovanda! Help!" Eva yelled and struggled until her throat was raw and she was completely immobilized. She soon became exhausted—barely able to lift her head to see who—or what—was making the footsteps that approached.

Eva recognized the lanky legs of the creature from the old Sanctuary. He now wore a wide-brimmed hat that shadowed his face. A hefty, cumbersome rucksack was strapped to his narrow shoulders. Numerous items hung from it, jingling with each step. The creature stopped and leaned on a carved walking stick. He snorted at the girl.

"Ovanda tateel! Please help me!" implored Eva in a hoarse voice. "You can keep my Omnipod. Just get me out of here." She could feel a burning sensation on the tops of her hands where the glistening tips of the plant held her tight.

The creature reached into a pocket on his rucksack and unsheathed a small sickle-shaped knife. He leaned down and severed the base stalks of the sticky plant clinging to Eva. She fell to the forest floor and rolled about trying to break free.

"Dat, dat, dat." He uncorked another bottle of his foul beverage and poured it on Eva's hands. The drink immediately dissolved the glue-tipped stalks and stopped the burning. He drenched the girl with more liquid from the bottle as she clawed her way free.

"Thanks," she panted. "Thank you."

He swallowed the remaining contents of the bottle and stood up, dusting himself off. "Beeta sa feezi," the creature said with a chuckle. Suddenly he dropped the empty bottle and froze, his gaze fixed behind Eva Nine.

"Daff effu Cærulean?" whispered a low guttural voice. A large silhouette crept from the under-growth and covered Eva in shadow. As she stifled a gasp, she recognized the familiar burly shape of last night's dark intruder towering over her. Its hum-ming weapon was pointed at the other creature's narrow blue head. With a low *woom* sound a short blast of vibration blew the lanky creature backward, where he landed on the ground, unmoving.

CHAPTER 9: SLICE

Eva opened
her eyes. She felt like her head was going to explode. Even her lungs were having a hard time keeping-ing enough air in them. Her right foot was worse. She couldn't feel it, or much of her right leg for that matter. She knew that when—or if—she got out of this, she was going to be sore for a long time. Her mind fuzzy, she tried to recall how she'd gotten into this predicament. . . .

With weapon in hand, the intruder had forced Eva back to its camp deep in the forest. She had hardly been able to take in the menagerie of creatures trapped there, when the brute had indicated that she should remove her satchel and jackvest. It had then thrown them onto a mountainous heap of loot.

After flopping the lanky blue creature off its shoulder and onto the ground, the intruder had

tied a noose around Eva's right foot and yanked her up into a tree, so that she was hanging upside down. As she'd swayed from a high bough, Eva's fingertips had dangled a meter off the forest floor. The swinging had slowed, and then she'd watched the intruder string up the other creature. Then, dizzy, she'd blacked out. . . .

Now conscious, she took in details of the camp from her flipped perspective.

The large campsite was set in a tree-lined glade, its perimeter ringed with tall poles, each with a variety of unlit lanterns. The long afternoon shadows pointed to the center of camp, where the pilfered loot was heaped. Parked next to the stolen goods was some sort of wavy-winged glider—large enough to carry the intruder.

A cacophony started as Eva scanned the area. The sounds came from the collection of animals and mobile plants that were trapped in all manner of ways around the camp. Large clear containers, very similar to the bins in her Sanctuary that had stored nutriment capsules, held a diverse assortment of bizarre insects. A pair of grounded birds flapped their finlike wings, trying to flee; like Eva, they were snared with a noose tight around their feet.

He is a huntsman, thought Eva. *These animals are his game. I am his game.*

On the far side of the huntsman's camp was his largest captive—an enormous six-legged behemoth with a rust-colored armored shell. Its shape reminded Eva of the holograms she had seen of sow bugs, albeit a mammoth-size sow bug. The behemoth was calling out in melancholy bellows that echoed throughout the forest. It too seemed to be fixed in place.

Eva was transfixed by the sheer size of the armored animal, and she soon realized that there were two—the smaller of which was hidden alongside the larger one. The huntsman appeared, stepping between the pair, his weapon now replaced with a long pointed lance.

The huntsman's wide, hulking shape was covered in bristly coarse hairs patterned in varying shades of gray—almost as if dappled light from the treetops were shadowing him. His cobby tapered head held two deep-set, piercing yellow eyes. His cold stare brought to mind the holograms Eva had seen of owls, or even certain types of dinosaurs. Strapped over one of his many broad appendages was an unusual haversack with electrical wires running to the back handle of the lance.

He traced his talons down the side of the larger behemoth, stopping to face both animals. Eva could hear the familiar humming sound as the huntsman's lance charged. The pair of armored animals shifted about nervously.

"Tuda neem," said the huntsman, placing the tip of the lance between the smaller one's bulbous eyes. He pressed the trigger. The animal let out a gagging cough and slumped to the ground.

The large survivor let out a long, mournful wail.

Eva clamped her dirty hands over her mouth, stifling a cry of shock. Her lashes gummed up as she continued watching.

With powerful arms the huntsman grabbed the slain animal by the legs and rolled it onto its back. After hopping on top of it, he removed the beast's head with one stroke of his humming lance. Viscous clear liquid drained from the body and stained the soil blue as it soaked into the ground.

Eva focused her vision on the burly huntsman as he began to slice the slain animal into large pieces with surgical precision. She wanted to close her eyes, but somehow she could not stop watching, mesmerized at how the humming sonic lance carved the flesh so effortlessly. It reminded her of Muthr cutting up spinach the night prior.

The huntsman flayed off the thick armored skin, peeling it away as though it were a wet blanket. Then he began carving the meat within. The thick, fatty flesh was tinged pink and was jiggly, like gelatin. He reached down, deep inside the chest cavity, and pulled out one of the creature's organs with his talons. He dropped the organ, what looked like a large dark cluster of grapes, into his toothy maw and gulped it down with relish. Eva closed her eyes as her stomach lurched.

The surviving armored behemoth pulled hard against its bind, which Eva could see was around one of its massive feet, and wailed again.

"Kap und gabbo. . . . Ta, broog iffa yu nabba," the huntsman mused in a soft tone.

"Oeeah. Te banga nee peezil," whispered a gruff voice next to Eva. The blue lanky creature had awakened and was pointing to the slaughtered animal.

"You're not dead!" Eva squealed, happy to see the creature alive. She pointed at the huntsman. "This monster is holding us both prisoner. We've got to figure a way out of here." With renewed vigor Eva tried lifting herself up to grab the snare around her foot. Unable to reach it, she flopped back so that she was upside down again.

"Dot, dat." The creature waved his thick finger

at Eva in a negative manner. Kicking with his free leg, he began to swing. Soon he swung faster and faster in growing arcs. Eva realized what he was doing and started doing the same. The creaking of the boughs above was smothered by the din of the other noisy captives. In moments the two crashed into each other. Eva clutched the worn jacket of the lanky creature tightly. She tried to ignore the sour stench coming from his mouth.

The huntsman stopped cutting for a moment, cocked his head, and listened.

Eva held her breath.

The huntsman returned to his grisly task, his back still turned to Eva and her companion.

"Peesa van shuuzu," said the lanky creature as he moved his hand in an upward motion toward the snare.

Eva tried to focus on what he was saying, despite the fact that her head was pounding. "I don't know what you mean," she whispered.

"Peesa," he said, repeating the gesture.

She pointed. "Up? You want to go up?"

"Ta! Ta!" He nodded. "Peesa."

"I tried that already, but I can't lift myself. I'm too—"

With great effort the creature grabbed Eva by

the waist and lifted her ever so slightly. As he did so, she could feel the tension of the snare loosen around her ankle.

"Pra! Dooma boffa!" the huntsman said as he slapped the face of the surviving armored animal. It shuffled backward, grunting in a miserable tone.

Eva and her fellow prisoner froze. She could feel that the snare had moved and was now wrapped around her sneakboot toe and no longer around her ankle.

"Peesa. Do it again," she whispered, and pointed up. Once again the blue creature lifted her up. This time Eva wriggled her foot inside her boot, causing her foot to slip out of the boot. She flipped down and fell to the ground with a soft thud.

As she lay on the forest floor, Eva could feel pins and needles as blood rushed back into her legs. She watched the huntsman sing to himself as he set his lance down and began sorting the slabs of meat. As the pain in her head subsided, she crawled below the lanky creature and tried to lift him.

"Dat, dat, dat." He pointed up toward his bare foot. Just below his thick, calloused toes a dark purple bruise ran around his ankle where the vine noose held him fast. "Te," he said, pointing to the pile of loot in the center of camp. Eva looked at the busy huntsman just beyond it, then back to the lanky creature. He was nodding, still pointing at the heap.

"What?" she whispered. "What do you want me to get?"

He responded by pantomiming one hand cutting his arm.

"Hit? Chop? What?"

He repeated the gesture once more.

"I don't know what you mean. You want me to cut your arm? Wait . . . cut! A knife?" Eva said. Her eyes got big. "*Your* knife! In your backpack!" She repeated his pantomime.

The creature nodded, grinning.

"Got it," she whispered. Ducking down, Eva soon found that her shoeless foot was numb and sore from having been snared. On hands and knees she scuttled over to the heaping pile of loot and sidled up next to the creature's large rucksack. With nimble fingers she opened up the pocket where the sickle-shaped knife was. In the pouch next to it was the unmistakable outline of her Omnipod.

Eva pulled it out and smiled.

Carefully she grabbed her satchel and jackvest from the mound of loot, her eyes screwed to the hairy thickset back of the huntsman all the while. As she turned to go, she spied a small item half-buried in the odd collection of spoils. She plucked out a small bright yellow component and read its label. "T6D9 Centurion Power Cell" was stamped in blocky letters on its dented side. Eva tucked the item into her satchel and rechecked the huntsman's whereabouts. He was still occupied with his meat carving, so Eva scooted back to help her lanky companion, undetected.

Little one.

A gentle voice wafted into Eva's thoughts, like old recordings she'd heard of songs. She looked around. *Is there someone else here? The air-whale?* Eva wondered as she scanned the area. The engrossed huntsman was now dressing his meat, while the collection of desperate birds bit at their binds. Her companion swayed, upside down and silent as he awaited Eva's return.

She scampered back and handed the knife to him. As he took it, the creature pointed to the woods behind him and whispered, "Tasha, zaata."

"No." Eva kept a wary eye on the busy huntsman. She shuddered at the thought of him chasing her through the woods again. *How can I escape him in the daylight? He's not going to chase after pellets again.* An idea tickled the back of her brain. She held up the Omnipod. "I'll help you. But you've got to help me, okay?"

"Bluh, sizzu feezi," replied the creature, rolling his eyes.

Finished with his butchering, the huntsman grabbed several large steaks and turned around, heading toward his glider. As he glanced up, he discovered that only one of his prisoners was left, hanging next to a lone sneakboot.

"Feezi meed!" he roared, throwing the meat down and grabbing his lance. "Ya battee meer de hagrim Ruzender. Wha seesha?"

High atop the tree with the snares, Eva could hear the huntsman shouting as he neared. She breathed into the Omnipod, "This is Eva Nine. Initiate Gym Buddy. Warm up to begin in fifteen seconds."

"Initiating in fifteen seconds," the device replied. "Fifteen . . . fourteen . . . thirteen . . . twelve . . ."

Eva hurled the Omnipod as far as she could out into the forest. The metal device went much farther than the little pellets had the night before. It landed out in the distance, spooking a gaggle of noisy birds. The huntsman dashed past the lanky prisoner, surveying the woods. Eva held her breath, counting silently.

Five . . . four . . . three . . . two . . .

"Who's ready to warm up with some jumping jacks?" piped a far-off voice.

The huntsman tore off after the decoy, ripping through the undergrowth. Eva climbed down the tree just as her companion stood up, balanced on one foot, knife in hand. The two of them hop-dashed toward the loot pile, where she helped him grab his things.

Little one.

Eva spun around, her heart fluttering. She shivered as a wave of hairs on her neck stood up. *Is there someone hiding here in the afternoon shadows?* The armored behemoth made a low groan, and Eva turned to look at him.

Little one. Help.

Eva gasped.

Help.

She stepped past the butchered carcass and approached the giant animal. Light-headed, Eva stared into its large protruding eyes. She could *feel* that the behemoth was not just gazing at her. Somehow, it *understood* her.

Free. Me.

She heard the song of its voice drift into her mind. Eva placed her pale palm flat on the behemoth's forehead between its bulging eyes. Its rust-colored skin was warm and pebbly, like it had been cast from the ground she had been trekking across. She felt a oneness with the animal, sensing its strength . . . its sorrow . . . its fear.

"Grazeet!" The lanky blue creature grabbed handfuls of stolen items and pushed them into his overstuffed rucksack. "Zaata! Zaata! Zaata!" he shouted.

I am sorry for your friend, she thought to the armored animal. *What can I do?*

The behemoth began to shuffle its six feet. It tugged forward against its binds.

Must. Get. Free.

Eva could hear her lanky companion approach her, but his voice sounded distant and muffled. The blue creature put his large hand on her shoulder and pointed to the forest excitedly. Nervously.

Hurry.

Ignoring her companion, Eva walked over to the behemoth's back leg. The pillar-size limb shadowed her as she knelt down and examined the snare that held it. Like her binds, it was simply a noose that was now pulled so tightly that it had cut the thick skin. The ground underneath it had become dark mud from the weeping wound.

Back, Eva thought to it, *step back.*

Hurry. Free.

Giving up on Eva, the lanky creature escaped into the woods. Still entranced, Eva put her hand flat on the behemoth's leg. It was thicker than her entire body.

You have to step backward, she thought. *Do you understand? Walk backward.*

Still the armored animal did not move in the right direction. Eva could hear the snare tightening around its foot. It let out another low bellow.

Call. Others. Free. Now.

Eva ran back around to face the animal and put both hands on its forehead. She began pushing it. *Back up,* she thought to it. *Move backward!*

Free.

Come on. She closed her eyes. *Please just move back and you'll be free.*

Others. Free. Run.

"Move!" yelled Eva. "You have to move back!"

The behemoth stopped. It started shambling backward. The tension on the snare around its foot loosened. Losing her balance, Eva tripped as she pushed, and fell flat on her stomach. Disoriented, she snapped out of her trance, and looked up.

On the opposite side of the campsite, the huntsman reappeared from the forest. He threw down the Omnipod and bolted straight toward Eva Nine.

CHAPTER 10: RUN

assa Ruzender Keet!" The huntsman leaped over the loot pile toward Eva.

Eva scrambled to her feet.

Run. Hurry. Free.

She dashed around the backside of the armored animal. As quick as lightning, the huntsman was on top of the behemoth's plated back, lance in hand as he searched for his quarry. Eva dropped, crawling between the massive legs under the animal's girth. Ducking under its thick, fan-shaped tail, which was tucked and hidden under its belly,

she grabbed the now loosened noose and pulled it off the behemoth's bloodied foot.

You're free now, she thought to it.

"Tista baffa fooh!" shouted the huntsman over the behemoth's bellows. He squeezed a lever and the lance began to charge, its hum growing loud.

Eva heard a loud *BOOM.*

She put her hands over her head, waiting for the weight of the dead behemoth to crush her—but the animal did not fall.

Instead she heard a familiar voice: "Ovanda say tateel?"

Eva opened her eyes and met the gaze of her lanky blue companion. He was kneeling down alongside the armored animal, his hand out-stretched. As he pulled Eva out from underneath the behemoth, she saw that he had the hunts-man's other weapon—the sonic rifle used on Eva's Sanctuary—in his other hand.

"Gabu Baasteel!" The creature spat, throwing the rifle down to the ground. He pointed up toward the orange sky. Eva saw that the sun was setting in the murky cloud cover.

The lanky creature hopped around the camp, cutting the snares of the other captives and free-ing the contained insects.

Eva walked over to the stunned and fallen huntsman. His massive arms were limp as he lay on his side breathing in a slow rhythm next to the carcass of the butchered animal. She felt a nudge from behind and a now familiar song in her mind.

Am. Free. Little one.

Eva's gaze traveled to the severed head of the slain animal. Its lifeless open eyes had clouded over and its beaked mouth was slightly agape. Flies danced on the dried white saliva that was caked on its chin and barbels.

Run. Free.

Yes, Eva thought back, *we must run . . . or . . .* She looked at the lance lying on the ground next to her feet. It was a thin ivory rod, much longer than the huntsman's rifle, and had a dark lever mounted at its midsection. The coiled electrical cables were tangled around one of the huntsman's legs. As she studied the bloodied tip, Eva thought about how easily it had cut through thick flesh. She thought about the knives in the kitchen and how they were tools.

Simply tools.

Now her kitchen had been destroyed and an innocent animal had been slain. She bent down to grab the lance.

No. Little one. Free.

"Feezi!" her lanky companion yelled. "Zaata! Zaata!" He pointed to the woods with his hat. With his walking stick as a crutch, he hopped toward her, grunting from the effort. Eva saw that his discolored foot was swollen and raised in such a manner that he could not put any pressure on it.

"Let me help you," she said.

"Dat, dat, dat," the creature said, shaking his head. Once again he pointed into the woods. "Feezi zaata." He turned and pointed in the opposite direction and said, "Ruzender zaata."

"No." Eva picked her Omnipod up from the ground. "You won't make it. And I don't know where I am. You said you'd help."

"Bluh," the creature said with a sigh, and threw up his hands.

A groan came from the huntsman's direction.

"Oh, no!" cried Eva. "He's waking up. Let's zap him again." She scanned the site for the sonic rifle. It was lying on the ground near the heap of loot. The behemoth let out a low hoot.

Free. Now. Run.

Eva looked over at it. The animal regarded her, hooting again.

I take. You.

"Zaata! Zaata! Zaata!" The lanky creature ambled over toward the rifle.

"Wait!" Eva said.

I take. You. I take. Him.

She nodded at the behemoth, then looked over at her companion. Balancing on his good foot, the lanky creature knelt down and grabbed the rifle. Eva heard a distinct hum as he started to charge it.

Groggy, the waking huntsman sat up, his lemon eyes blinking rapidly. "Grasset de fugill Ruzender!" he bellowed.

"No!" Eva ran over to support her companion. "Use me as a crutch."

The bristling huntsman grabbed his lance. He pulled himself up, charging his weapon.

Hurry. Little one.

The lanky creature aimed the humming rifle at the huntsman as he and Eva stumbled toward the armored behemoth.

Get. On. Little one.

The huntsman was now on his feet, snorting loudly. The combined charging hum of both weapons rose to a grating pitch.

"We'll make it," Eva said as they reached the behemoth. It knelt low to the ground, and she grabbed on to the armored plating, pulling herself up.

"Come on! Hurry!" she shouted with her hand held out.

With an unsteady aim the huntsman pointed the lance at them as the lanky creature climbed up. The humming was so loud now that it vibrated Eva's entire body. She ignored the noise as she helped her lame companion scramble up onto their mount's armored back. The lanky creature fired the rifle. It was so charged that it kicked out of the creature's hands and its blast toppled a stack of cages behind the huntsman.

Jump. Free. Hurry.

"Go!" screamed Eva.

The huntsman released the lever on the sonic lance. The intense sound wave was so loud that it rocked the surrounding forest. The huntsman's lanterns exploded, and several trees in the line of fire were reduced to heaps of green shredded pulp.

Eva's eyes watered, and long tears streaked backward over her cheeks as cool wind buffeted her face. The behemoth descended through the dusky light in a gigantic leap, like a humungous grasshopper. Though Eva was holding on to the animal for dear life, she had a giddy smile on her face.

Despite its immense size, the armored animal

landed gracefully in a clearing and tucked its thick, fanlike tail underneath its body.

Free. Jump. Again.

"Hold on!" she said to her lanky companion saddled alongside her on the animal's back. With a feeble grin he held tightly on to the behemoth's armored plates.

With tremendous force the animal snapped down its tail, sending them all soaring up into the sky. Birds and other flying creatures flapped about, screeching from the disturbance. The behemoth arced over a copse of wandering trees and landed more than a hundred meters away. In moments the trio had cleared the woods completely and now found themselves on the rocky plain right at the forest's edge.

Safe. Now. Little one.

"We did it!" Eva threw her arms around her companion.

"Ewa seetha tadasha," he replied, patting her on the back. He let out a long sigh of relief, and pulled a bottle out of his rucksack. After uncorking the top, he offered a drink to Eva.

"Um. No, thanks." Eva could smell the curdled scent wafting out of the bottle.

Her companion shrugged and took a swig, and then smacked his lips in delight. "Ta! Feezi!" He held up one finger as an idea dawned on him. "Zuzu, zuzu," he mumbled as he rummaged around through his rucksack. Eva realized that their armored mount was quiet, grazing on the lichens that grew along the forest edge.

Thank you, she thought to it, watching twilight soak the landscape. *Is it time to join your others?*

Not now. Quiet. Rest.

"You've been through a lot." Eva slid off the back of the animal. "We all have."

"Oeeah!" The lanky creature found what it had been searching for. He dismounted, joined Eva on the mossy ground, and reached for her hand. Into her palm he dropped a heavy metallic ball. "Kip!" he said.

Eva inspected the object, furrowing her brow. She glanced back up at her companion.

"Kip! Kip!" he repeated, pointing to his whiskery throat.

"What? Do you want me to eat this?" Eva weighed the sphere in her hand. "I don't think I can eat metal."

"Dat, dat, dat, feezi," said the creature, moving Eva's hand with the ball closer to her mouth. "Doot, doot . . . ba kip!"

"Talk?" Eva said. As she spoke, the ball lit up in a

pattern of tiny micro-lights. "Wow. What is this?"
She watched the illuminated pattern dance across
the small device. A miniscule cloud puffed out of
a tiny pinhole at the top of it. Eva moved it away
from her face. "What's it doing?"

"Dat," whispered her companion. "Peesa tobondi
feezi, ta kipli." He moved Eva's hand back to her
face, the dust cloud drifting toward her. He sat
back and inhaled deeply, then pointed to Eva.

"You . . . you want me to breathe this dust in?"
Eva grimaced. "I . . . I don't know. Thanks anyway,"
she said, handing the ball back.

Shaking his head, the creature muttered, and
blew the dust into Eva's face.

"Ugh!" She coughed repeatedly. "What are you
doing? Are you trying to kill me?" She could taste
metal in her throat and feel it in her sinuses.

The creature sat back and chuckled.

"Oh, it's funny, is it?" Eva threw the metallic
sphere at him. "Well, you can just keep your stupid
glow ball! I have to get back to my wrecked home
now." She walked away in a huff.

"Tes, continue kipping," said the creature.

"Wait a second!" Eva stopped, turning back in
his direction. "Did you just say 'continue'?"

"Zazig. I try to peebla foo," her companion said,

picking up the ball. It was speckled in wondrous tiny lights.

Eva took it back, mesmerized. "You—you want me to talk more, don't you?"

"Yes, continue kipping," he answered with a toothy grin.

Eva blinked in astonishment as she put it all together. "You want me to talk into this ball, right? Because it is recording my voice, and if I do—" The sphere chirped and startled Eva, who dropped it to the ground.

"If you do," repeated the creature, picking her sphere up again, "you hret graaveem my speech."

"It's a translator! I get it! It allows you to understand what I am saying." Eva squealed with joy as she grabbed it.

"Understand." The creature nodded. "Geefa. I now understand." He opened his other hand. It held an identical device, also aglow with numerous tiny lights.

The cerulean creature with backward-bending legs held up his palm. "I am Rovender Kitt, an old creature in a new world."

"I am Eva . . . Eva Nine," said Eva with a smile, mimicking his gesture. "I am a new creature in an old world."

End of
PART I

PART II

So the weird-

tasting dust, that's what's allowing me to understand you?" Eva Nine had been hiking behind Rovender as they journeyed along the forest edge. She carried her remaining sneakboot in her hand.

"Yes, yes. The 'dust' is actually tiny transmitters. They send the signal to the ball, the vocal transcoder, which I gave you," Rovender answered. He hobbled along through the muted moonlight as if he were searching for something. "Most everyone has one. Keep that transcoder near you at all times, and you'll understand whomever you encounter."

"Wow. Everyone, huh? Can I talk to the trees with it?" Eva looked at the tiny transcoder, excited.

"Don't be ridiculous," Rovender said. "Everyone knows that the trees here speak a language only they understand." He squatted down on his good foot and inspected a clump of moss growing on the twisted roots of an immense tree. He pinched off a sprig and brushed it over his nose, which Eva could see was nothing more than a pattern of pores on his narrow snout. "Let us stop here for a few moments," he said.

Rovender pulled off his rucksack and eased down into a sitting position under the tree. Eva flopped down on the padded ground next to him.

"So, who was that big scary guy? Why is he after us?" she asked. Still a bit shaken from her escape, Eva was nonetheless excited to be speaking with another living being that was not a hologram or a robot.

"Ah, the Dorcean?" Rovender yanked up a handful of the moss. "His name is Besteel. He claims he hunts for the queen. He's a ruffian and a thug as far as I'm concerned." Rovender paused. He raised his ragged ear as he listened to the forest's nocturnal sounds. His ear dropped and he returned to his task of gathering moss.

"Why did he destroy my home? Why is he hunting us?" Eva furrowed her brow. She shuddered at the memory of Besteel eating the organs of the slain animal.

"Us? I don't know if he's after *us*, Eva Nine." Rovender shook the dirt from the clutching roots of the moss. "I believe he's after *you*. For some reason he thought I was luring you away from him."

Eva let out an incredulous gasp. "After me! What?" Her eyes went big. "I didn't do anything to him! This doesn't make sense."

"I wish I could tell you more," Rovender said as he opened up his rucksack. "But there is nothing more to tell. Besteel is not one to disclose such things."

Eva turned away. She could feel that coil of dread slither down and settle in her stomach. Disregarding it, she watched as the armored behemoth approached them at a slow, steady gait.

Rovender glanced up from rummaging through the belongings in his pack. "I think you have a new friend," he observed.

"Oh, Otto?" Eva said, smiling at the behemoth. "He told me he's watching over me in return for setting him free."

"Ot-to? Told?" Rovender blinked in astonishment. "Does he speak to you?"

"Oh, yes. Can't you hear him?" Eva fanned her ears with her hands. "His voice is like a soothing song in my head."

"I cannot. But *he* told *you* his name was Otto?" Rovender eyed her, seemingly suspicious. He pulled out a ball of twine from his rucksack.

"Naw, I named him that," Eva said with a smile. She gazed over at Otto as he scratched his ear with his back paw. "I have always wanted a real, living pet, and now I have one."

"A pet! That?" Rovender exclaimed. "Eva Nine, I have heard stories of beasts telepathically imprinting onto others—like wild dargs becoming tame for frint farmers—but what you call a 'tardigrade' is no pet."

"I didn't call him that. I told you that's what the Omnipod identified him as: a species of tardigrade, also known as a 'water bear.'" Eva waved the Omnipod at Rovender for emphasis. *It also said water bears are microscopic,* she thought. *Why is everything so gargantuan? Have I somehow shrunk in size?* She dropped the Omnipod back into her satchel and pulled out a handful of nutriment pellets.

"Well, Otto should return to his herd. He'll be safer there." Rovender grabbed a bottle from his pack of belongings.

"I told him he could leave, but he refused," Eva said, popping the pellets into her mouth, like candy. They tasted like potatoes. She glanced back over at Otto, who was now cleaning his wounded foot. Eva continued, "He said he was separated from his herd, and they have moved on, far away from here."

"Bluh, so you say. He should leave anyway. Besteel will easily track you otherwise," Rovender said as he unwound a length of the twine. It spooled down next to the gathered moss and the bottle that lay near his swollen ankle. Eva could see that Besteel's snare had left a raw, open lesion cutting through Rovender's thick calloused skin.

"Are you going to make a fire?" She picked up a clump of moss. "I can help."

"A fire? No." Rovender took the moss from Eva and set it on his wound. "I need my ankle to heal so that I may lead you back to your home, and continue on my way." He uncorked the bottle. Eva saw Rovender wince as he soaked the moss, letting the cloudy liquid run over the cut on his ankle. After blowing on the wound to lessen the sting, he took a drink and grabbed the length of twine. He began wrapping it around the makeshift dressing.

"Um, I think there's probably a better way to tend to that injury," Eva remarked. She watched him lean over and cut the twine with his peg teeth, finishing with an elaborate knot to hold the dressing in place.

"I am fine, Eva Nine. This will do." Rovender admired his handiwork.

"Hold on." Eva pulled out her Omnipod. "This is Eva Nine. Initiate IMA," she said.

The device flickered on. "Individual Medical Assistance initiated. Is this an emergency?" it asked.

"Ha! I remembered it!" said Eva, grinning. "Now I've got to figure out how you do the rest of this." She scanned through a few menus within the program. "Hmmm . . . It's not an emergency. . . . I just want to add a new patient."

Rovender settled back and grabbed a pouch full of seedpods from his pack. He offered some to Eva.

"Naw, I'm okay." She continued fiddling with the program. "Aha! Here it is! New patient registration. Maybe I can figure out how to heal your foot."

"Don't worry, Eva Nine," said Rovender. "Really, I will be fine." He wriggled his toes. Eva ignored him, focusing on the Omnipod. Rovender dropped a handful of seeds into his mouth.

"New patient," Eva said to the Omnipod. "Name: Kitt, Rovender. Age: uh . . . How old are you?"

"Almost eight trilustralis," he answered, spitting seed husks out of the side of his mouth.

"Trila . . . How do you spell? Wait, how long is that?"

"Ah, there must be no word for it in your language. You see, if the transcoder cannot find a suitable translation, it will use a similar word from your root language, whatever that may be," Rovender explained.

Eva stared at him, confused.

"Never mind," he continued. "The celestial time

for my clan must be recorded differently than it is for yours. I am not sure what moon and star cycles your clan uses, but our trilustralian cycle is the same one that our ancestors used for generations."

Eva set the Omnipod down. "Isn't your home in that old Sanctuary where I . . . um, *met* you today?"

"That abandoned cave?" Rovender spit the rest of the husks out. "That was just shelter for the night. No, my home was quite far from here."

Eva looked out into the night. She didn't feel as vulnerable and scared as she had during the day. In the dark, things appeared closer. Cozy. More comfortable. And now she was no longer alone, just like in the picture on the WondLa. She thought of Muthr. "Do you have a family back home, Rovender?"

"A family?" He took a drink, swallowing audibly. "No family. Not anymore." Rovender's voice sounded distant. Lonely.

Eva sat quietly for a moment. She didn't want to pry and upset him, or give reason for him to abandon her again. "I never had a family," she said softly, watching Otto. "I always wanted one—but I never got one."

"Then you are lucky, Eva Nine." Rovender gathered his things and stood, pulling his rucksack back over his shoulders. "Come. It is time to go."

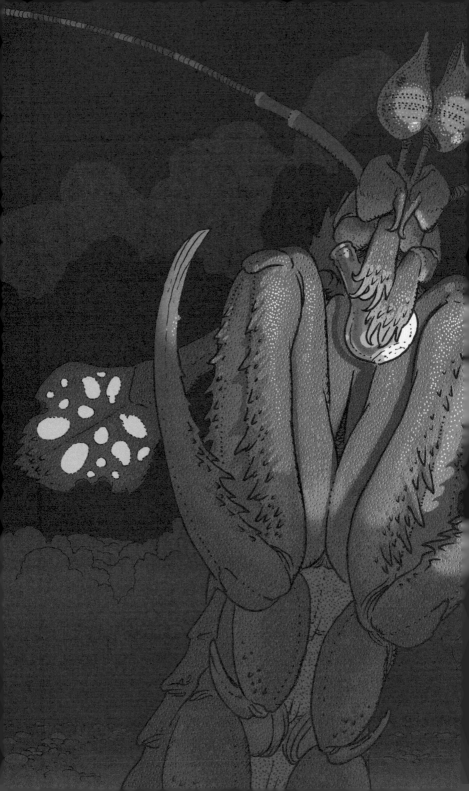

CHAPTER 12: SAND-SNIPERS

We need to

go that way." Eva stood at the forest edge, pointing across the plain. She could no longer see the line of trees on the opposite side, for the crescent moon was now hiding behind thick clouds, soaking the world in blackness. However, the Omnipod softly illuminated her face, and Rovender's, as it displayed a detailed map of the surrounding area. A blinking dot indicated where her Sanctuary was located.

The Omnipod drew an arrow on the map. "Walking at a leisurely pace," it said, "you should arrive at your destination in approximately one hour and thirty-seven minutes."

"If we can get to Muthr, she can help us find the others," Eva said, tracing the holographic trail on the Omnipod with her finger.

"Us?" Rovender broke his gaze from the device. "I will lead you back to your home. From there I must bid you farewell, Eva Nine."

"But we escaped together." She looked up from the Omnipod. "I thought we were friends."

"Indeed that was a bit of excitement this afternoon," Rovender said, placing his hand on Eva's shoulder. "And I am richer for our paths crossing, but my journey continues in a different direction from yours."

"Is it because of Besteel?"

"No," Rovender said. "But when we split up, he will no longer be able to track us as easily. Which is good for us all, Otto included."

Eva studied his face as best she could in the pale glow of the Omnipod; however, like Muthr, he appeared stoic.

"Okay, then. Fine. Let's go. I'm sure Muthr is waiting for me." She started across the dark flat field of gravel and stone.

Rovender grabbed her arm. "No, no, no," he said. "We cannot travel over this ground." Otto clucked in approval.

Eva scoffed. "Why not? I 'traveled' all over it today."

"This dried riverbed is thick with sand-snipers," he declared.

Eva stared at Rovender for a beat. She put the Omnipod near his mouth. "Sand-what? Can you repeat that?" she asked.

Rovender pushed the device away. "Sand-snipers are vicious carnivores that live underground in deep tunnels. They mostly hunt at night and use surface vibration to capture their prey."

"I saw a pit today. I wonder if one lived there?" Eva thought back to the mysterious hole, its entrance surrounded by unusual ivory-colored rocks and branches. . . . Perhaps they had not been rocks after all.

Tunnel biters. Yes. Look.

Otto's words drifted into the girl's head.

"Otto tells me there's one out there now," Eva said as she scanned the dark landscape. She saw nothing.

"Really? He *tells* you more things, does he?" Rovender cocked his head at the giant water bear.

"Let us see if Otto, and you, are correct." He threw his empty bottle out onto the dark plain. Eva could hear it ping as it bounced on the bumpy terrain. Suddenly a far-off pattern of wondrous blue lights emerged from the ground. The lights dashed across the open area toward the direction of the unseen bottle.

"Oeeah!" Rovender looked at Otto. "You tell the truth. Perhaps this Otto does speak to you after all."

"I told you," Eva said, crossing her arms.

The bioluminescent markings did little to reveal the shape of the sand-sniper, but Eva could see that the monster was big, possibly longer than Otto. Its lights shifted in color from blue to a brilliant green, and it clicked aloud as if speaking in code.

Eva aimed the Omnipod at the sand-sniper, recording its calls.

"Tell me, Eva Nine," Rovender said with a chuckle, "what is *this* monster saying to you?"

"Ha, ha—very funny." Eva bristled. "Let's get a better look at this thing," she said. With the Omnipod still aimed at the sand-sniper, she said, "Please enter lumen mode."

The Omnipod's central eye created a brilliant white beam of light that cut through the blackness straight toward the sand-sniper. Eva sucked in her breath as the light revealed the towering visage before her.

Multiple cordlike antennae crisscrossed in the center of the sand-sniper's face. Orbiting above, two large bowl eyes scanned the night, moving independent of each other. Below the confluence of antennae an array of hooked claws and bristled graspers flexed in a steady rhythm. Its snapping maw spit out Rovender's bottle and clicked in cadence.

"Eva!" Rovender scolded her. "Shut that light off!" He pushed the Omnipod down, forcing the beam to the ground.

Visibly shaken, Eva watched the sand-sniper's glowing lights diminish.

"Are you trying to get us killed?" Rovender barked. "Thank the stars they don't venture into the woods. We'd be done for."

"I'm . . . I'm sorry." Eva said, still in shock. "I had no idea."

"No idea? How is it that you do not know of these fiends?" Rovender said, aghast. "I have encountered several here on these grounds. *These grounds* that surround where you say your home lies."

Eva shut the Omnipod off. "I . . . I have never

been up here on these grounds before. Ever."

"Up?" Rovender cocked his head, studying the girl. "You mean to say you have just hatched?"

"Hatched?" Eva raised an eyebrow at him. "No. I didn't *just hatch*. I don't even hatch. I'm twelve. I live in an underground home, a Sanctuary—just like the one you were camping in."

"Unbelievable," Rovender replied, rubbing his whiskered beard.

The moon had reappeared through the cloud cover, illuminating the world with an eerie, dim smile. Eva saw no sign of the sand-sniper.

Otto spoke to her. *You. Home. Come.* He stepped out onto the open plain.

But what about the sand monster? The tunnel biter? Eva thought to him.

Not hurt. Me. Ride.

"He wants us to get on," Eva said to Rovender. She grabbed on to one of Otto's massive armored scutes and pulled herself up. Looking down at Rovender, she continued, "He says the sand monsters won't bother him."

"Does he?" Rovender examined the giant water bear, still rubbing his beard.

"Yes, he does." Eva enjoyed knowing something Rovender didn't.

At last he nodded and climbed up. "Very well. I will trust what he tells you. Ask him to follow the forest edge, so that we may still hide if necessary."

Otto began shuffling along the edge of the open plain. Rovender pulled out another handful of seeds and dropped them into his mouth. "This may be a good idea, Eva. I am tired, and my foot could use the rest. However, we must still keep a wary eye out for Besteel."

"Besteel? Will he find us?" Eva scanned the darkness, wondering what else was lurking around out there. Hunting.

"Perhaps." Rovender spit seed husks out to the

ground below. "The Dorceans are very skilled hunters and trackers. Is your home well protected?"

Eva looked down at her hands in the pale moonlight. Her nail polish was mostly chipped off—replaced by dirt and grime. "Our home? No. He broke in and destroyed it last night."

Rovender studied Eva, chewing. "'Our'? Are there others who live with you?"

"No. Just Muthr—my caretaker. But she's just a robot. She's not real."

"Like the light images that come from your device?" Rovender pointed to the Omnipod.

"No, not a hologram. I mean, she's a robot . . . you know, not alive . . . like you and me." Eva felt a little flustered.

"I see," Rovender said, still watching her.

Eva stared ahead, in the direction of her Sanctuary buried in the dark woods.

I wonder if the Sanctuary is even there anymore, she thought.

I wonder how Muthr is doing. Is she looking for me?

Why does a robot take care of me? Why not another person?

Eva also wondered why she had not been taught exercises on dealing with bird-eating trees, giant water bears, and burrowing sand monsters. Or evil huntsmen.

She confessed, "You know, I had hoped that there were people like me living in these Sanctuaries. A *lot* of people like me. But I don't see any. Where are they?"

Rovender leaned in close to her. "Eva Nine, I have traveled to many lands and seen many wondrous things. A creature such as you, I have never seen."

Eva closed her eyes. She wished for all the world that she had not heard this.

We are close,

Rovender said, eyes closed as he stood on top of Otto's large plated back. Eva watched as he summoned the night air, fanning it around his face. "I can detect a smoldering scent that is neither a burned animal nor a burned plant. We should continue from here by foot." He grabbed his rucksack and dismounted.

Muthr is neither an animal nor a plant. . . . I hope she's okay, Eva thought as she slid down Otto's side to join Rovender. She felt some regret on how she had described Muthr to Rovender earlier. She flicked on her Omnipod. "This is Eva Nine. Please check for messages."

"Greetings, Eva Nine. You have no new messages—voice or otherwise," the device chirped.

I stay. Otto spoke. *I wait.*

Thanks, Otto. Eva patted him on the head.

"Come, come, come." Rovender ushered Eva into the mysterious woods. "We don't want to risk Besteel seeing us. He will likely be returning to this area."

"Returning? Why?" Eva clipped her satchel to her jackvest.

"Because he is clever." Rovender put on his heavy pack. He gazed up, scanning the cloudy midnight sky. "We may be doing the very thing he is expecting us to do—I don't know. But I would suggest you retrieve your robot mother and depart as soon as possible."

Eva followed him into the woods, using the soft radiance of the Omnipod to light her way. "She's not my mother. She just takes care of me."

Rovender chuckled. "Well, she must have her hands full. You are much to take care of, Eva Nine."

Eva fumed, saying nothing.

"So tell me, Eva," Rovender said as he wound his way through the thick trunks of moss-laden trees. "If this robot is not your mother, what became of your mother? Of your family?"

"You tell me first," Eva said, a hint of insolence in her voice.

Rovender was silent as they trekked deeper into the woods. From unseen forest-dwellers Eva could hear chortles burbling in rhythm over her footsteps.

Finally, Rovender spoke. "My life mate, my partner, became very ill when a sickness crept into our village, infecting many." Eva heard him clear his throat. "She left this world, taking our unhatched offspring with her."

Eva said nothing as she followed him through the undergrowth. *I've never really been sick before,* she thought. *I didn't know an illness could be so deadly.*

"So what about you?" Rovender paused, looking at Eva over his shoulder. "If the robot is not your mother, what became of her?"

Eva answered, her voice like a lone tinkling bell in an orchestra of nighttime noise, "I never knew my mother or my father. I've only known Muthr." She remembered the robot pushing Eva up the exhaust shaft in the kitchen just the night before.

Rovender studied Eva in the moonlight. "Let's get back to her, then, okay?"

Eva nodded in agreement.

They continued on in silence for some time, winding their way deeper and deeper into the forest. At last Rovender stopped. "I believe your home lies just ahead, Eva Nine."

A humming sound drifted down from the night sky.

The shadow of a large bird zoomed overhead.

"Sheesa!" Rovender hissed, pushing Eva into the shadows of a wandering tree. "I knew it!"

"What? What is it?" Eva's eyes went wide as she looked up through the canopy.

"It's Besteel." Rovender spit. "I should have sabotaged his glider when I had the chance. Now he is searching for us from above."

Eva could hear the hum of the glider. It was very low and distant, then it grew louder.

"He is circling," Rovender said. He craned his neck, catching a glimpse of the glider as it soared over them. "We shall let him go by again. Then we will run for it. Okay?"

"Won't he see us?" Eva rotated her sore foot, readying it.

"He can sense heat, but it is cool tonight. So if we can get underground in time, he may not detect us," Rovender answered, keeping his eyes on the dark sky. The thin moon went back to sleep behind the clouds. The sound of the glider diminished, then began to increase. "He's coming back," Rovender said, crouching in the shadow of the tree. "Get ready."

The glider whooshed by.

"Go! Now!" The two hop-dashed across a small

clearing toward the entryway of Eva's Sanctuary. As they neared, Eva tripped over the heavy ply-steel entrance door lying on the ground. Rovender yanked her inside. The two nearly toppled down the staircase that led down to Eva's home.

While she caught her breath, Eva watched Rovender inspect the sky from the cover of the battered entry-way. "Besteel is circling over once more," he reported. "Ah, good. Now he's moving on." Eva could hear the eerie hum of Besteel's glider fade away.

"We are safe for the moment," Rovender cautioned. "So we should hurry. Go, go, go."

Eva descended the staircase. She had never taken these stairs before—stairs that she had known existed, even though she was not supposed to. Below, electric lights flickered inside the control room—another place she had been forbidden to enter. Eva hesitated.

"Perhaps I should go first to make sure it is safe," Rovender said.

"No, it's okay," Eva said as she continued down the stairs. "I know where I am. Besides, you have to leave, right? Now I'm on my own?"

Rovender peered down from the top of the stair-well. "Perhaps I can, at least, help you find your robot mother."

Eva nodded. "Okay. Thanks."

With his walking stick supporting his weight, Rovender hobbled down past Eva, leading her into her Sanctuary.

The stairs ended at the back wall of an empty white control room, Muthr's quarters. Of course Eva knew of this room. Muthr had told her all about where she went at the day's end, and the Omnipod had showed the room in its entirety when Eva had viewed the omniscient floor plan— but still, she'd never been *in* this room. Expecting an arsenal of high-tech equipment, Eva found only a damaged holo-puter projecting images of the many chambers in the Sanctuary. The images flickered in an unsteady rhythm as they floated in the center of the room.

"How do you enter?" Rovender studied the locked door leading to the Sanctuary's main hub.

"Hold on," Eva said, scanning the numerous displays. In these she was able to look into each room.

Room 1: The Control Room. Eva could see the overhead view of herself and Rovender looking at the holo-images.

Room 2: The Holography Chamber. Eva could see the main projector lying on the scorched floor.

Pieces of it were scattered and submerged in puddles from the extinguishers.

Room 3: The Gymnasium. The exercise equipment was toppled and thrown about. A sizable piece of debris was lying at the bottom of the half-drained wading pool.

Room 4: The Greenhouse. This was black. The camera must not have been working for this room.

Room 5: Eva's Bedroom. This seemed the most damaged of all. Blackened and distorted clumps of the girl's possessions were melted into a sprawling heap, while cooling pipes bled water everywhere.

Eva stared at the projection in total shock. *Is everything I own gone?* She pulled her eyes from the appalling sight and continued her search for Muthr.

Room 6: The Kitchen. This was also black. Eva assumed the camera was not working here either.

Room 7: The Supply Room. This was ransacked. All the shelves were toppled, with the goods spilled out onto the floor.

Room 8: The Generator Room. The other "no access" room was also black. Eva could see that the camera was working, but the lights were off in the room.

"That's where I left Muthr," Eva said, pointing to

the blank kitchen screen. "Let's try there first." She tapped the green glowing button next to the door, but the door did not open. Eva tapped it again, harder. Nothing.

"Is it not working? Perhaps there is another way in?" Rovender asked.

"Let me see if it is damaged." Eva walked over to the holo-screen for the control room. She attempted to interact with the Sanctuary's menus, but the Sanctuary would not respond. "That's weird. It's not letting me access anything," she said. Eva looked up and announced in a clear voice, "This is Eva Nine. Are you there, Sanctuary?"

The familiar calm voice of the Sanctuary replied. However, static was mixed into it, causing it to sound fuzzy and far away. "Earth in Vitro Alpha Nine, to reenter Sanctuary you must proceed with an authorization code."

"Code?" Eva looked up at the camera in the ceiling, the Sanctuary's eyes. "I don't know any code."

"Reentry into HRP underground facility five-seven-three is strictly prohibited without proper authorization," stated the Sanctuary through the static.

"Prohibited? I *live* here. You know that," Eva said, looking around at the various screens. "Please let me back in. I need to find Muthr."

"Multi-Utility Task Help Robot zero-six is unresponsive. Therefore, her location is undetermined. The integrity of said Sanctuary has been compromised. Please return to the surface and send distress signal from Omnipod to HRP underground facility fifty-one," the Sanctuary stated.

"I did that already," Eva replied, her tone stern. She waved the Omnipod at the camera. "But there are no humans out there. Instead there are monsters—giant sand monsters and trees that eat you. I need Muthr's help. Please let me in so that I can get her."

"Multi-Utility Task Help Robot zero-six cannot leave Sanctuary premises, Eva Nine. Please return to the surface and—"

"I told you I did that already!" Eva's frustration grew. "You have to let me in!"

"Terminating communication. Good-bye," the Sanctuary said. It shut off the holo-puter, causing all the screens to evaporate. The control room went dark.

"No! No! NO!" Eva yelled. She paced the room, furious.

Rovender leaned on his stick. "I never trust a talking machine," he said.

Eva flopped down at the foot of the stairs and

held her Omnipod in both hands. It shone on her furrowed face.

"It would seem"—Rovender looked around the darkened room—"that you have been presented with a puzzle, Eva Nine."

"A puzzle?" She looked up.

"Yes." Rovender inspected the door's manual keypad. "A riddle that you may solve. Now, you can solve this puzzle in a variety of ways. You can solve it with power, like Besteel did, and force this door to open." Rovender pointed to the scorch marks that pocked the door. He continued, "You can solve it by asking nicely, which you have already done, and received no results." He approached Eva. "Or you can solve it by answering the query."

"The authorization code? But I don't know that," Eva whined.

"So who would?" Rovender asked.

"Muthr would, but she would never—" Eva paused, a thought flitting through her mind. She recalled the inscription that had been scrawled into her dresser drawer . . . the one that had allowed her access to the Sanctuary's secrets.

"Sanctuary," Eva said, standing. "This is C-P-zero-one."

The Sanctuary was silent for a moment. *Won't it know it's just me?* Eva wondered.

She picked at the scab on her thumb with her finger.

"C-P-zero-one," the Sanctuary responded. "Access password, please."

Eva looked over at Rovender. She then glanced up to the unseen camera mounted in the ceiling. "Omniscient," she said.

"How may I be of service, Cadmus zero-one?" the Sanctuary asked.

Rovender looked at Eva. "Who is Cadmus?"

Eva shrugged her shoulders. "Open control room door and allow Eva Nine and Rovender Kitt access into main hub, please," Eva commanded.

With a low grinding sound the door unlocked. It opened only halfway, clearly damaged from Besteel's siege.

Before she could enter, Rovender put a hand on Eva's shoulder. He said, "The real question one should ask when presented with a puzzle is, 'Should I solve it? Do I really need to know the answer?'"

"I do. I need to know the answer," Eva said, and stepped into the burnt remnants of her home.

CHAPTER 14: ASHES

She had seen the images, and she knew the place was wrecked. But when Eva Nine stepped out into the main hub of her Sanctuary—her home of twelve years—she went numb. The main hub was now dark, no longer illuminated by the hologram vistas of beautiful landscapes. The holo-projector that had created the vistas now dangled from the ceiling by wires as it spurted sparks like a severed artery.

Most of the doors, usually hidden behind holograms of mountains and skies, were torched and pried apart. The greenhouse door opened and closed, banging into a watering can lying in the entryway.

The electronic sounds of birds singing and rivers running were now replaced with the angry hiss of cracked thermal pipes and fractured, bleeding water ventilation ducts.

"It is unfortunate that all of this is destroyed," Rovender said, picking up a fork from the debris. "So much can be garnered by simply asking for an invitation."

Eva stepped through the precarious damage in the main hub, and headed to the kitchen. She took a deep breath as she crossed the wrecked doorway, using the Omnipod to light the darkened room.

The refrigeration unit was wide open, disemboweled of all its foodstuffs and shelving. The sink faucets ran like tears onto a heap of broken dishes and utensils. Other dishes were scattered in ivory jagged shards on the countertops and tiled floor. With the light of the Omnipod, Eva peeked over the counter to the front of the stove—but the robot was nowhere to be found. "Muthr?" she whispered, and she peered up the exhaust shaft that had provided her escape. "Muthr, where are you?"

Eva wandered back out into the main hub, wondering which room to search next. "Rovender?" she called out.

"Right here, Eva," he answered as he popped his head out of the supply room.

"Do you see any sign of her?"

"I don't believe so," he replied. "Though, in truth, I don't know exactly what your mother robot looks like."

"Oh, she looks like this." Eva turned the Omnipod flat and brought up a projection of Muthr.

"Can't your device locate her?" Rovender knelt close to study the hologram.

"Not if she is off-line, which the Sanctuary said she was," Eva said. She pointed to the blown-out entrance of the gymnasium. "Why don't you check in there, and I'll try next door?"

"Okay." Rovender trotted across the hub toward the gym, his rucksack jingling with every step.

Eva entered the greenhouse, stepping over the watering can. Inside, the fluorescent grow lights flicked off and on, illuminating the hydroponic irrigation system, which lay in a heap like a pile of broken bones. The carbon dioxide generator hissed at Eva as she searched the aisles of upturned

fruit and vegetable plants. Once more there was no sign of Muthr.

"Eva Nine, come quick!" Rovender shouted.

Eva dashed back out into the main hub, tripping over the watering can. "Is it Muthr? Did you find her?" she asked.

Rovender called from the adjacent gymnasium entrance, "This way!"

As with the rest of the items in the wrecked Sanctuary, the gymnasium's exercise equipment was bent at odd angles and completely destroyed. The wading pool bottom was somehow cracked, with half of the water drained out. In the deep end of the pool was a familiar cylindrical shape.

A shape Eva had known since birth.

Muthr was lying like a dead log at the bottom of a clear chlorinated pond.

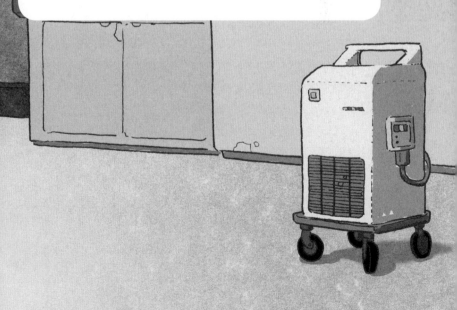

Muthr!

Eva screamed, jumping down the steps of the drained pool and scrambling to the deep end. She felt a slight electric shock as she waded into the water and tried to pick the robot up. Eva called out to Rovender, "Help me!" He slid off his rucksack and hopped into the pool, splashing Eva in the process.

Slowly the two of them rolled the unresponsive robot back to the shallow end. With great effort they then hoisted Muthr up onto the ply-steel deck. Her orblike eyes were glossy black without the slightest hint of an amber electric glow.

"There was a little light blinking when I first saw her here," Rovender said, pointing to a light on Muthr's braincase. "But it has stopped."

"She's got water in her," Eva said as she ran her fingertips over Muthr's smooth metallic shell. She stopped at a small plate on the back of the robot's torso. "One other time, during swimming lessons, moisture got on her power cell. I just need to dry it off and she'll be fine." Eva furrowed her brow while she jammed her fingernails at the seam of the closed panel. "Come on!" she grumbled.

"What is the problem?" Rovender watched Eva scrabble at the closed power cell hatch.

"I can't get this open. It's stuck!"

"There must be some simple way to—"

"No!" Eva pounded on the hatch. "Open! Come on! Open!" The force of Eva's fist unlatched the inner lock, and the small hatch opened. Pool water poured out of it.

The power cell was missing.

"What? Where can it be?" Eva sat back, dumb-struck.

"What is the matter? Has her spirit been stolen?" Rovender asked.

"I don't understand. Why is her power cell miss-ing?" Eva said, staring at Muthr. Discolored scorch marks ran down one side of the curvy robot lying motionless on the deck. All of her mechanical arms were drawn into her body like a dead spider's.

"Wait!" Eva rummaged through her satchel, and then finally pulled out the power cell that she had found at Besteel's camp. Eva snapped the dented cell into place and then leaned over to watch the familiar glow return to the robot's eyes—but they remained black.

"Oh, no! Why isn't this working?" Eva swal-lowed down the coil of panic.

Rovender placed a hand on her shoulder. "I know this is not what you want, but you should leave soon, Eva Nine. Besteel will return."

"Hold on! Maybe that one is just damaged. There are more power cells in the supply room. I'll be right back!" Eva ran out of the gym, across the hub, and into the supply room. Jumping over the toppled shelves, she scanned the discarded piles of water purification tablets and broken holo-bulbs. Out of breath, Eva asked, "Sanctuary, where are the power cells?"

"Hello, Cadmus zero-one. May I help you find something?" The static-filled voice of the Sanctuary crackled over the intercom.

"Who? Oh!" Eva remembered that the Sanctuary thought she was someone else. "What shelf would the power cells be on for Muthr?"

"T6D9 centurion power cells are in row five, top shelf," the Sanctuary replied. "However, supplies are exhausted. Acquisition of new cells must be arranged through sibling Sanctuaries."

Eva heard a hiss behind her. The door that led to her secret place opened into the darkness beyond.

"Eva Nine," Rovender's voice echoed through the main hub. Eva hopped back out of the supply room and found him rolling Muthr's rigid body on her wheel through the debris, leaving a watery trail behind them. "The light has started blinking again," he said. Eva saw a tiny red light on Muthr's braincase pulse in a steady rhythm.

Eva addressed the house. "Sanctuary, Muthr has been found but is not responding. Please advise us as to what we should do next."

"Bring Multi-Utility Task Help Robot zero-six

into the generator room," the Sanctuary answered. "Access is through the control room."

Eva and Rovender wheeled the robot into the control room, where an unseen door slid open next to the stairwell. Eva nodded to her companion, and they pushed Muthr into yet another room that Eva had never been in.

Overhead, lights flicked on in the solid white room, revealing a wall of glass cabinets that held a variety of petri dishes and test tubes. A squat cylindrical freezer breathed icy fog in the corner, while a series of immaculately clean glass tubs and tanks dominated the opposite wall. Eva shivered as a tingle ran up her spine.

"Clearly Besteel did not find this room," Rovender said, viewing a row of widemouthed jars filled with a reddish liquid.

"This is the generator room? It looks more like a lab," said Eva.

"Accessing data banks of Multi-Utility Task Help Robot zero-six. Please stand by," the Sanctuary announced.

Eva looked over at Muthr. The light on the robot's ash-covered head blinked in a rapid pattern. Eva's eyes traveled down Muthr's scorched body, and rested on a cluster of worn Beeboo stickers just above the wheel casing. Eva remembered sticking these onto Muthr when she was a toddler. Some of the stickers still worked, dancing and smiling in an animated fashion.

The Sanctuary instructed Eva, "Carefully remove Muthr zero-six's head in a counterclockwise direction. When you have done so, place it here." At this, a large robotic crab-shaped form rose from the seams in the white tiled floor. The form had an empty socket at its center. Eva and Rovender eased Muthr down, laying her face up.

"You remove it, okay?" Rovender whispered.

"Okay." Eva knew that Muthr could come apart; she'd seen her do it once before for a routine cleaning. But Eva hadn't liked watching—for it had only reminded her that it was just a machine raising her.

The red light on Muthr's forehead stopped blinking and she let out a tiny electronic chirp. Eva watched as the clamps that held the head and neck assembly in place unlocked.

Counterclockwise, counterclockwise, Eva said to herself. She rubbed the sweat off her palms onto her tunic and grabbed the head and turned it—but it did not come off.

"It's not working." An icy chill of nerves coiled in Eva's stomach. *Am I going to fail this exercise too?*

The Sanctuary repeated the instructions, "Carefully remove Muthr's head in a counterclockwise direction and place it here."

"I think, perhaps, you should try turning the other way. It may work better," Rovender said in a gentle tone.

Eva exhaled out the iciness that had seized her. Focused, she rotated Muthr's head in the opposite direction. It turned smoothly and slid out of the torso. Eva stood, wavering at the added weight of the robot's heavy head, and walked over to the large mechanized crab form. She set the head in the socket at the center of the crab body and locked it into place.

"Oeeah!" Rovender whistled as he stood next to Eva. "Do you have to remove your head as well to recharge your spirit?"

"Rovee! My head doesn't come off!" Eva giggled, jabbing him playfully.

"Look!" Rovender pointed.

A warm amber glow returned to Muthr's eyes. "Eva Nine!" the robot said. "My child, you are alive."

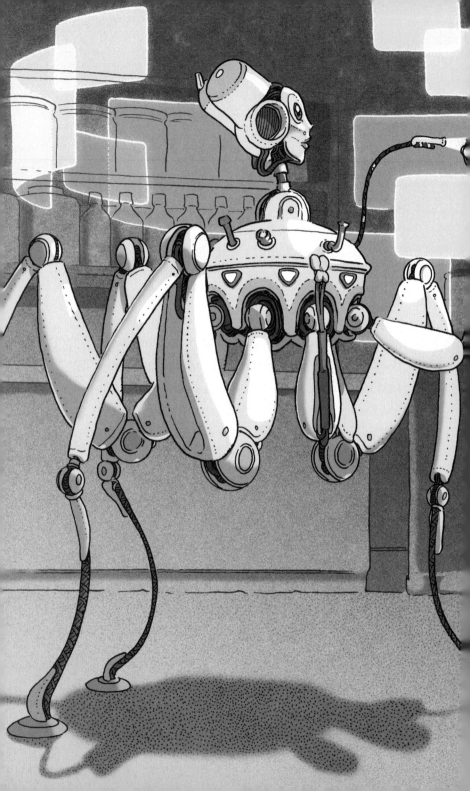

CHAPTER 16: PUZZLE

I am so glad you escaped successfully," Muthr said. She had numerous electrodes snaking from her head, giving her the appearance of a wire-haired Medusa. All of the electrodes' cables were connected to a port on the Sanctuary's central computer.

Eva was sitting in one of the empty glass tubs, her bare feet raised and her jackvest balled up behind her head like a pillow. She paused from sipping a container of blue-tinted drink. "What happened to you?" she asked.

With her new thick crablike appendages, Muthr grasped her headless original body and raised it. "Well, after you were gone, I was able to slip out of the kitchen through the chaos." A giant plug descended from the ceiling, locked into the neck socket of the old body, and hoisted it up farther. "At that point the entire house was filled with smoke. Half of the Sanctuary caught fire when the holo-projector exploded."

Eva watched a bundle of wires snake down from the top of the room, followed by directional lamps, which extended outward on mechanized arms.

Muthr attached the numerous probes to her old body and continued, "The intruder grabbed me in the haze and I struggled, toppling over the burning rubble. When I righted myself, I realized my cell hatch had popped open and my power cell had fallen out. With little reserve power I tried to get here, to this room. However, I realized I was covered in burning debris and aflame."

"So you dove into the gymnasium pool to put the fire out," Eva concluded. Wall-mounted arms emerged from hidden panels and began servicing Muthr's original body.

"Honestly, Eva, the extinguishers here were not designed for such a siege," Muthr said, watching her old headless body move and jerk back to life. "I needed to douse the flames before I could come in here, and before any of my inner workings were damaged."

"And?" Eva pulled a handful of nutriment pellets out of her satchel and began eating.

"The computer is running diagnostics on me right now," Muthr said. She was surrounded by a dazzling array of holo-charts and menus that were projected at a dizzying rate. The entire display flickered, and Eva realized that the Sanctuary's main computer had been somehow affected by Besteel's raid.

"So tell me about this stranger you have brought back with you," Muthr said, reading the statistical data.

"Oh, Rovee?" Eva said. "His full name is Rovender Kitt, and he's great. He helped me escape from—"

"Eva Nine?" Rovender's head popped in through the doorway. "Are these what you need?" On his backward-bending legs he brought a new pair of sneakboots and socks to her.

"Yes! Thanks so much for doing that for me," she said. Eva took the shoes and set them next to her discarded soiled socks. "I didn't want to go in there and see how destroyed my bedroom was."

"There is not much left to see," Rovender said, pointing at the shoes. "I could only find one in gray and one in white."

"That's okay," Eva said. "They'll both get so dirty up there that they'll match. As long as I'm not barefoot again."

"Good," Rovender said. After glancing up at Muthr's hanging body, he returned to the doorway. "I am going to check for Besteel. If the area is clear, we best get moving."

"We?" Eva asked, smiling.

"Yes," Rovender replied flatly. "I need to get on my way and so do you. Do you understand?"

Eva nodded in agreement. She saw Muthr watch Rovender slip out of the room and go up the stairs in the main entryway. Eva also noticed that the Sanctuary was running Identicapture, in an attempt to identify her lanky companion. Muthr turned her gaze back to Eva and asked, "How is it that you understand the language of this stranger, Eva?"

"I told you, he's not a stranger. He's a friend," Eva said as she fished around in her satchel. "And I can understand what he is saying because he gave me this." She held up the vocal transcoder.

"Interesting." Muthr extended one of her many arms. "May I?"

"Um, sure," Eva said, handing the transcoder over. "Just be careful. We are going to need it."

"Of course. Oh, and Eva?" Muthr spoke in that old-timey movie voice. "Can you please wash your hands? They are filthy."

"Are you serious?" Eva jumped out of the empty tub. "You're asking me to wash my hands after what I've just been through?" She stomped over to a small basin. Water trickled down over her grime-covered fingers.

Muthr held the transcoder up while the Sanctuary computer scanned it with a red laser. "Do not be dramatic, Eva. I know you have had some setbacks with your surface exercises, but otherwise you have handled yourself quite well. Besides, I trained you for worst-case scenarios. It's not like there are species of venomous snakes waiting for you in every clearing." Muthr examined the transcoder, bringing it close to her many eyes. "I was just preparing you to be ready for any dangers that you may encounter."

"Dangers?" Eva shook her hands dry. "Muthr, do you have any idea how scary it is out there?"

"Of course I do. With the aid of the Sanctuary I am the one preparing your exercises," Muthr replied in a matter-of-fact tone. She turned to the door. "Well, hello, Mr. Kitt."

Rovender stood in the doorway, holding a half-empty bottle. "The area is clear, as far as I can tell," he reported. "Besteel is still gone for the time being. But he will likely circle back here within one or two days. You do not want to be here when he does."

Muthr faced him. "What is he saying?"

Rovender disregarded Muthr. "You should leave now, Eva Nine. You need to put as much distance as you can between yourselves and Besteel."

"I don't understand." Eva's brow furrowed. "Why do you think he'll come back after me?"

"As I told you, I do not know." Rovender swallowed his drink. "But, obviously, he is collecting as much quarry as he can capture."

"Will you please tell me what is going on, Eva?" Muthr's voice was higher in pitch. "What is he saying?"

Eva took the transcoder back from her and put it into her satchel along with her food and drink. "He's says it's time to go. Are you ready?"

"Why is it that we need to leave in such a rush?" Muthr addressed Eva, yet still faced Rovender.

"Because Besteel, the intruder, *the monster* who demolished the Sanctuary, will be back," Eva answered. She unrolled her socks. "And for some insane reason, he is hunting after me."

"Besteel?" Muthr repeated while yet more holo-charts and graphs fluttered around her head. "Tell me this, then, why is it that there is no record of a 'Besteel' in the main computer? Or, for that matter, an animal such as Mr. Kitt?"

"Exactly—welcome to my world." Eva snorted under her breath.

"Enough, Eva!" Muthr snapped. With her crab-like body the robot closed in on Rovender. "It is not that I am accusing Mr. Kitt of being in company with the intruder who attacked us. However, when my omniscient computer system cannot identify this stranger, or his devices, well, then—I grow concerned for the safety and well-being of my child."

"I am not a child!" Eva snapped. "I—"

Rovender interrupted. "What is it that has your mother robot so aggravated?"

"She can't identify you on the Sanctuary's omni-scient computer," Eva replied. "Therefore, she doesn't know if she can trust you."

Rovender snorted. "Your answer is obvious, Eva Nine." He took another swig from his bottle. "Your 'omniscient computer' is wrong." He stepped out of the room and went back up the stairs.

"What did he say?" Muthr kept her gaze on the

empty doorway where Rovender had stood.

Eva sat down on the edge of the tub and pulled her clean socks on. "He says the computer is wrong. And I would say that he's right."

"Nonsense," Muthr said in a haughty tone. "The expansive library in this system is state of the art. It has every organism known to—"

"Muthr! We need to leave," Eva said. "You've seen what Besteel can do, so get yourself back together and let's go!" She pulled her sneakboots on.

"Distance traveled: zero kilometers," the shoes announced. Eva bent over and activated the odometer in the sneakboot's heel. She looked back up at Muthr. "Come on," Eva said. "We have to hurry!"

"Muthr zero-six cannot leave the premises," said the Sanctuary.

Eva paused for a moment, looking up at the intercom speakers.

"I am sorry, Eva, but I cannot go up there. I was not designed for such things," Muthr added. She reached a hand out to the girl. "My place is here, in this Sanctuary."

"What?" Eva said, grabbing her jackvest. "I came back for you! You're coming with me."

"I cannot. . . . I wish I could." Muthr moved closer. "Now, what I need—"

"No!" Eva backed away, pointing to the robot's suspended body. "You *have* to come! What I need is you."

"Again, I apologize, dear, but my programming prohibits me from doing so. I would if I could . . . but I cannot." Muthr looked down.

Eva reached for her satchel while her jackvest tightened itself snugly around her body. "I can't believe you're saying this," she said. "I can't believe this is happening."

"Sanctuary," Muthr said aloud, "this is Muthr zero-six. Have you assessed domicile damage yet?"

"Sanctuary five-seven-three has received 84.53 percent damage, 76.8 percent of which is irreparable. Emergency transmission for immediate retrieval has been sent," the report came over the intercom. Even with the static, Eva hated how calm the Sanctuary sounded while spouting off how ruined her home was.

"Based on the absence of return transmissions from sibling Sanctuaries, what do you suggest?" Muthr asked while looking at holograms of charts and maps floating in front of her.

"Remain in Sanctuary for thirty days. If retrieval does not occur, then begin shutdown process and send ward to the nearest settlement, HRP underground facility fifty-one."

"Remain?" Eva yelled. She fastened her satchel

straps to her jackvest. "That's ridiculous, Muthr. I will not do that. You will not do that. Rovee and I will get you out of here."

Muthr was silent. Unmoving.

Eva pulled her hair up in a wad and wrapped it tightly with one of her braids. "Come on. I will help you up the stairs, and we'll go to Sanctuary number whatever together . . . okay?"

Muthr spoke. "Eva, listen to me—listen!"

Eva stopped and looked at Muthr's face, hoping for a sign of real emotion in the silicone rubber and circuits. She blinked back the tears that burned her eyes. Muthr was just a robot, but she had also taken care of Eva since birth. Trained her. Protected her.

"Eva." Muthr's voice was low. "I cannot come with you because *I am not supposed to.* My programming prevents it. You see, I am only meant to live here to instruct you on how to survive and prosper on the surface. Once you are ready, and of age, then you no longer need me. That's the way the program works."

"But I'm not ready." Eva sniffed. "I need you."

"But *you are* ready, dear. Look—you exited prematurely and you survived." Muthr brushed away Eva's bangs. "Do as the Sanctuary instructs and you will be fine. I wish I could be there with you, but my place is here."

"Here? In this mess?" Eva wiped her eyes with her sleeve. Once again the Sanctuary—*her Sanctuary*—was not cooperating.

It was puzzling.

Eva pulled out her Omnipod and handed it to Muthr.

"Why are you giving me this?" Muthr asked, taking the device. "You will certainly need it where you are going."

"Omnipod," commanded Eva, "please open Identicapture and show Muthr, and the Sanctuary, the life-forms living on the surface."

An array of holograms flickered in front of the robot's glowing orbs. Many-winged birds. Wandering trees. Weeping bird-catchers. Giant water bears. Sand-snipers. The Dorcean huntsman.

Eva addressed both Muthr and the Sanctuary: "Please identify these organisms and advise on how I should interact with them."

There was a long pause. Finally the Sanctuary spoke. "All said organisms are classified as unidentifiable because of insufficient data. Interaction cannot be deduced at this point. Proceed with caution."

"Now do you think I am ready?" Eva asked, taking the Omnipod back.

"I—I do not know," Muthr replied. For the first time ever Eva heard hesitation in the robot's voice.

"Then you *have* to accompany me. The Sanctuary is unsafe, and the surface is unsafe. I am not yet ready for life on the surface alone." Eva fixed her gaze directly on Muthr and said, "Sanctuary, this is C-P-zero-one. Based on new information, please analyze whether Muthr zero-six should accompany Eva Nine to the nearest settlement."

"Analyzing. Please wait," the Sanctuary said.

"C-P-zero-one?" Muthr asked. Eva shushed her.

The Sanctuary announced, "Cadmus zero-one, Multi-Utility Task Help Robot zero-six is relinquished from her Sanctuary duties. She would be best suited accompanying Eva Nine to neighboring HRP underground facility fifty-one." As the Sanctuary finished speaking, Muthr's refurbished body descended to the floor and was released from the ceiling hoist that held it. All of the maintenance equipment retracted back into its hidden compartments within the walls.

The old body rolled over to Muthr's temporary body. As the crablike form sank back into the paneled flooring, the robot's original body grabbed the head and placed it back onto its torso. Muthr was whole again.

"Yes!" Eva hugged Muthr, holding her tightly. Rovender reentered the room, and she smiled at him. He nodded back to her.

"I—I can leave?" Muthr sounded genuinely shocked.

"You can leave! You're coming with us!" Eva squealed, squeezing her tighter.

"Thank you, Eva," Muthr said. "Though, I am still perplexed that there are no records in our exhaustive data library for organisms like these."

"Weird, right?" Eva looked around at the holograms floating in the room. "I guess there is still much to learn about all of Earth's inhabitants."

"Eorthe?" Rovender mispronounced the word. A look of confusion grew on his whiskered face. "Is this a place?"

"Yes. Of course," Eva replied. "Here. Where we are. *This* planet is called Earth."

The lanky creature laughed out loud. "This makes much more sense to me now," he said.

"What's so funny?" Eva asked.

Rovender's smile disappeared. "You are not on this planet you call 'Earth,' Eva Nine. You are on a planet named Orbona."

CHAPTER 17: DOORS

On planet

Orbona? What?" Eva exclaimed.

"Orbona?" Muthr repeated. "There is no planet in the Milky Way galaxy by that name. Though there are numerous planets yet to be identified, Mr. Kitt, you must surely be mistaken."

"Shh! Hold on. Muthr, be quiet for a sec," Eva said, closing her eyes. Something vague and distant wafted into her thoughts.

"What?" Muthr asked, alarmed. "What is happening, Eva?"

Rovender knelt close. "What is it?"

"I think it's Otto," Eva answered, her eyes still shut. "But he's so far away that I can barely hear him."

"Concentrate," Rovender said, his voice soft. "Open yourself to his call."

"What is Otto?" Muthr asked. "Can you please tell me what is going on here?"

The hunter. You. Home.

Eva opened her eyes wide. "It's Besteel. He's here!"

"Sheesa!" Rovender lifted an ear toward the staircase.

Even Eva could hear the hum of the glider's engine shut off. "We can't go out the main entryway," she said.

"How did you escape before?" Rovender asked.

"Back to the kitchen exhaust vent," Muthr said, taking Eva by the hand. The robot led them out of the generator room. "Let us go!"

As they dashed through the robot's control room, Eva glanced up and saw a shadow darken the top of the stairwell.

"Come! Come! Come!" Rovender hopped behind them, shoving Eva and Muthr into the main hub. "We must hurry!"

"Hold on!" Eva yelled, halting in front of the scorched kitchen doorway. "This way won't work. Muthr can't go up the shaft."

"Eva, dear," Muthr said. "It is all right. I—"

"It's *not* all right," Eva barked. "We came back for you, and you're leaving with us!"

"Whichever path we choose, we need to choose

it in a hurry." Rovender's tone was antsy as he looked over his shoulder into the control room. Dark gray claws grabbed the half-open door of the room. With tremendous strength they pried it open, revealing the sinister, predatory face of Besteel.

"Ruzender Keet," he hissed in a heavy accent. "You has something that beelongz to me!"

"This way!" Eva yanked Muthr into the storage room. "Into the next Sanctuary!"

"Wait, do you need more provisions before exiting?" Muthr asked as she was pulled through the maze of overturned shelves and spilled supplies. Rovender followed, limping fast with his walking stick.

Eva turned to see Besteel bound across the main hub.

"Rovee! Hit the red button!" she yelled, standing in the doorway of the secret hallway. Rovender banged the door's manual pad with the bottom of his stick as he hopped by. The damaged doors creaked as they attempted to shut, but they could not close all the way. Once more Besteel wriggled his clawed hands into the gap between the doors and began wrenching them apart.

"Come on!" Eva ushered Muthr through the back door hatch while Rovender hobbled closer. Behind him, Besteel's immense arm groped about for the control panel of the half-open doors. Then he withdrew his arm and replaced it with the bulbous muzzle of his rifle. The distinct hum of the charging weapon vibrated in Eva's ears.

"Let's go!" She pushed Rovender inside the secret hallway.

"Sanctuary, please lock down sibling corridor hatch," Muthr commanded. Her amber eyes glowed in the dark hallway. The door slid shut behind them and locked into place. Beyond it Eva could hear the hum of Besteel's rifle rising higher and higher in pitch.

"Go! Go! Go!" Rovender pushed them down the hallway.

Besteel fired his rifle. The intense sonic wave battered the back wall of the supply room. Dust and rubble pelted Eva, followed by a low, straining creak.

"What's that?" She looked up from her cowering position in the darkness.

"It is the support structures," Muthr's voice echoed through the hall. "They have been damaged."

"Move!" Rovender yelled.

A loud rending sound erupted as the ceiling over the trio gave way. Rovender and Eva scrambled forward, toppling over Muthr. Behind them a deluge of rock and rubble poured into the hallway, blocking the path.

"Are you all right?" Muthr asked.

Clearing her throat, Eva pulled herself up to sitting position. "I'm fine, thanks," she answered. Eva tried brushing the dirt and dust off her clothing, but all she managed to do was smudge it around. "How are you?" She could see that one of Muthr's extended arms was bent at an odd angle.

"I tried to brace my fall with arm three," Muthr said, holding up the bent metal rods that had been her forearm. "Though the arm sustained permanent damage, I believe all else is intact." She retracted the remaining wires from the damaged arm into her torso.

There was a coughing behind them. "Rovee!" Eva cried, kneeling down next to her companion. "Are you okay?"

Rovender dragged himself out of the rubble with a groan. "I will be okay, Eva Nine. Many gratitudes," he said, slumping against the wall. "That cursed boomrod rifle of his does more damage than an angry male grall in a bayrie's crystal nest." He sneered as he lit his lantern and pulled out a bottle. "Where are we?"

Eva looked over at Muthr. "Good question. Tell us, Muthr, where are we?"

"Apparently you already know, Eva. So why don't you tell Mr. Kitt," the robot answered, still examining her damaged limb.

Eva pulled out her Omnipod and brought up the hologram of the Sanctuary's entire floor plan. "We are in a connecting corridor that will take us to a neighboring Sanctuary," she said. "A Sanctuary, for some reason, I was never allowed to go to."

Muthr looked over at her. "That is correct, Eva. Of course, this was based on a decision made by our Sanctuary and myself. A decision made as a safety precaution, which you obviously disobeyed."

Eva fumed. "Oh, really! I don't think—"

"Eva Nine, Mother Robot"—Rovender stood up between the two—"let us put this decision aside and proceed to this adjoining Sanctuary. Hopefully, there we shall find shelter for the night and refuge from Besteel." He set off, his many belongings tinkling together on his rucksack as he went. Muthr looked at Eva for a beat, her eyelids clicking loudly. She wheeled behind Rovender, dropping her severed forearm. Eva followed, trudging slowly as the three journeyed down the dark corridor.

"Heart rate BPM acceleration detected, Eva Nine," her tunic announced. "Please—"

Eva shut off the tunic before it could finish its report. Her damp palms gripped the Omnipod tightly as she journeyed farther down the hallway.

The trio would soon be arriving at the end of the hall—the location of Eva's secret place. There was nowhere else to go. This was the only path out.

"Muthr?" Eva's voice was hushed. She kept her eyes down on the Omnipod's glow.

"Yes, dear," the robot answered, rolling behind Rovender.

"Um . . . there is something you should know. Something I should have told you."

"And what is that?" Muthr asked.

"You were right. I've been sneaking out of the Sanctuary and into here."

Muthr was quiet as she slowed down to match Eva's reluctant pace. They were nearing the half-way point in the corridor.

"And . . . well," Eva said with a gulp. "I've been bringing stuff here, my old stuff, the stuff you told me to get rid of."

"I know," Muthr whispered.

"You—you do?" Eva looked up and stopped walking.

Muthr turned to her. "It is all right, Eva," she said. "You needed your space. Even living in that big, lonely Sanctuary, you still required a place where you felt truly alone. Solitude."

Eva looked down, processing this. "But if you

knew, why wouldn't you let me go find the kids in the other Sanctuary?"

Muthr put her arm around Eva. She could feel the warmth of the robot's body permeate her clothing. Muthr's voice was gentle. "Eva, our Sanctuary told me that the surrounding Sanctuaries, including this Sanctuary up ahead, were nonfunctioning—with a ninety-eight percent chance of non-occupancy. Now, if we enter and there are people present, I will be the first to apologize and tell you how wrong I was in keeping it sealed off. All right?"

Eva nodded, saying nothing more. They continued onward to the end of the hallway.

"Oeeah! I'd say you've been bringing things here, Eva Nine," Rovender exclaimed, shining his lantern light on the accumulated objects that surrounded the door. "This is quite a collection."

Muthr slipped past him to approach the damaged controls for the door. She lifted up the manual control plate and connected several of the door's wires to herself. The red and green lights on the control panel flickered on. "Are you ready?" she asked, turning to Eva.

"Is there anything you want to bring with you?" Rovender bent down, examining the altar of possessions. Eva knelt next to him and picked up her stuffed Beeboo doll.

"I gave you that for your third birthday," Muthr mused. "Do you remember?"

"I do," Eva said, nuzzling the grungy doll as it winked and smiled at her. As she did so, its wobbly head rolled off, spilling yellowed stuffing out of it. Rovender gasped.

Without a word Eva set the Beeboo doll back in its special spot. With a delicate hand she picked up the doll's head and placed it back on top of its body. "You take good care of everyone, okay?" she said to it.

As Eva's eyes took in every detail of her collection one final time, she paused on a lone item—the item not given to her by Muthr. She plucked the WondLa up from her hoard.

"What is that?" Muthr extended her neck to get a better view.

"Nothing really," Eva answered, showing her the deteriorated image. "It's just something I found . . . something I hope to find again." Eva tucked it into her satchel and took a deep breath. "Okay," she said, "I'm ready."

"Okay," Rovender echoed.

"Okay," Muthr said.

Eva stepped past her collection and walked through the doorway of the adjoining Sanctuary.

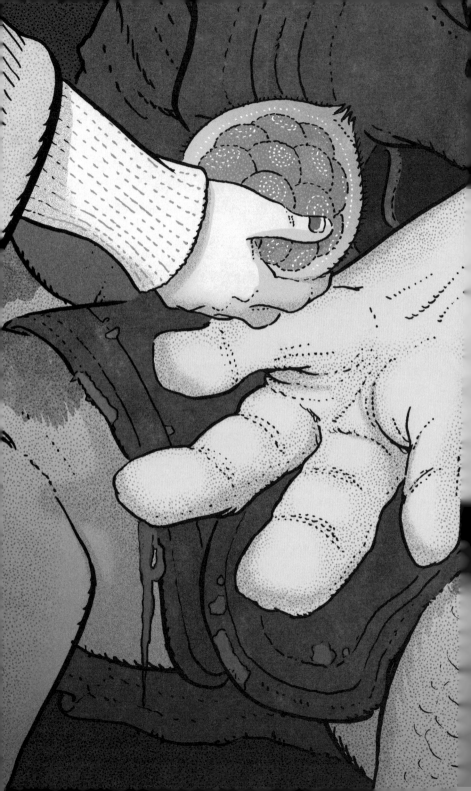

CHAPTER 18: SUSTENANCE

The first thing Eva noted was the smell. It was the dirty earthen scent of damp potting soil. She recognized it from her many "hands-on" horticulture exercises held in the greenhouse. But Eva wasn't standing in this Sanctuary's greenhouse. She was standing in the main hub.

Roots from unseen trees above had wriggled their way down, cracking the Sanctuary's ply-steel roof like an eggshell. Through the open doors of the bedroom, Eva could see that the ceiling had partially collapsed, opening up to the night sky above. Unusual fungi and lichens covered walls that at one time had held holo-projectors and geothermal heating units.

Muthr turned to Eva, her amber eyes dim in the Sanctuary's darkness. "I am sorry, Eva. I truly wish I had been wrong about this place," she said.

"It's okay." Eva sniffed. "I'm sorry I didn't believe you."

"Do not worry." Muthr hugged Eva tightly. "We shall continue searching."

"The main entrance has caved in," Rovender observed, pointing to the remains of the control room. "We cannot exit through there."

"Let us journey on to the next Sanctuary," Muthr said, scanning the doorway of the old supply room with a laser. "Or we could stay here for the night. How are you feeling, Eva?"

"I do want to see the other Sanctuary," Eva said, glum. "But maybe it would be good to take a break. I'm tired."

"Very good," Muthr said.

"We should rest, Eva. You've had quite a day," Rovender concurred, looking up at the ceiling. "However, we should retire in a more concealed chamber. Let's check the other rooms."

Eva translated for Muthr, and the trio split up, exploring the overgrown Sanctuary.

From the gymnasium doorway Eva was greeted by a

large growth of jade green mushrooms projecting outward toward her. She heard the mushrooms inhale and exhale as their caps expanded and contracted. Their breathing was in rhythm with a trickling sound that echoed from within the overgrown gym.

"Are you all right?" Muthr asked as she approached Eva.

"Yeah," Eva replied, shining her Omnipod light around the room. "I just wonder if we will find any other humans here at all."

Muthr's gaze followed the cluster of mushrooms growing rampant over most of the gymnasium walls and corroded equipment. She whispered, "Only time will tell. Though, I must say, I find it hard to believe that we are truly on another planet. Even if the Omnipod classifies everything here as unidentifiable."

"I know. I can't even believe it either," Eva said, watching water drip down from the ceiling into the pond that had once been the wading pool. The pond's surface reflected the soft glow of the Omnipod in green rippled rings. Tall sphere-topped reeds towered in clumps at the pond's edge.

"Believe it." Rovender joined them. "Good work, Eva Nine. You've found our camp for the night."

"Really?" she said, looking at the fungi growing over the tiled floor.

"Yes." Rovender slid off his rucksack and set it down next to the pool. He leaned over the edge and slurped up the water.

"You're drinking that?" Eva watched as Rovender splashed his face.

"Sure," he replied, pulling an empty bottle out from his sack. He skimmed it along the surface of the pool. "As long as I drink the freshly fallen water here, just below the surface. See?" He held up the bottle, now full of mostly clear liquid.

"But what's that?" Eva pointed to dark particles swirling around in the bottle.

Rovender chuckled. "It will settle to the bottom, Eva Nine. Do not fret. This water is good."

"Perhaps he can drink that, Eva, but not you," Muthr said, her red laser penetrating the bottle.

"Muthr says I can't drink it." Eva's tone was apologetic.

"Bluh." Rovender shook his head and sat down next to the pool. Eva flopped down next to him, watching as he submerged his bandaged foot in the water.

"Eva, I would like to further study the details of the organisms you recorded on Identicapture, if you do not mind," Muthr said.

"Sure, no prob." Eva unstrapped the Omnipod from her wrist and handed it to Muthr.

"If you need to rehydrate, have more Pow-R-drink, dear," Muthr said as she took the device.

"Okay." Eva pulled the plastic bottle out from her satchel.

"Eva Nine, can you bring me the fruit that grows on top there?" Rovender asked as he pointed to the spindly reeds growing on the far side of the pool.

"Over here?" Eva said, hopping up and walking over to the slender reeds.

"Yes, yes," Rovender said as he unstrapped a bedroll from his pack. "Those are the ones."

Eva gathered an armful of the translucent spherical fruit that grew on the tips of the sturdy stalks, only dropping one on her return trip back to the makeshift camp.

"Many gratitudes to you," Rovender purred. "These look ripe too." He was now sitting on his bedroll, patting an additional roll he had laid out for Eva. She sat down and dropped the armload of fruit into his lap.

"These are voxfruit," he said, grabbing one and ripping the rind off. "They are not often found but are very tasty. I will have to remember this place." The inside of the fruit was full of bright green berries, which the creature devoured with relish. Rovender handed the other half of the fruit to Eva.

She studied the berries. "I don't know, Rovee. . . . I could get sick."

"Yes. You could get sick," Muthr echoed, her gaze still on the Omnipod.

"Do I look sick?" Rovender asked through a mouthful of fruit.

Eva pulled open the lid on her drink container and took a sip.

"I am curious," Rovender said as he peeled another voxfruit, "what is it that you are drinking?"

"Pow-R-drink?" Eva replied. "It's, you know . . . like juice."

"It is a pH-balanced vitamin-enriched water solution," Muthr answered.

"With gum flavoring," Eva added as she translated to Rovender. "And look!" She stuck out her blue-stained tongue.

Eva's lanky companion drew back, unsure of how to react.

"Here. You wanna try some?" She passed the bottle to Rovender. Muthr paused from studying the Omnipod to watch the interaction.

Rovender sniffed the contents of the bottle. He then gulped some down, made a sour face, and spat the liquid out over his shoulder. "Bluh! It tastes like chemicals."

Eva heard Muthr chuckle. Rovender glared at the robot.

"If you are thirsty, you should have this instead." Rovender swallowed down the water he had collected.

"Um, yeah, thanks anyway, but I don't want to puke," Eva said, taking another sip of her drink.

Muthr added, "Eva, please remind Mr. Kitt that his water is not purified. It is likely filled with all sorts of bacteria. You could become quite ill from it."

Rovender narrowed his eyes at Muthr. "This water has been filtered through the soil of Orbona, Eva Nine. It tastes of the sky and the land it originated from. The land you both are now a part of."

Eva pondered this for a moment while she picked at her fingernail.

"Eva, you have your hydration kit," Muthr said. For a moment it appeared as if she understood Rovender's statement as she returned the Omnipod to Eva. "And I have packed a quantity of purification tablets, should you need to drink the natural water here. However, I do not believe it will come to that. We shall rendezvous with inhabitants of our neighboring underground facilities soon enough."

"What about your robot mother?" Rovender pointed at Muthr with a voxfruit rind. "What food and water does she drink?"

"Muthr doesn't eat," Eva answered. "She's just a robot."

Muthr added, "Though I am a manufactured hybrid biocomputer, and contain what some may consider 'living organs,' I use no metabolic processes to gain energy. Instead I derive all my power from a replaceable centurion power cell."

Eva translated all of this to Rovender as she finished her drink.

"One who does not drink or eat, who tells the other what she must eat and drink . . . Curiouser and curiouser," Rovender said, and stared at the girl and the robot.

Eva returned her empty drink container to her satchel. While doing so, she spied the WondLa. She pulled it out and studied it by a flickering lantern light. She thought it odd to have the WondLa with her, away from its secret place.

"Is this the thing you took from your collection, Eva Nine?" Rovender threw another rind into the pool and scooted close for a better look. "Of all the things you left behind, why did you choose to keep this?"

"This?" Eva answered, her eyes fixed on the crumbling picture. The little girl in the depiction was happy. Smiling. The robot beside her was also smiling. Along with the headless adult, they were holding hands and walking together, moving forward.

They were one. They were a family.

"I call this my WondLa," Eva whispered.

"Wond-La?" Rovender repeated.

"Why?" Muthr asked.

"If you look closely, they're the only words left on it that you can read. It's the only thing I own that didn't come from our Sanctuary. I thought it came from the people living here, but I guess I was wrong." Eva let out a long, dejected sigh.

"You are correct, Eva," Muthr said. "I have a record of all inventory within these Sanctuaries and it did not come from here."

"But it had to come from somewhere," Eva replied. "I think another human left it for me."

"But it is not in our inventory," Muthr said, looking down at the WondLa. "Perhaps it was left by the likes of Besteel or Mr. Kitt."

Eva rubbed her thumb over the image of the little girl.

"It looks very old. Very dirty," Muthr added. "Are you sure you want to bring it?"

"Don't you get it, Muthr?" Eva said, affronted. "Look at the girl and her parent. Look at their robot. See how happy they all are? When is the last time you and I smiled like that?"

"Actually, we did so three hundred and seventy-eight days ago when you beat me in a game of holo-gammon," Muthr replied. "But still, there was a reason this was not in our home. It is covered in mildew and contaminated with bacteria."

Eva rolled her eyes. "Have you ever seen anything like this?" she asked, handing it to Rovender.

"Like this?" Rovender wiped his hands on his tattered jacket before taking it. "No, Eva Nine, I have not. But I have seen similar objects in the Royal Museum in Solas." He handed it back.

"The where?" Eva perked up.

"The Royal Museum. It is in the city of Solas." Rovender lay down on his mat, resting his head on his large rucksack. He closed his eyes. "It is ruled by Queen Ojo. Perhaps there you might find someone with answers about your village."

"Can you take us?" Eva asked.

"What is he saying?" Muthr said.

"He says there is a museum with other items like this," Eva held up the WondLa. "He's going to take us there."

"Take you? I did not say that, Eva Nine." Rovender opened one eye at the girl. "What I did say was that Besteel is on our trail. We'd be better off if we split up."

"We will no longer require Mr. Kitt's services

once we reach the surface," Muthr said. "With the Omnipod, we should be capable of locating a safe route to the next underground facility."

"You'll see how useless that thing is once we're aboveground," Eva muttered.

"Eva, let us not—"

"Not now, Muthr!" Eva barked. She looked over at Rovender. He appeared to be asleep.

Muthr sighed. "I think I shall check the structural integrity of this Sanctuary and keep watch for any signs of the intruder," she said as she exited the gymnasium. "Try to get some rest, Eva. Tomorrow we shall continue our search."

Eva lay back on her bedroll, staring up at the rivulet of water on the cracked ceiling above. She heard the ceiling weep—*drip, drip, drip*—into the green pool next to her. It reminded Eva of holograms she'd seen of caverns. Dark caves had always appeared mysterious and spooky when she'd explored them in the holo-chamber, yet here she somehow felt secure. Safe.

"Rovee?" she asked aloud.

"Yes, Eva Nine."

"Do you really think we might find other humans in the city of Solas?" She turned on her side to face him, her head propped up on her hand.

"I cannot say, but it is a big city. There are many sorts that dwell there."

"Muthr's never been aboveground before. And the Omnipod is not really working right. . . ." Eva swallowed. "Could . . . could you take us there? Then we'll leave you alone, I promise."

The lanky creature remained still with his eyes closed. "There is a fishing village, Lacus, that's about a two-day hike from here if we journey east through the Wandering Forest," Rovender said. "I will guide you. Once in Lacus, though, you will be on your own."

"How will we get to Solash from there?" Eva asked.

"Solas," Rovender corrected her. "You can take a ferry across Lake Concors, which will bring you directly into the main port."

"Thanks, Rovee." Eva lay back on her bedroll. "Thank you so much."

"Get some rest, Eva Nine." Rovender crossed his large hands over his narrow chest.

Eva took off her jackvest and balled it up into a pillow. As she settled down, she spied Muthr standing silently in the gymnasium doorway, the robot's silicone skin glowing in the pale lantern light.

Eva tucked the deteriorating WondLa into the inside pocket of her tunic, next to her beating heart, and closed her eyes.

Eva winced

as the late-morning sunlight danced across her face. Once again she was aboveground deep in a forest—the Wandering Forest, as Rovender had called it, before he'd walked off to relieve himself.

Compared to the previous day, her morning had been uneventful. Normally Eva would have enjoyed the tranquility, but she had been excited, hopeful that they would find other residents living in the neighboring Sanctuaries.

After rising and eating a quick breakfast, the trio had opened the hatch leading to the next adjoining Sanctuary. To Eva's dismay, she'd discovered it was more overgrown than the previous one. A sense of wonder, mixed with sadness, had fallen upon her as she'd walked through the familiar structure. It was

laid out exactly like her home, but had disappeared under thick carpets of bizarre fungi, lichens, and moss. The main entryway to this third Sanctuary had been wide open and covered in small bulbous growths. With each step that Eva had taken as she'd helped Muthr ascend toward the surface, the growths had whistled, puffing their spores.

"Well?" Eva asked now, watching Muthr. At present the robot was quiet, save for her blinking eyelids. Dappled light glimmered upon her through the canopy. All around, a concert of forest voices chirped, buzzed, burbled, and chortled. A sweet scent wafted through the air, mixing with the familiar smell of wet potting soil.

Eva noticed a bright pin light blinking on the back of Muthr's head—a light she had not noticed before. She neared Muthr, grasping one of her rubber-tipped hands.

"Eva, I cannot fathom . . ." Muthr's voice drifted away and she appeared lost in thought. Eva wondered how the codes and programs that allowed Muthr to operate were processing all of this new information. Muthr turned as a tiny, thin leaf landed on her lacquered metallic torso. The leaf walked in slow strides, then hopped off. It landed on the moss-covered trunk of a tree and became inconspicuous.

"It is more vivid, more alive, than I expected," Muthr said. "In fact, my optical sensors may be overloading. There seems to be an error in my programming."

"Are you okay?" A look of concern settled upon Eva's face.

"It is odd," Muthr continued, "but the emotional replicator program that I normally use for interaction with you is sending me mixed signals: both of wonderment and of fear."

"Wonderment and fear? That's weird," Eva said, perplexed.

"That's called being *awestruck*," Rovender said, returning. He slapped Muthr on the back. "Welcome to the real world, Mother Robot, a beautiful and dangerous place. Now you can truly begin to live."

"What was that?" Muthr asked.

"He said you're awestruck," Eva replied. "By the beauty of living in this dangerous place."

"Awestruck. So it may be," Muthr said, her voice quiet.

Rovender pulled his large rucksack over his shoulders, causing his numerous items to jangle together. "Okay, Eva, we need to keep moving if we want to make it to Lacus by tomorrow night." He grabbed his walking stick and set off. "Come, let us continue. And stay alert—like I said, it can get dangerous here."

"What did he say?" the robot asked Eva.

"Hold on a second, Muthr," Eva said. "Rovee, can I ask you something?"

"Yes, Eva Nine," her guide paused, turning to her.

In a hushed voice Eva asked, "If it does get dangerous, shouldn't we all be able to speak to one another?"

"What? We are—"

"Muthr," Eva whispered. "She needs to be able to understand you, and I am getting tired of translating. Don't you have another vocoder thingy?"

Rovender looked over at the robot. Muthr was aiming the Omnipod at the tiny walking leaf, recording it. "I do not have another transcoder," he said. "I gave you my last one."

Eva let out a frustrated sigh. "Okay."

"Wait." Rovender whispered. "She can also use yours, as long as the device is near you both. So you'll have to stay close, understand?"

"Really?" Eva smiled. "Thanks!"

"And, Eva," Rovender added, "she has to ingest the transmitters for it to work. Press the silver button, then have her hold it near her mouth."

Eva nodded. She remembered how suspicious she had been of the transcoder when she had first been presented with it. She walked up to Muthr's back as the robot studied the hologram of the walking leaf on the Omnipod. Eva pulled the transcoder out of her pocket. "What did you find?" she asked in an innocent tone.

"I thought it to be a species of insect," Muthr said, turning to Eva, "perhaps even one of the genus—what are you doing?"

"I need you to let this thing, the transcoder, work on you."

"Eva, I do not know if I should allow that. It could compromise my programming," Muthr replied. She glanced over Eva's shoulder to Rovender.

"Listen," Eva said, "if we encounter any of the creatures I showed you on the Omnipod, it could get dangerous. You need to be able to understand exactly what Rovender is telling us about this planet."

Muthr's eyelids clicked. "You are right, Eva. What do I need to do?"

Eva pressed the button on the bottom of the transcoder. A tiny cloud of transmitters puffed out. "Start speaking," Eva said with a smile.

Eva and Muthr followed in single file behind their guide. For the remainder of the morning they traveled along a winding animal trail through the thick brush. Eva and Rovender chatted while Muthr recorded endless data with the Omnipod.

They spooked a covey of birds, which flew overhead, warbling aloud to one another.

"I've seen these before. What are they?" Eva asked.

"Turnfins," Rovender replied. "They are everywhere, and eat everything. Feed one of them and soon you're feeding the entire flock. That makes catching them easy."

"Turnfins," Muthr repeated as she entered the data into the Omnipod.

Eva watched the birds disappear into the shadows of the forest. "Catch them? For a pet?"

Rovender chuckled. "No, Eva Nine—for food. They are actually quite delicious if prepared properly."

"For food?" Eva thought of the turnfins that had greeted her the first morning of her escape, roosting on the wandering tree next to her. She thought of the weeping bird-catchers capturing and devouring them. She thought of herself captured, just like the pair of turnfins, in Besteel's camp. She shuddered at the memory of the brute cutting up the giant water bear and consuming its organs. Her stomach twisted.

Rovender turned back to Eva, smiling. "Maybe we'll catch some for dinner tonight, eh? I know a delicious recipe."

Eva's stomach curdled at the words Rovender

had spoken. "How could you do that? That's just like something Besteel would do!" she said.

Rovender stopped, turned, and seized Eva by the arm. "*Never* say that I am like Besteel," he growled. "That brute is a monster who kills for sport. I only take what I need from the forest, when I need it to survive."

"Yeah, but—"

"You do not understand, Eva Nine," Rovender said with restraint in his voice. "There may come a time when you, too, will have to live off of this land. Those pellets you carry around won't last forever."

"They should last for more than a month," Muthr piped up as she approached. "Thirty-four days, to be exact. Please take your hands off her, Mr. Kitt."

Eva looked up at Muthr, then back at Rovender. The lanky creature let go of her, saying nothing.

Muthr continued, "That should be adequate time for us to reunite with other humans at the next settlement."

"I will tell you, Mother Robot, the same thing I have told Eva: I have traveled all over this landscape, and I have yet to see another like *either* of you." Rovender turned away and started back down the trail.

"Well, then, perhaps we should head toward the coordinates that the Sanctuary gave instead of this city you speak of," Muthr replied.

Rovender stopped and shook his head. "I was better off when I couldn't understand her," he grumbled.

Eva put her hands over her mouth, subduing a snicker.

"What is that?" Muthr asked.

Rovender approached Muthr. "Very well. Show me this place where your machine has told you to go."

Muthr kept all five eyes fixed on Rovender. "Of course," she said. In seconds a large holographic relief map of the surrounding terrain floated above the Omnipod's central eye.

"Our location is approximately here," Muthr said, pointing to a wooded spot on the edge of a wide river. "So the nearest human underground facility is on the other side of this river. About a twenty-seven-day hike from here if we keep a steady pace for eight hours a day."

"Twenty-seven days!" Eva looked at the map. The location looked much closer when everything was shrunk down. "Twenty-seven days of walking is a long time—especially with all of the scary stuff out here trying to eat us."

"We shall be fine." Muthr handed Eva the Omnipod. "And if we ration accordingly and follow our practiced survival skills, we should arrive safely. How about it, Mr. Kitt?"

"Is there anyone even there?" Eva stared at the holographic map.

"I have sent them a distress signal and am awaiting a reply," Muthr said. "However, their communications may be disabled and faulty, as ours were."

"Or perhaps it no longer exists," Rovender said.

"Mr. Kitt, will you or will you not lead us there?" Muthr asked. Eva's eyes locked with Rovender's for a beat, then she looked down.

Rovender snorted. "If that's where you want to go, then I will bid you both farewell." He pulled out one of his bottles and continued his trek. He called out over his shoulder, "Oh, and by the way, Eva Nine . . . according to your map, Besteel's camp would have been underwater in the middle of your river. Good luck with your journey."

Eva studied the holo-map. She could see the glowing pin dot that was her Sanctuary. It was nestled next to a wide river.

"I think he's right," Eva said, pointing to the map. "The only thing I saw yesterday, besides a lot of forest, was a big empty area full of rocks and gravel. I didn't see a river or any water at all."

Muthr was silent. Calculating.

Eva spoke. "We want to find the other humans, right? If we go to this city, there's bound to be somebody there who can help us." She glanced over as Rovender rounded a wandering tree. "Let's see where he takes us, Muthr. Please?"

"All right, then, let us travel to Solas. It is closer than the nearest facility, and perhaps there we may learn how best to proceed," Muthr said.

Eva smiled. "Good idea."

"But, Eva." Muthr's voice was hushed. "I do not trust Mr. Kitt. There are no records of planet *Orbona* in the Omnipod. We must remain observant. Understood?"

"I understand. But so far he's been really helpful. Right?" Eva said.

"Only time will tell." Muthr patted Eva on the shoulder. "All right. Let us go."

Eva jogged ahead, catching up with Rovender. On a single wheel, Muthr rolled along behind her as they ventured deeper into the forest.

It soon became clear to Eva Nine that the farther they trekked into the forest, the more peculiar the life-forms became.

"Extraordinary," Muthr exclaimed as she passed a tall cup-shaped plant. The plant was covered in thick hairs waving about, collecting bits of pollen and other airborne particles that seemed to swim about in the cool, damp air. "It reminds me of holograms I've seen of undersea organisms."

A large, tufted, floating insect drifted down from the treetops near the cup-plant. As the plant's cilia swept the insect into the plant's circular mouth, the cup collapsed around the fuzz, creating a chorus of hoots in the process.

"Rovee, what is that?" Eva aimed the Omnipod at it.

"Some species of chimera," he replied, trudging through the bush. "Don't get too close. They can be temperamental."

"A chimera, like the monster?" Eva looked at the holo-model of it.

"A chimera can mean also that it is a hybrid, somewhat like me," Muthr answered as she watched the cup open back up.

"It contains traits from both plant and animal kingdoms," the Omnipod added.

The trio made their way through the grove of chimeras, arriving a few moments later in a small moss-laden glade.

"This may be a good place to camp for the night,"

Rovender announced. "I have seen no wandering trees for some time, so we should be safe."

"Hey, can I make a fire?" Eva asked, waving her Omnipod.

"Good thinking, Eva," Muthr replied. "See if you can locate some kindling. I will determine the proper location, far from any trees."

"No fires," Rovender said, pulling off his rucksack.

"Why ever not?" Muthr asked. "Eva could use the hands-on experience."

Rovender unstrapped his bedrolls from his pack. "For one thing, we are near the heart of the Wandering Forest. The wandering trees would stampede if they sensed danger."

Eva looked over at the thick-trunked trees that ringed the glade. The last rays from the setting sun tinted their tops in a vibrant golden hue.

"And another thing," Rovender continued. "Besteel hunts by heat detection. You might as well send a beacon straight to him. No fires."

The trio camped under dark heavy cloud cover, as the moon made no appearance that night. Rovender tended to his ankle and turned in early. Muthr patrolled the perimeter of the camp, recording every nocturnal sound produced within the forest.

Eva checked the odometer on her sneakboot as

she pulled it off. It read fourteen and a half kilometers. As the climatefiber warmed her tired body, she fell into a deep, restful sleep.

The following morning the trio continued their trek into the thick wood of the Wandering Forest. Eva was quiet as she took in the scenery, recording many of the forest inhabitants on her Omnipod.

"Eva Nine, come here! You must see this." Rovender loped ahead from the shadow of heavy growth that they were traveling through and into a sunlit field of waist-deep bracken. As Eva neared, she found her guide standing in front of a thick knobby spire that towered high above him.

"This part looks like the holos I've seen of pineapples," Eva said, pointing to the perfect pattern of nodules at the the base of the spire.

"No, no, Eva. This is a signpost. A portent," Rovender said as he walked around it and pointed to several more looming nearby. "Should you come across these, be wary."

"A sign for what?" Eva craned her neck up to see the blunt tip of the spire.

"Who put it there?" Muthr asked as she joined them and inspected the towering spire. Eva could see that the signpost was more than four times the height of the robot.

"We are at the edge of the forest's heart," Rovender whispered, kneeling down next to the base. "See here, Eva Nine? The eyes all look in toward the center. Toward the heart."

Eva leaned down next to where Rovender was indicating. She saw dark shiny round growths on the tips of the nodules.

"Those?" She peered at them. "Those are eyes?"

"Trust me," Rovender said. He stood, pointing in the direction that the eyes appeared to be staring. It was into a tight copse of enormous interwoven trees. Their canopy was so dense that Eva saw nothing beyond their green-hued veil. Rovender spoke in a hushed tone. "It is told in my clan that you do not enter there unless you are pure of spirit."

"But who put the signs here?" Muthr asked again.

"The forest did," Rovender replied. "Now, let us continue."

"Hold on a second." Eva furrowed her brow. "You mean the trees did it? Or perhaps some large creature."

"No, Eva, not the trees and not another creature," Rovender replied.

"Well, that doesn't make sense. So what do you

mean by saying that the forest put it there?" Eva asked.

Rovender continued across the field of bracken. "I mean exactly what I say: The forest has placed warnings to let you know you are to be careful, to be considerate, while journeying through it. Do you understand?"

"Not really." Eva stopped, and looked at the trees surrounding her. Heavy clouds, dirty with rain, rolled overhead. "I am still confused. How can a forest do anything? I mean, a forest is just land with a bunch of trees growing on top of it."

"Agreed," Muthr said.

"Perhaps on your planet of origin, Eva Nine— but not here." Rovender banged a second signpost with his walking stick. As he did so, the post next to Eva also rattled. The multitude of dark nodules blinked, and the eyes rotated in the direction of the disturbance. They then peered around in unison, their gaze resting on Eva for a moment before they returned to their original position. Eva blinked in astonishment at the signpost, then looked to her guide for further explanation.

Rovender leaned on his staff. "You see, here the forests are alive. They watch. They move. They feed. They have a heartbeat. Just like you. Just like me. Just like everything."

This is a good

place to rest," Rovender announced as he pulled off his rucksack. The trio had emerged from the Wandering Forest and found themselves on the edge of a vast dried lake bed. The ivory sand caked on the ground was cracked into an endless interlocking pattern that continued out toward the horizon.

"We can follow the forest edge," Rovender said, gesturing to behind them. "It will lead us north to the shore of Lake Concors, where Lacus is located. We should be there by nightfall."

Eva's eyes followed the line of trees as it vanished into the horizon. In the distance, she could

make out a small circling flock of turnfins. Below them an enormous rust-colored shape was steadily ambling toward them.

You. Safe.

"It's Otto!" Eva squealed, taking off toward the giant water bear. "Muthr, come meet him. You are not going to believe it."

The behemoth shuffled on his six legs toward Eva. She could hear him hoot and sing as he approached. She ran up to Otto and stretched her arms over his wide rugged face, hugging him. A large, pebbly tongue licked her in greeting.

"Oh, Otto! I am so happy to see you!" Eva could feel warm comfort emanate into her body from him. *Thank you for warning us about Besteel.*

You. Safe. Good.

Muthr rolled up alongside them. "My word, Eva. It is the size of an elephant."

"The Omnipod said he was a species of tardigrade, or water bear." Eva climbed up onto the top of his giant head. "Otto helped Rovee and me escape. And he's the one who warned me when Besteel returned to our Sanctuary."

"Did he?" Muthr looked him over. "And how is it that you understand his calls and I do not? Does the transcoder not work on him?"

"No, he sings to me and I get 'impressions' in my mind." Eva scratched Otto behind one of his heavy, floppy ears. "Pretty amazing, right?"

"Telepathic impression," Muthr said as she rolled closer to Otto, her laser scrutinizing every centimeter of his armored body. "How interesting."

The giant water bear caught a glimpse of the laser and pounced after it. Muthr scooted back and dropped the beam to the sandy ground, where Otto chased it as if it were a brightly glowing toy.

Eva giggled. "He thinks it's a glowfly! Keep doing it!"

"That is enough for now, Eva." Muthr turned the laser off. "We best get you some lunch before we continue."

As Eva led Otto back to Rovender, Muthr rolled alongside her. She tapped the shoulder patch on Eva's tunic.

"Why is AnatoScan disabled? When was the last time you checked it?" Muthr asked.

"I dunno," Eva replied, petting Otto's side. "It was bothering me with its 'please hydrate now' and 'please urinate now,' so I shut it off."

"Shut it off?" Muthr sounded aghast. "Eva, you must leave it on. The program is designed to keep you in top shape. Stop for a second and let me reactivate it."

Eva stopped, letting out a noisy sigh and rolling her eyes.

"Oh, come now. It is not that bad," Muthr said, turning the shoulder patch on.

Rovender approached them as they neared his temporary camp. He greeted Otto with a scratch under the chin between his barbels.

Eva's tunic reported in a cheerful tone: "Heart, lungs, brain activity, and other functions are within healthy margins. However, fluid intake is low, Eva Nine. Please consume fluids immediately. Thank you."

"Just take a break and rehydrate, all right, dear?" Muthr said.

"Okay, okay," said Eva, flopping down next to Rovender's rucksack. She opened her satchel and pulled out her hydration kit. From it she plucked one white hydration tablet and then placed it in a round metallic mesh infuser. The infuser had a thin chain attached to it, which Eva now held as she spun the infuser in the air, like the holograms she'd seen of ancient hunters using a bolas. The tablet within began to hiss, and she stopped, catching the mesh ball in midair. Eva hung the infuser inside of her drinking container, like a tea ball, as water began to trickle from it.

"Well done," Muthr said. "You properly started the reaction required to pull the moisture from the air and did not lose a single drop."

Eva looked up at her and smiled. She had practiced making water uncountable times in her Sanctuary, but this was the first time she'd done it in the wild. She glanced over at Rovender.

He stared at Eva, then at the partially filled bottle, mouth agape. "You pulled water from the air?" he said. "Eva Nine, I am impressed."

"See? I couldn't do that if I had just hatched," Eva said with a grin as she rummaged in her satchel, producing a Pow-R-drink tablet. She dropped the tablet into her drinking container, where it stained the water blue.

"Eva, may I see the hydration infuser?" Muthr asked. "I will go ahead and collect more water for you while we rest here."

"Sure." Eva pulled the empty infuser from her container and handed it, along with her hydration kit, to Muthr. The robot rolled out into the open plain and began filling bottles. Otto followed her, seemingly curious about Eva's robot caretaker.

Rovender pulled out some voxfruit from his pack and began peeling it. He eased down next to Eva, offering a piece to her. "Try it," he said, "you might like it."

Eva took the fruit and sniffed. It had a citrusy scent. She aimed her Omnipod at it. "Initiate Identicapture, please," she said.

Eva watched Rovender eat as he glanced at the hologram of the voxfruit rotating over the device.

The Omnipod chirped, "This could be a species of chlorophyte plant known commonly as a Volvox. If so, it comprises a community of microorganisms. There is more information, including life cycle, ecology, and human importance. Shall I continue?"

"Wow. For once you sort of knew what this was," Eva said. "Is it poisonous?"

"Negative," the Omnipod replied.

"Will it walk away?" she asked.

"Whether the plant that produced this fruit is sentient enough for voluntary locomotion is undetermined at this time. More data is required."

Eva looked over at Rovender.

"It isn't going anywhere," he said.

"Hey, I don't know," she replied. "The spinach on my planet doesn't walk around and eat birds." Eva peeled back the translucent rind and plucked out one of the berries within. She sniffed it, licked it, and finally nibbled off a piece. The voxfruit was tangy yet sweet, reminding Eva of the taste of gooseberries. She popped the whole berry into her mouth, savoring it.

Rovender smiled as green fruit juice ran down his whiskered neck. He wiped his whiskered face with the back of his large hand. "Well, Eva Nine? Are you dying yet?"

Eva giggled and ate her entire voxfruit. "It's different from the fruit we grew in our greenhouse," she said, "but I do like it more than nutriment tablets."

"How do those taste?" Rovender took a drink from the water he had collected at the Sanctuary pool.

"Like . . . like nothing," Eva said. "I think they're just starch."

"Why eat them, then? Where is the pleasure?"

"Because I have to," Eva replied. "Just like you."

"Bluh." Rovender popped another berry into his mouth. "Sure, I eat because I *have* to. But I also eat because I *want* to. It is one of life's few pleasures."

Atop Otto's large back, Eva and Rovender watched the trees at the forest's edge creep about in a great gigantic herd. Just below, Eva could hear the crunch of the sandy grit under Muthr's knobby rubber wheel. Instead of riding alongside Eva, the robot had chosen to roll next to the giant water bear, scanning the surface terrain and listening to the data stream from the Omnipod. Eva could hear the device reporting in its chirpy tone, "This plain is, in fact, a salt flat created from a dried lake bed and likely extends to the shoreline. . . ."

Even though she was out in the open flats, and a considerable distance from the forest edge, Eva somehow felt a comfort radiating from Otto. Of course, it was also reassuring to have Rovender and Muthr with her. As she rode along, Eva began weaving a braid from some of the fibers that had come loose from her tunic and the top of her sock.

"What's that you're doing?" Rovender was cleaning the scab from the rope burn around his ankle.

Eva looked at him sideways. "Something. You'll see."

Rovender peered up at the horizon as the dim sun began to sink. Clouds were converging into a mountainous thunderhead over the great lake. "It may rain tonight," he said. "I can smell the air changing."

"Really?" Eva followed his gaze to the massive gray clouds. "I'd love to feel actual rain fall from the sky."

Rovender gave her an incredulous look. "Feel . . . rain? You never have?"

Eva shook her head. "No. I grew up underground. How could I?"

"You can pull water from the air, yet you have never felt rain. Unbelievable," he said.

Eva finished braiding her string, leaving the ends frayed. She paused, then rummaged through her satchel and produced a small laser nail clipper. "It's weird, I know. But isn't the rain just like taking a shower?"

"No. But I believe it will be cleansing for you in many ways." Rovender pulled out a handful of seedpods and began eating them.

Eva brought the laser clipper up near her head as she grasped a wad of hair. In a quick slice she lopped off one of her many thin braids. She returned the nail clipper to her satchel and pulled the hair braid apart.

"What are you making?" Rovender asked once more.

Eva wove the hair into the braid of fibers from her clothing. "I told you, you will see." She changed the subject: "So tell me, Mr. Kitt, what are we going to do once we arrive at Lacus?"

Rovender spit seed husks over his shoulder. "I will show you where to secure a good room and a ferry that will take you across the lake to Solas. As for myself, I will likely continue north along the coastline, a region I have yet to explore."

"Why don't you stay with us?" Eva kept her eyes on her braiding. "You've been so amazingly helpful, and, despite the fact that I can pull water from the sky, we'd be totally lost out here without you."

Rovender chuckled, his gaze drifting off into the distant clouds. "No, Eva Nine. I must keep moving. Keep searching."

"Searching? For what?" Eva stopped.

"Solace."

"The place where we are going?" she asked.

"No, not there." Rovender closed his eyes. His face appeared etched with pain. "After my partner passed, I could no longer stay at my village. I could no longer stay anywhere." He opened his indigo eyes, blinking the memory away. "And so I packed all our belongings and I left." He patted his rucksack. The numerous items dangling from it jingled in unison. Rovender opened a pocket and pulled out a piece of jewelry. To Eva it looked like an ornate necklace made of jeweled seashells. He contemplated it as he held it in his calloused hands.

"That's beautiful," Eva said.

"So was my partner," Rovender replied, and put the necklace back into his rucksack.

"So you left . . . to go where?" Eva asked.

"Anywhere." Rovender looked out at the horizon.

Otto stopped walking. He shifted his weight from foot to foot and let out a low growl.

"Mr. Kitt!" Muthr looked up from the Omnipod. She pointed back over the Wandering Forest. "Up there!"

Above the treetops soared a large bird emitting a low hum.

"Sheesa! That's Besteel!" Rovender sneered as he grabbed his spyglass hanging from his pack. He peered into the eyepiece. "He is on his glider, combing the forest."

The giant water bear let out another low hooting sound.

"We have to take cover now!" Rovender lowered the spyglass. "He'll have trouble spotting us in the wood."

"Head for the trees, Otto," Eva said aloud. *And hide us as fast as you can,* she thought to her mount. Otto turned and made his way toward the tree line, letting out a low, creaky call that sounded like branches rubbing together.

"He's not going to make it in time," Rovender said, grabbing his rucksack. "We need to make a run for it."

"Hold on! Otto will make it." Eva kept a wary eye

on Besteel. The huntsman circled over the forest, then headed in their direction.

"I don't know what Otto has in mind, but tell him not to leap, Eva," Rovender said. "Besteel will discover us for sure."

Muthr spoke over the whine of her motor as she raced alongside them, "Mr. Kitt, Eva, what is that?"

Several large wandering trees broke from the forest and barreled across the flats straight toward Eva and her companions.

"I have no idea. Eva, what's going on?" Rovender asked.

Protect. Hide. Safe.

"Don't be afraid," Eva said. "They are here to help."

Within moments the trees had surrounded Eva's party. Under thick green cover, the travelers were escorted back into the dense forest. Besteel's glider hummed as he circled over them. Everyone flinched.

"Oeeah," Rovender said in a soft tone as he looked up through the dense limbs. "This is something I have never seen before."

"What is it?" Eva whispered.

"Look." Rovender pointed. "He is transporting something large in that cargo net there."

Eva peered up at the glider as it flew out over

the flats. Multiple sacks were strapped to the wings, and a hefty net swung about below it. "I wonder if he is leaving the forest. Maybe he's going to Lacus too?" she observed.

"Not with that cargo." Rovender peered through his spyglass.

"He is moving away," Muthr said in her calm voice as she studied the radar on the Omnipod. "He is crossing the lake bed and is far from us now."

As Eva and Rovender looked down at Muthr, they saw Otto strip off a sheet of lichen from one of the tree trunks with his short beak and consume it.

"And here also is something else I have never seen." Rovender nodded down at the giant water bear.

"What? That the trees and Otto are friends?" Eva was puzzled.

"And you and Otto are friends." Rovender pointed to the girl.

Eva furrowed her brow, confused.

"Do you not see, Eva Nine?" Rovender gestured at the greenery around them. "The forest is alive. Here it has protected one of its own. One that is pure of spirit."

Eva blinked as it sunk in. "Me?"

"Yes." Rovender smiled a toothy grin. "Now let's get moving. We are almost to Lacus."

CHAPTER 21: FOG

By dusk,
a heavy fog had fallen upon the land, concealing it as far as Eva could see. From her vantage point atop Otto, she thought the mist below looked like a dark treacherous sea, and her mount was her faithful ship, *The Mighty Otto*. Even in the dense murk she could still see Muthr, for the pale light of the Omnipod illuminated the robot's form as she rolled alongside them.

"We are getting close," Rovender said in a quiet tone. "Can you smell the lake?"

Eva inhaled deeply. The air had a damp mineral scent. It was like nothing she had ever smelled before, though it did faintly remind Eva of freshly watered plants in the greenhouse of her Sanctuary.

"Look there." Rovender pointed ahead. "Do you see it?"

Eva squinted in the twilight and focused in the

direction he was indicating. She could barely make out the tiniest glint of lights off in the distance. The thunderclouds that had formed all afternoon hung huge and heavy above them. From time to time lightning snaked through the sky, but never reached down to touch the lake.

"The Omnipod indicates that there are quite a large number of life-forms in the colony we are approaching," Muthr declared. "Are you sure we will be safe here, Mr. Kitt?"

"Yes," Rovender replied. "I have been to this village many times. The local folk, the Halcyonus, are friendly and trustworthy. They live entirely off the water."

"And here we may find news of other humans?" Muthr asked.

"Perhaps, Mother Robot," Rovender said. "Occasional travelers come through here, so you may be able to learn more. I will introduce you to a friend who perhaps can help."

The smell of the lake became more distinct as Eva and her companions approached its windy shores. The lapping of the waves against the shoreline was a sound she had heard before in simulations. Now, as Eva heard actual water caressing the land, she couldn't wait to explore.

Otto stopped abruptly, and Rovender gathered

his belongings. "We are here," he said, dismounting the behemoth.

Eva grabbed her satchel and slid down the side, landing on the pebbly beach. Dark water swirled around her rubber-soled sneakboots. Distant calls of turnfins, carried on the lake's chilly breeze, filled the night sky.

Eva looked out at the great lake. Its dark rippling vastness stretched so far out that it merged with the dense fog on the horizon. As lightning flickered high above, Eva spied what looked like gigantic towers perched on top of a low-lying island.

Muthr was still and silent facing the lake and its windy breath, the little light blinking on the back of her head. Eva approached her.

"Can you believe it? A real lake," Eva said, taking one of Muthr's warm hands. "It's so huge. I never thought we'd see something like this."

Muthr recited,

> *"O'er the glad waters of the dark blue sea,*
> *Our thoughts as boundless, and our souls*
>   *as free."*

Eva looked up at her as she finished. Muthr stroked Eva's cheek with silicone-tipped fingers.

"The bridge to Lacus is up ahead. Are we ready?" Rovender lit the lantern hanging from his rucksack. Through the lapping waves, he made his way over to Eva and Muthr. "Eva Nine, you should send Otto on his way."

Eva balked. "What? No!"

Rovender knelt down, looking Eva in the eyes. "He cannot come where we are going."

"But he's my friend . . . just like you are."

Rovender took off his hat. "I understand. However, he will find safety from the likes of Besteel in the numbers of his herd. He must go."

Eva nodded in agreement and traipsed over to Otto at the lake's edge. He raised his massive head and let out a cheerful hoot as he watched her approach.

Little one. Protect.

Eva leaned her forehead against his. *I am safe now, thanks to you,* she thought to him. *You must go and find your herd, where you can also be safe.*

No. Others. Here.

You have helped us all, Eva replied. She pushed down the rising tide of her tears. *I will miss you, but you need to find the others like you. That is what I am doing too.*

Little one. Safe?

Eva peered out at the great lake. The reflection

of the village lights was swallowed up in its inky undulating surface. She glanced over at Muthr, who was asking Rovender more questions about Lacus. Rovender seemed fidgety, perhaps even a bit nervous, as he pulled a threadbare tattered brown wrap from his rucksack.

Am I safe here? she thought to Otto.

Not. Sure.

Then can you stay a little longer? Eva thought. *Hide. If I need you, I'll call you.*

Little one. Protect.

I'll protect you, too.

Eva sniffled loudly as she walked over to join her companions. "Otto says he's going to rest for the night. He'll leave at dawn," she said to them in a glum tone.

"Good. Otto has been a tremendous help. Please tell him he has my utmost respect," Rovender said, handing Eva and Muthr fabric wraps of their own. "Cover yourselves in these."

"What for?" Muthr asked, taking the wrap.

"As I said, they get occasional travelers here," Rovender replied, "but it may be best to keep you both hidden until we find out if Besteel has also been coming here." He draped his loose cloak over himself, shrouding his head in a baggy hood.

"Very well," Muthr said. Eva helped Muthr cloak herself in the coarse fabric, then did the same.

Rovender then pointed ahead along the shoreline with his walking stick. "Okay. We shall go this way."

Eva and Muthr followed the lanky creature along the beach to a wide, swaying footbridge that stretched out over the water's surface. As they started to cross, Eva realized that the town was not on an island at all but was suspended somehow over the lake's depths.

As lightning danced through the sky, she turned back and saw Otto entering the lake, slipping silently under the mist-covered surf. Distant thunder rumbled.

Eva felt jittery, clammy, and giddy all at once. As they continued across the bridge, now far out over the water, patches of fog dissipated, revealing the utter expanse of the inland sea. She held Muthr's hand tightly, feeling the climatefibers in her tunic constrict to warm her from the crisp, briny air.

Eva looked up in awe at the bowl-shaped tower that they were approaching. On closer inspection, she realized that the building was composed of small globular huts stacked upon one another in a haphazard fashion. The entire cluster was supported by a gigantic piling, thicker in width than the Sanctuary, holding its inhabitants high above the water. Multiple footbridges, like the one she was crossing, radiated out from the edifice and connected with others. Every nook and cranny was filled with roosting turnfins. Even in the dim light Eva could see drips of dried guano all down the sides of the huts.

From her vantage point Eva counted five of these towers altogether, though the fog was so thick that she couldn't be sure if there were others.

Muthr pulled her close as they continued behind Rovender. Thunder rolled over the night sky. Taking everything in with her eyes wide, Eva Nine slipped her free hand into the inside pocket of her jackvest. Finding a familiar flattened shape, she ran her fingers over the WondLa and made a wish.

End of
PART II

PART III

Tinkling shells,

suspended in a large wind chime, greeted Eva and her companions as they made their way through the entrance of Lacus. An archway, made from driftwood, oars, and a hodgepodge of previously sunken objects, stood, steadfast, over the suspended walk. A clustered assortment of golden glowing globular lanterns flickered as they swayed in the chilled breeze coming in from Lake Concors.

"We shall find a place to rest for the night," Rovender said, turning to Eva and Muthr. He stopped and pulled their wraps up over their heads, creating hoods. "It will be best that you remain as inconspicuous as you can until we find out if Besteel is also here."

"I certainly hope he is not," Muthr said. "That marauder has wreaked enough havoc as it is."

Rovender began to lead them around the perimeter of the first gigantic piling on the rickety boardwalk. As they rounded the towering structure, they approached several long-limbed locals peering down into the dark depths below. They looked similar to Rovender in general body shape, though their stature was smaller and their legs were thinner and longer, like the holograms Eva had seen of storks and herons. Bright markings colored their wedge-shaped heads and surrounded their large russet eyes.

One of the locals was holding a handful of thin cords. Eva followed the cords with her eyes and saw that they were tied around the necks of a gathered bunch of turnfins. She pulled out her Omnipod.

"No, no, no, Eva." Rovender pushed the device down. "We are incognito, remember? Put it away for now."

The locals stopped, eyeing the trio as they neared.

Rovender nodded to them as they passed.

"Rovee," Eva whispered, "they sort of look like you."

"Yes. They are the Halcyonus, the resident species of Lacus. They, too, are from my place of origin."

"Are those turnfins their pets?" Eva looked back as one of the Halcyonus untied the cords and placed the birds in round woven cages.

"No, they are fishing." Rovender led them along the boardwalk as it spiraled around the colossal piling. Eva could see more fishermen below her, down near the waterline. One of them was holding a bright glowing round lantern just above the water. Several more drew the turnfins in by their leashes as the birds paddled about on the inky surface.

Rovender pointed to the next tower with his walking stick. "My friend resides at this next rookery. Let us continue." He led Eva and Muthr onto another low, swaying bridge. They left the first tower behind and made their way toward a much larger one. As lightning twisted through the clouds, Eva could see that the second tower was top-heavy with numerous rounded huts, even more so than the first.

Nearby, a lone fisherman stood at the lowest dip of the sagging bridge, centimeters above the water's surface. A large turnfin hopped up onto the bridge and squawked. Eva could see that there was something large stuck in the bird's throat just above the tight knot around its neck. The fisherman reached into the turnfin's mouth. He pulled out a brown fish with spidery legs and threw it into a bucket.

"Good evening," Rovender said as they passed him.

The fisherman looked up, blinked at the strange trio, and nodded in salutation. He fed the turnfin a small slender fish, and the bird jumped back into the water.

"The Halcyonus have gathered their food from the water in this way for more than a millennium," Rovender explained. "They have a unique relationship with the turnfin."

Lilting music wafted from high atop the second tower and mixed with the melancholy rumble of distant thunder as it settled down upon Eva. She found that the combination of sounds soothed her nerves as she crossed the lengthy footbridge over the open water. It almost sounded as if someone were calling to her. Beckoning her.

They entered the base of the tower through a high archway with stairs spiraling up through it. Rovender pointed to one of the many colored lanterns illuminating the passageway.

"Oeeah! Look, there are green lights. That means

there are vacancies, should my friend not be able to accommodate us. Come." Rovender led them on.

The threesome made their way up the abandoned spiral stairway inside the tower and emerged in a circular courtyard. They were surrounded by a proliferation of round huts built upon one another in an irregular manner. There were so many of these shacks and shanties stacked high overhead that the dwellings formed a conical bowl that towered up toward the moody sky. In the dim glow that emanated from the numerous windows, Eva could tell that the bottom huts were storefronts and that the travelers had arrived in the middle of an open-air marketplace. Many of the shops were closed, their colorful cloth signage swaying quietly on the abandoned plaza.

"What simple domiciles," Muthr said, observing the architecture. "Yet there is an exquisite intricacy in how they are all intertwined with one another."

"It's amazing!" Eva's voice rang through the quiet square as she captured holograms with her Omnipod. "Can we look around?"

"Not until we find out about Besteel, and put that infernal device away!" Rovender barked.

"What?" Eva dropped the Omnipod so that it hung from her wrist. "I'm not doing any harm."

"I know." Rovender stared up into the pitchy night. "But Besteel may be able to sense the electrical charge that your device emits. Now stay close. We are almost there."

He scanned the area, then ushered Eva and Muthr to a shaky staircase that led up to a lighted circular doorway on the second tier of huts. Rovender appeared anxious as he helped Muthr up the last few steps. He waved his hand over a blue light embedded in the door, and it switched to yellow. A voice within replied, "Enters." Rovender swung the thick door open, and the trio stepped inside.

A smell like wet rotting flowers permeated the air as they entered the cozy, dimly lit home. The antechamber was constructed from a series of wooden circular archways woven together to form the ceiling and walls. A curtained doorway separated the trio from the rest of the home, and Eva could hear several voices chatting behind it. A lone Halcyonus emerged through the thin curtains into the lighted entry, allowing Eva to take in the creature's physical details. The individual was draped in brightly patterned fabric, which only enhanced the distinct markings of its skin. Eva also realized that the Halcyonus had two mouths—one on top of the head below the nostrils, which she could hear breathing, and one lower, which she soon learned was used for speaking.

"Rovender Kitts!" said the female, for that is what Eva determined she was. "So good to sees you agains."

"Hostia Haveport." Rovender approached her with his hand raised. Both pressed their flat palms together in a greeting. "It does my weary spirit good to see you again. Tell me, how is your family?"

"They are all well. Holds on," Hostia said. "Zooze! Zoozi! Rovender is here!"

A squeal could be heard from within the house, and a Halcyonus fledgling hopped out from behind the curtain, holding a hand-carved puppet tied to the end of a long rod.

"Rovundeerz!" he squeaked, wrapping his arms around Rovender's lanky leg.

"My little Zoozi." Rovender patted the fledgling's head. "How have you been?"

"Good!" Zoozi replied. "We are playings puppets! Wants to play?"

"Of course. Let me introduce my friends first—Oh, look! Here's Mægden. My, you're getting tall . . . and more beautiful," Rovender exclaimed.

The colorful Mægden poked her head out into the entry room. Eva could see that she was a juvenile Halcyonus but older than Zoozi. The young lady smiled at Rovender but said nothing as she studied Eva and Muthr. Behind her, a colorful male, dressed similar to the fishermen the trio had passed, entered the room.

"Fiscian." Rovender held his palm up in greeting. "How are you, my friend? Are the fish still biting?"

"Rovender Kitts," the fisherman replied. "There are always smiles in this house when you arrives. Come in!"

"I will, I will," Rovender said, "but first I must introduce you to my friends."

"Please do," Hostia said. She studied Muthr and Eva with brilliant orange eyes. "Who are your concealed companions?" she asked. Though larger, the hostess appeared less colorful than Fiscian and the fishermen that Eva had seen.

"Before I introduce them"—Rovender addressed the family in a hushed voice—"I should tell you, there is a Dorcean hunting after these two."

"Who is its?" Hostia asked. "Anyones we know?"

"His name is Besteel. He claims he's working for the queen," Rovender replied.

"Besteel?" Fiscian repeated. "Somes of the others here have seen a Dorcean glider traveling backs and forth across the lake."

"It could very well be him," Rovender said, looking

at Eva and Muthr. "I am not sure what he is up to, some sort of game trade, perhaps."

"A Dorcean huntsman." Hostia's scarlet eyelids blinked as she studied Eva. "Why these two?"

"They are unlike any others I have encountered in all my travels," Rovender said. He looked down at the scar around his ankle. "Which may be why Besteel is after them. That huntsman is a reckless and dangerous spirit. If you would not want us here, we would understand."

"Well, let us meet them and we shall see." Hostia gestured for Eva and Muthr to remove their cloaks.

Rovender lowered Eva's hood first. "This is Eva Nine."

"Sheesa!" Mægden exclaimed. Her father jabbed her with his bony elbow.

Hostia's eyes went wide. "I haves never seen any a thing like this!" She helped Eva unwrap her cloak. "Tell me, Eva Nines, where is it that you comes from?"

"Um—," Eva began.

"Me helps too!" Zoozi said, yanking Muthr's cloak off. The entire Haveport family gasped.

"And this is Eva's mother," Rovender explained.

Hostia stared at Muthr, then back at Eva. "Do theys metamorphose when theys become adults?" Hostia asked.

"No." Rovender chuckled. "She provides the child's upbringing."

"They've never seen a robot before?" Eva whispered.

"The Halcyonus and the Cæruleans, my clan, do not make such things," Rovender answered.

"Where is it that you comes from?" Hostia asked Muthr.

"We are from HRP underground Sanctuary five-seven-three," Muthr answered, her amber eyes glowing brightly. "Do you know, or have you heard of, the whereabouts of any other such human facilities?"

Hostia blinked, clearly bewildered, and looked to Rovender for a translation.

"They are looking for their clan. Would it be at all possible to procure a space for the evening?" Rovender asked.

Zoozi ran over to Muthr and ran his stubby fingers over her sleek metallic sculpting. "She is a beautiful toy, Mamus."

"A toy?" Muthr's tone was aghast.

"You are right," Rovender said, patting Zoozi on the head. "She is a big toy to this young lady. But both the toy and the girl must remain a secret to all in the village."

"Because of Besteel?" Hostia asked. She and Fiscian exchanged glances.

"We've had some narrow escapes from his tireless pursuits," Rovender admitted. "As I have said, we do not want to cause any jeopardy to you or your family. They'll be on a ferry to Solas by morning."

Outside, the thunderhead banged its immense drum, sending a tremor through the midnight sky. Hostia grasped Eva's hand and stared at her with penetrating orange eyes. "May I?" she asked.

Muthr began to speak, but Rovender stopped her.

"Um, sure," Eva replied. She watched as the Halcyonus rubbed Eva's hand on the top of her head, near her nostrils and secondary mouth. Hostia closed her eyes and inhaled deeply. She took in the scent of Eva.

The composition of Eva.

The electricity of Eva.

"Yours spirit is good, and you are friends of Rovender. You may stay," Hostia announced, still holding Eva's hand. "You all may stay."

"Many gratitudes," Rovender said, pulling off his rucksack.

Hostia led Eva by the hand and addressed them all, "Our homes is your home. Come in."

CHAPTER 23: WEAVE

As she stepped through the curtained doorway, Eva entered the main living room of the Haveport family. Wide colorful pillows and brightly patterned blankets were arranged along the perimeter of a circular, tightly woven floor. A round curtained window looked out into the quiet central market below. An array of dimly lit lanterns hung, like a cluster of large fruit, from the center of the room. Hostia reached up and rubbed one of the round glass-blown lanterns with her hand, and the entire bunch flickered and then glowed brightly.

The lights illuminated an iconographical painting that covered the ceiling. It looked like invented star constellations with a large planet and several moons rendered in great detail. On the planet, which Eva assumed was Orbona, an immense rocket lay on its side, with a line of figures entering it. The inside of the rocket was filled with these figures, and an eye—with a horizontal iris—was painted on the nose of the ship. Enchanted by the mural, Eva banged into a tray sitting atop a low table.

"Sorry," Eva said, pushing the decorated tray back. She realized it was covered with a buffet of finger foods. Bright vegetables and fruit lay sliced in a row next to what appeared to be spiderfish skewers. A myriad of sauces and dips circled an ornate bowl in the center of the table that held a small flame.

"It is no problem, Eva," Hostia said. "Everythings is fine. We can enjoy this before suppers. Haves you eaten?"

Muthr answered, "No, thank you. We—"

"They have eaten already," Rovender finished. "But,

you know, I am always hungry for your cooking."

"Ofs course, but first a family drinks to our guests," Hostia said, walking toward the back of the room. A decorated sack was mounted to the back wall, with faded streamers hanging on either side.

The sack looked heavy with some sort of liquid. Several rods and tubes dangled from the bag, reminding Eva of the holograms she had seen of bagpipes. From a basket below it Hostia pulled out three tiny fluted glasses. The hostess filled the glasses with squirts of liquid from the various tubes, tapping in powders contained at the ends of the rods.

"What is she making?" Eva asked.

Rovender explained. "It is a tradition among the Halcyonus that you have a drink from the *heart* of the house—the family cask. Just as no two homes are alike, no two homes make the same drink."

A smiling Hostia handed out the drinks to the trio. Rovender drank his down in one shot. "Much appreciation and gratitude to you," he said with a nod, handing the glass back.

"And to you," Hostia replied. She looked at Eva.

Eva sniffed the contents of the glass. An enigmatic whiff of otherworldly spice whirled around her face. She looked over at Muthr, who

was analyzing her drink with a laser.

"It seems to be a combination of distilled herbs and spices," Muthr said. "Their basic compounds are similar to anise, cinnamon, and perhaps coffee beans. Add a water purification tablet and you should be fine, Eva."

"No," Rovender whispered. "Just drink it."

"Yes, drink!" Hostia said, still smiling. The other family members had now leaned over to get a better view of the curious interaction.

"You will insult them if you tamper with the drink in any way," Rovender added in a whisper, nudging Eva's glass closer to her face.

"I understand, Mr. Kitt. However, I—," Muthr began.

"Oh, Muthr," Eva cut her off. "They are allowing us into their home. Remember?" She consumed the drink in one gulp. Warm herbs and spices tingled her insides as the liquid made its way down her throat. "Much thanks and gratitude," Eva said, mimicking Rovender's gesture.

"And to you," Hostia said, taking the glass. She looked at Muthr.

"Oh!" Eva grabbed Muthr's drink. "Don't worry about her. She does not eat or drink. She's a robot."

"What is a robots?" Mægden asked.

Hostia studied Muthr, cocking her head to one side. "Why doesn't it drinks?"

"She just doesn't. She runs on power cells," Eva said, handing the drink back. Rovender intercepted it and gulped it down. He wiped his mouth with the back of his hand. "It is true. The mother is a machine. A contrivance."

"She is a toy, Mamus. Remembers?" Zoozi asked.

"That's right," Rovender replied with a grin. "You don't feed your toys, right?"

"Ah, yes." Hostia nodded in understanding. The rest of the family did the same.

"Come and sits," Fiscian said, spreading the large pillows out onto the floor. "Tell us of your journey."

"Yes, it's been some time since you haves been here, Rovenders," Hostia added, sitting down on the pillows. Mægden brought pillows over for Eva and Muthr to relax on.

And so, Eva and her companions enjoyed the hospitality of Hostia and her family. They all listened as Rovender recounted his story of the strange creature he'd encountered named Eva Nine. Rovender described a daring escape from the vicious huntsman, Besteel, and he told of the surprising companionship of Otto, the giant water bear.

Afterward Fiscian taught Eva a traditional Halcyonus fishing song. After she entered the words into the Omnipod, Eva joined everyone in singing:

> *"Oh, the wind was at our back*
> *and the tide up to our knees.*
> *As we gathered up our gifts*
> *from the green and giving seas.*
>
> *"Both my feet are cold and wet,*
> *but I walk without a care.*
> *Very soon I shall be home,*
> *where my family waits there.*
>
> *"Mother cooks a tasty meal*
> *as my children all hug me.*
> *Please don't thank me for my gifts.*
> *Thank the green and giving sea.*
>
> *"Sing! Sing! Sing!*
> *For the green and giving sea."*

"We appreciate all that you are doing for us, Hostia," Rovender said, carrying his heavy ruck-sack behind Eva. She and Muthr were following their host as she led them up a ramshackle staircase lined with fishing equipment, to an empty loft above the house. Eva could hear roosting turnfins chortling softly from within their baskets.

"You know, Rovender, our home is always welcomes to you," Hostia said, opening the round door and entering. "All ofs you."

"Much gratitude," Rovender said as he held the door open for Eva and Muthr.

"Thank you," Eva said, nodding to Hostia as she entered.

"Your hospitality is much appreciated, Mrs. Haveport," Muthr added, extending an open hand. Hostia studied the wire-veined hand and gave it a quick pat.

The loft was a smaller version of the main living area, though there was an accumulation of fishing baskets nestled under the low window. Though empty, the baskets filled the room with a salty scent. Hostia reached up, lighting the lanterns in the room, and then pulled a single drape over the window. She grabbed three large pillows, larger than those used in the living area, and laid them out on the woven floor.

"There is a comforts station one door down," she said as she unfolded a blanket. "Would anyone care for any more foods or drinks? Seabrine tea, perhaps?"

"No, thank you, Hostia. You've done enough. Oh, and I almost forgot . . . ," Rovender said as he reached into his pack and pulled out his remaining voxfruit. He handed them to her. "I brought Zoozi his favorite breakfast."

"Much appreciations and gratitudes to you," Hostia replied, taking the fruit. "Zoozi will be so excited."

Rovender smiled a toothy grin as Hostia went to leave. She paused at the door and turned to Eva. "You do not haves to leave by morning. You all are welcome to stay as long as you like."

Eva's eyes widened. She thought of exploring the market in the morning, meeting the locals, and learning how to fish. She thought of herself and Muthr living here with Hostia and her family.

Hostia continued in a solemn tone. "However, you should know that a Dorcean on your trail is likes a turnfin chasing a spiderfish—no matters how far down you swim to hide, he always catch his prey." She waved. "Safe journeys, Eva Nines and Mother Robot." Hostia left, closing the door behind her.

"Well, that was not very reassuring," Muthr said, rolling to the window and peering down into the vacant plaza below. "Do you suppose Besteel is, in fact, here, Mr. Kitt?"

"I do not think so." Rovender pulled out one of his bottles and began rearranging the pillows. "The Halcyonus are a tightly woven community. If he'd been spotted here, Hostia would have heard about it." Eva saw him look over at her as she pulled off her satchel and jackvest. "We are safe for the night as long as we stay put, and remain inconspicuous," he said.

"Then what?" Eva asked as she pulled the Omnipod off of her wrist. She slipped off her sneakboots and socks and dropped the Omnipod inside a boot. She flopped down onto a squishy red-patterned cushion. It felt good to wriggle her toes in the cool open air.

"Tomorrow morning I'll take you to the ferry docks and see you off." Rovender propped up a pillow under his legs and examined the scab on his ankle.

"Despite our differences, Mr. Kitt," Muthr said as she wheeled toward the center of the room, where Rovender and Eva were relaxing, "I will be the first to say we could not have come this far without your guidance. And so, I thank you."

"Yes, Rovee, thank you!" Eva scooted close, threw her arms around him, and gave him a peck on the cheek. A befuddled-looking Rovender remained rigid. "Oh! That reminds me!" Eva said as she crawled over to her belongings and pulled something out. "I wanted to give you this." She unrolled the braid that she had made earlier.

Ivory threads from her tunic, along with the thick climatefibers of her knee socks, were woven into dirty-blond strands of Eva's hair, and the braid was accented with colorful beads. "Hold out your hand," she instructed, draping the braided strand in her lap.

Setting down his bottle, Rovender watched. Eva took his large, calloused hand, palm up, and placed it on top of the braid. She looped the loose ends together and began tying them around Rovender's wrist.

"I learned how to make this from one of my holo-shows," she said. "It is a special bracelet, a *friendship* bracelet, that I've made for you to wear. That way you'll never forget about us. And you'll know that wherever you are—wherever you go—we'll be friends. Always." She sniffed as she finished tying the bracelet. "There," she said, admiring her handiwork. "It looks good, right?" Eva's pale green eyes were glassy. Misty.

Rovender held up his hand and stared at the bracelet wrapped around his thick wrist. He glanced over at the girl and the robot, both quiet and looking back at him. Grabbing his ratty cloak and bottle, he stood and made for the doorway.

"I am going to do a sweep of the village tonight to be sure of your safety, Eva Nine," he said. He draped the cloak over his head, opened the door, and looked back over his shoulder. "Get your rest. You have a busy day tomorrow." With that, Rovender Kitt slipped out into the night.

Distant thunder grumbled as the village of Lacus went to sleep.

Calling turnfins awoke Eva Nine from her deep slumber. Through the undulating curtain she saw the lavender predawn light drift into the room. Her blanket still wrapped around her, she crawled over to the window to view the waking village.

Down below, one group of Halcyonus fishermen gathered gear for their morning outing, while another was in the center of the open-air plaza arranging small mats in a circular layout. Eva wanted to get dressed and explore before she left; she couldn't wait to see everything in the daylight.

Muthr was in sleep mode, standing stationary in the shadows of the room with her eyelids closed. Eva's jackvest and satchel were next to her. Rovender's rucksack was still in the room, but the lanky creature was nowhere to be seen.

I'd love to get some holos of Lacus before we leave, Eva thought.

As quietly as possible Eva slipped on her thick socks and reached for her sneakboots.

"Walking distance traveled: thirty-four kilometers," the shoes announced. Eva shut off the odometer in the sneakboot's heel. The ever-vigilant robot awoke.

"Good morning, Eva, dear. Did you achieve restful sleep?" Muthr asked.

"Good morning, Muthr. Yes, I slept great," Eva said as she pulled on one of her boots, feeling it contract around her foot to hold it snug. "Where is Rovee?"

Muthr rolled to the window and peeked out. "Mr. Kitt departed early this morning to secure our ferry to Solas. He said he would return shortly to bid us farewell."

Eva slipped her other foot into its sneakboot. As she did so, she felt the Omnipod still tucked inside. She removed the Omnipod, snuck it into her tunic pocket under her blanket, and then put the sneakboot back on.

"And where are you off to?" Muthr turned toward Eva. "Mr. Kitt specifically told us to remain here."

Muthr is not going to let me explore at all. I'll have to think of a good excuse.

"Oh, I just have to use the . . . um, comfort station." Eva pointed to the shoulder patch on her tunic as she walked to the door. "You know, before AnatoScan kills me."

"Of course. Let me come with you." Muthr rolled close.

"I'm okay. Seriously—you don't have to come with me," Eva said.

Muthr stared at her, her eyelids clicking with each blink.

"Besteel's not here, remember?" Eva wrapped her blanket around herself and pushed the door open. A misty morning chill swept into the room. "Hold on to my stuff," she said, pointing to her jackvest and satchel. "I'll be right back. Okay?"

"Very well. Hurry right back," Muthr said with a sigh.

"I will. Don't worry. I'll see you in a sec." Eva smiled as the door closed.

I'll have to be quick, she thought.

Standing at the outdoor walkway of her room, Eva watched the morning light paint Lacus in a golden varnish. The rings of interwoven globular huts that comprised the village rose up toward the dawn sky like a gigantic bowl. Stretched across the diameter of the structure were strings full of long colorful pennants, waving and twisting in the day's early breeze. From every residence Eva could see the citizens of Lacus emerging as the village came to life. A shiver ran up her spine, and she trotted over to the neighboring hut where the comfort station was located. Eva pushed the door open, and spied two Halcyonus locals inside, chatting to each other.

"Hi! I'm Eva." She raised her hand up.

One of the Halcyonus whispered to the other, and both scurried past her out of the station. Eva relieved herself in the simple bathroom and exited. "I hope the others in this village are more like Hostia's family," she said to herself as she pulled the Omnipod out from under her blanket.

As she captured holograms of the village and its inhabitants from the walkway, Eva heard music—the same lilting music from the night prior—drifting down.

Eva paused and closed her eyes, mesmerized by the wondrous fugue.

"Human child." She heard a breathy whisper within the song. Eva opened her eyes and looked around. A flock of turnfins fluttered across the square above her as villagers below began to open their market stalls. Eva searched the locals milling about: She saw the party of fishermen heading down to the bridges below, a street sweeper cleaning, and a group of yogis stretching on their mats, but no one addressing her.

"Human child," the song whispered again. "Eva the Ninth. Nine Evas. The child human."

"Who are you?" Eva scanned the multitude of windows across the plaza, trying to locate the source of the music and the whispering. High above, the flock of turnfins circled and squawked, as if they were pointing down to a tiny hut nestled between two larger shacks at the topmost tier of the village. As her eyes traced the latticework of stairs that led to it, Eva started toward the remote location. She paused for a moment at the door to her room, but the mysterious melody danced in her ears. Entranced, she pocketed the Omnipod and headed toward the tiny hut.

CHAPTER 24: GIFTS

Eva crept

along the rickety walkway that circled past the many homes of Lacus. With each step she ascended higher and higher into the towering village. More than once she had to dodge a bewildered resident as the locals emerged from their huts for morning chores.

"How do you know me?" She looked up at the slew of windows still high above her.

"I know many things," the song murmured back to her. "Many things I know."

"Are you like me?" Eva squinted up through the sun's morning glare to check her bearings.

"I am like you," the voice whispered, "but you are not like me."

Arriving at the topmost tier of houses, Eva stopped in front of a large round hut where one of the cables holding the pennants was anchored. The closest flag, a faded orange streamer with stars and symbols painted on it, danced and twirled in the wind—revealing a narrow stairway alongside the home. Eva edged up the steps as the music drifted down over her, tantalizing her and leading her along.

She crossed a narrow swaying footbridge that led to the entrance of a small woven shanty. The music was coming from inside. Eva waved her hand over a blue light embedded in the door—as she had seen Rovender do—and the light changed color to yellow.

"In. Come," the voice sang in a soft hush. "Come in."

"Hello," Eva said, pushing the door open and stepping into the shadowy cramped abode. A hazy, heavy scent of burning soap and spices greeted her. Above, a knot of thick drapes and curtains hung down from the ceiling in a radial pattern like the holograms she had seen of a spider's web. Looking at the maze of drapery, Eva bumped into something small, which startled her so that she almost tripped and fell.

The floor was covered in a vast array of objects. Boxes, vases, containers, and canisters covered every centimeter of the walk space.

"Gifts given," the raspy voice intoned. "Given gifts. Watch where you venture, Eva the Ninth."

Eva treaded slowly through the hoard of gifts,

careful not to upset anything. Among the assemblage on the floor was the object creating the music. An illuminated vase flickered in time to the otherworldly tune it emitted through a lengthy contorted horn. Behind it, heavy tasseled curtains closed the entry room off from the remainder of the hut.

"Do not fear me," the whisper said from behind the curtain. "Fear me not. And do enter."

Eva gulped, reached up, and pushed the curtain aside.

The remainder of the small dwelling was also dark, save for the wan beam of sunlight shining through the large window. And this did little to warm the morning chill still trapped within. The mixed scent of flowers, spices, and oils was much stronger in here, causing Eva to feel nauseous. The flood of gifts concealed the creaking floor. The weave of the rounded walls was decorated in a simple pattern, which continued up to the roof. As in the entryway, dark drapes led the way in, toward the shadowy recesses of the shack, where Eva spied the source of the voice.

Sitting in the gloom, away from the sunlight, was a round, fat, pale being. It was larger than Eva, with numerous stumpy arms. It sat—perfectly balanced—on a one-legged stool.

The two regarded each other in silence, as the fat

being fanned itself in a lazy manner. Next to it a tentacle ending in three pincers hung from the shadowed ceiling; the tentacle was depositing clear eggs into a bowl. One of the being's runty arms stretched out and grabbed an egg, passed it to another of its many hands, and slipped it into its large mouth. Eva could see something tiny and wriggling inside the clear eggshell before it was consumed. Her stomach lurched.

"Gadworm eggs," the fat being said, though its mouth did not move. "Eggs of the gadworm. You know, they always lay twenty-three. As long as I keep eating them, she'll keep laying. Three and twenty. Twenty and three."

Eva glanced up. The endless tapering worm was suspended throughout the entire house on the cords that held the curtains. Eva's eyes followed the snaking body for a moment, but the worm's coils led her gaze back to the mysterious fat being. It watched her with two glittering slits set far apart on a wide head. "I am Arius. Arius am I: the one who sees."

"You . . . You're not human." Eva kept her distance. "I thought—"

"You thought only a human, a being such as you, would reach out." Arius hummed in the music. "Reaching out is not only a human thought."

"I know." Eva was crestfallen. "I'm sorry. It's just that you said you were like me, so I thought you were . . . you know . . ."

"Like you I am." Arius ingested another egg in her toothless maw. "But you are not like me."

Eva furrowed her brow.

"I have siblings. Siblings that I know. Yet siblings that I hide from," Arius sang. "You have siblings. Siblings you don't know. Siblings you've been hidden from."

"Siblings?" Eva was excited and confused all at once. "A brother or a sister? How do you know?"

"As I said, I see many things," Arius replied, reaching for another gadworm egg. "Many things I see, and yet, many things you do. You have yet to do many things."

Eva stood silently for a moment, trying to understand Arius's strange speaking. Was she just making all of this up? Was it the truth? Eva felt dizzy.

"Perhaps you'd like to know more?" Arius passed an egg from one hand to another. "To know more like you, perhaps?"

"Do you know if there are other humans here?" Eva pulled the blanket around her tighter.

"Usually I ask for a gift. *A special gift.*" Arius gestured to the multitude of trinkets heaped upon the floor. "A special gift to answer what you ask."

"I—I don't know if I have anything to give." Eva shifted her weight. She thought of the Omnipod in her pocket. Muthr would blow a gasket if Eva gave the device away.

"Not to worry. You are a gift in and of yourself, Eva the Ninth," Arius purred. "That is why I summoned you here. And here you are: a gift."

"I am not sure I understand." Eva took a step back, glancing down at the offerings piled all around Arius. *Does she even open these presents?* Her mind flickered to Besteel's menagerie of captured animals. "Can't I just leave and bring back something else for you instead?"

"Nothing more can you bring instead," Arius chimed. "You have brought the thing I want."

"I think I should go," Eva said, shuffling back to the curtain separating the room from the entryway. The music vase continued its enigmatic song.

"You must know that I see time. Time to me is like a rope." Arius stared at Eva with her tiny slits. "A rope where the past unravels behind us. A rope where the future weaves together to form the present."

"How does that make me a gift?" Eva stood in the entrance of the room, ready to run.

"You, like I, are a fiber of this rope." Arius ate

another egg. "This rope is made of fiber from me, from you, from everything. And you, human being, can affect the weave. I want to see what could be. To do that, I need you. You need me."

"Can you tell me where the other humans are? Or when I'll find them?" Eva stepped back into the room.

"Come closer and you will see." Arius gestured with one of her runty arms. "I will see if you come closer."

Cautiously Eva stepped through the trove of offerings into the dim sunlight. She felt sweat run down her neck under the scratchy blanket she was bundled in, but she didn't loosen her grip on it.

"Closer still," Arius said as she fluttered her fan. "Still closer."

Eva studied her. The being had no legs to speak of, just plump useless tentacles that hung limp from under her rolls of fat.

She couldn't catch me if I were to run, Eva thought.

Eva continued, step-by-step, until she was standing right in front of Arius. Her ivory skin had the texture of a mushroom, and Eva could see strange glyphs imprinted on each of her many arms. She could smell the fermented sweetness of the eggs on her breath.

As quick as lightning one of Arius's many hands shot out, clutched Eva by the wrist, and held her fast.

Let me go!

Eva shrieked. "Please, Arius, please!"

The fat being closed her tiny slit eyes and chanted:

"The ancient hive returns again,
to claim a land no longer to claim.
A nymph, born of the earth, forged by
    machine,
will lead a way through hate, through fear,
    through war.
The heart will be thy ally, and the feast will
    come to an end."

Eva stopped struggling, entranced by the intonation of Arius's voice:

> "From the west a mighty machine does run.
> Stars will bring one dream, while another
>   dream dies.
> In the sands of time, the nymph will find
>   the answer
> to the question that has plagued thy very
>   soul,
> but the answer will not suffice—
> and, put in motion, an equation begins,
> a powerful equation with many, many
>   answers."

Eva's eyes fluttered and her body went numb as Arius held her tightly and finished:

> "You will be chased to the ends of the earth,
> but the end will reveal all that you seek.
> But first the ruler of a great city will hold
>   you in court.
> The past will face the future—
> but neither will recognize that they are
>   their own reflection.
> A sibling will set you on your path.

*Go forth, human child, and foster your wit,
for even the most wicked have a family
that loves them."*

Arius released her steely grip, and Eva fell backward into the pile of offerings. She scrambled up and scuttled through the hoard and back out into the entryway, where the strange, lilting music played. Eva thrust the door wide open and dashed across the swaying footbridge from Arius's shack. She rushed down the stairs and back out into the main walkway that ringed the topmost tier of huts.

As she caught her breath, Eva rubbed her left wrist where the soothsayer had grasped her. In the reddish bruise she could see a mark forming in her skin. It was a perfect circle with another, smaller circle in it—a mark identical to one Arius had on one of her arms.

"What the—?" Eva pushed her bangs away as she studied the marking in the sunlight. Amidst her ragged breathing, she heard a sound above her.

A familiar sound.

The humming sound of a glider.

Besteel floated down inside the circular tower and hovered just a few meters in front of Eva.

"Heart rate BPM acceleration detected, Eva Nine." The chirpy voice of her tunic was muffled under the blanket. "Please begin meditative relaxation to decrease BPM. Thank you."

"Finally, Besteel gets heez elusive prize." The huntsman jumped from his glider and landed right in front of Eva. He seized her with his many talons.

"Let go of me!" Eva tried to wriggle free. She realized that Besteel was only clutching her by the wrapped blanket, so she dropped down. Eva slipped out of his grasp and ran as fast as her legs could carry her.

"Sheesa!" Besteel roared and threw down the blanket as he leaped back onto his glider. Eva glimpsed her wrap as it fluttered down several stories and then landed, tangled on one of the many lines holding the pennants that crisscrossed the plaza.

She bolted away from Besteel down the rickety walks, which were now teeming with Halcyonus locals. Eva tried to locate Hostia's home in the myriad of huts. As she sprinted past a large streaming banner, she heard the unmistakable hum of Besteel's charging weapon.

A low *woom* was heard, and the walkway

behind her blew to pieces from the sonic wave blast. Pedestrians scattered in all directions. In the chaos, Eva slipped into one of the nearby homes and slammed the door behind her.

A family of Halcyonus stood, seemingly dumbfounded in their entry room, as a panicked Eva faced them. "Please," she pleaded in between gasps, "I need to hide. Can you help me?"

The inhabitants yelled and hollered as they pushed her back out the front door. Besteel caught sight of Eva and brought his glider close, boomrod at the ready. Eva rushed down the circular walk, trying to put some distance between her and his weapon. Once more she heard the sonic vibration. The boardwalk in front of her burst into splinters. A stack of fishing baskets tumbled down to the tier below.

Eva spun around and ran back the way she had come. She had run several meters when yet another section of the walkway shattered from Besteel's sonic rifle. She was now cut off in both directions.

As fast as a whip Eva turned back and ran toward the gap. With all of her strength she jumped across it, landing flat on her stomach on the other side. The damaged boards underneath her began falling away as Eva grabbed at the fragments of walkway still intact. Her legs and feet dangled free while she dug her nails into the wood, clinging on for dear life. Over her shoulder she saw Besteel hovering close on his glider, his boomrod aimed right at her head. She risked a glance down at the numerous pennants and flags fluttering, with her blanket, in the morning breeze far below.

"No need to move, leettle one," Besteel purred. "Besteel will geet you."

Eva gulped. She could feel her grip loosening on the boards. The huntsman was almost within reaching distance. "That iz it. Stay steel."

Eva let go of the walk and dropped down a story to the walkway below. Landing hard on her right side, she shrieked as her arm and shoulder were jolted with pain. After pulling herself up with her left hand, she was soon under the shadow of Besteel's glider as it dropped down from above.

With a running leap Eva hurled herself off the walkway and into the middle of the open courtyard. She plummeted down many stories through the flags and pennants, her arms flailing about.

As she fell through the twisting banners, her hand caught hold of something and she hugged it close to her. Eva clutched on to a flag, even as the force of inertia jerked her body down, causing pain to surge through her right arm. She struggled to pull herself up to the transverse cable that held the bigger-than-bedsheet flags and banners. Besteel had yet to locate her as he navigated his descending craft down through the flapping pennants, his humming weapon charged and ready.

Eva looked over and saw that she was perhaps nine meters away from where the cable was anchored to the base of a walkway. Blocking out the throbbing in her arm, she began swinging hand over hand toward the cable mount. Besteel spotted her and closed in.

"Help me! Help!" Eva shrieked. She saw local bystanders on the walkway run with hands extended toward the cable she was hanging from.

Eva pushed through the pain in her shoulder, swinging faster. She heard a high-pitched creaking sound as the cable's anchor gave way under her additional weight. The entire line—flags, Eva, and all—plunged down toward the plaza square.

She held on to the cable as she fell on top of a vendor's pushcart, strewing baskets of fresh fish all over the ground. In seconds, flocks of turnfins descended on the havoc, gobbling the free meal from the wrecked cart. Villagers came out with brooms and sticks to shoo the birds away. Besteel hopped down from his hovering glider, locating Eva in the mayhem.

Disoriented, Eva stood up on wobbly legs, trying to focus. She shook off her dizziness and realized she was not far from Hostia's home. She ran toward the hut. She'd soon have help.

Muthr was there.

Rovender was there.

Hostia's family was there.

Eva thought about what Besteel had done to her home.

She changed direction, dashing down a narrow alley. A loud sound wave erupted, and the wall next to Eva shattered into shards of clay and wood. Dodging the rubble, she continued racing down the winding alley. As she heard grunts and groans behind her, Eva realized Besteel could not fit through the alleyway.

The alley emptied out onto a boardwalk, which went around the immense piling that held up the entire village. For a split second Eva looked over her shoulder to see where Besteel was, but saw no sign of him.

He dropped from the footbridge above, landing right in front of her.

"Gotch you." Besteel sneered and aimed the humming boomrod at Eva. She fell backward onto the walkway, her hands covering her face. A cluster of angry fishermen grabbed Besteel from behind, throwing off his aim, and the shot fired up into the air, blasting off a piece of the foundation above. Without a moment to lose, Eva scrambled up and sprinted down the nearest footbridge.

The huntsman threw his assailants off his back and charged after her. Eva made her way to the next footbridge that led out over open water toward the next tower of homes. She took off in that direction, ignoring the burn of exhaustion in her legs.

She saw that there was another bridge above her, and one below—full of morning fishermen. In an instant Eva jumped from her footbridge down to the one below, sending a flock of turnfins squawking up into the air, and then she ran faster than she'd ever run before. She looked up and realized that Besteel had taken the bridge above her and was gaining ground. There was no way she could outrun him.

With her attention focused on her pursuer, Eva ran right into a fisherman. Both toppled down onto the bridge, with the fisherman yelling at her in an indignant tone.

Panting hard, she struggled to get up. "Please! Please help me!"

A loud crash exploded behind them. Eva turned to see Besteel rising up behind her from broken planks—he had jumped more than twenty meters down to her bridge. As she pushed the angry Halcyonus fisherman aside, Eva heard the hum of Besteel's charging rifle. "You are mines, leettle runner." He aimed the weapon at her.

Eva stood, facing the towering huntsman, trembling. "Why are you chasing me? What do you want?" she yelled.

"You are a prize worth all this running about," Besteel said. The boomrod's muzzle was centimeters from Eva's chest.

"I am not a prize! You'll never catch me!" She spit into the predator's face.

Stunned at her ferocity, Besteel blinked the spittle out of his eyes. It was only for a second, but it was all that Eva needed—she dove off the bridge and plunged down to the bitter green depths below.

As the emerald surface of the lake rushed toward her, Eva's mind replayed Hostia's warning about hunting turnfins, diving spiderfish, and never being able to hide.

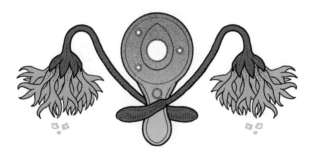

Perhaps it was

the cold temperature of the water that knocked the girl unconscious. Or perhaps it was the fear that filled her heart as she plummeted down, down, off the bridge and hit the lake's surface like a doll.

Eva Nine sank into the blue-green depths of the great lake, the sun's rays reduced to pale dancing ribbons of light playing above her. A large shadowy form emerged from the dark gloomy deep to claim her limp figure.

A behemoth.

Otto's legs propelled him up toward the surface. Paddling like an enormous many-legged turtle, he gently came up under Eva's body and carried her toward the sunlight.

Breathe. Little one. Air.

Eva lay, unmoving, upon the large armored back of the water bear as he swam about under the footbridge.

She did not see the fishermen on the bridge lowering ropes to rescue her.

She did not see Rovender jump down into the water and swim toward her.

She did not hear Muthr scream, louder than a robot should, for her daughter.

And she did not feel the large arm of Besteel grab her up as he flew over Otto in his glider and carried the girl far, far away.

Eva blinked her eyes as white light burned into her retinas.

Am I back home in the Sanctuary? she thought.

A smell, of chemicals and acid, assaulted her nose.

No, I am not.

Groggy, Eva sat up. A sting of pain shot up from her elbow in her right arm. She rubbed her shoulder.

I think it's just bruised. I'll check it later. She felt

the Omnipod still tucked safely in her pocket.

Eva rubbed her eyes with the heel of her hand and checked her surroundings. Every direction she looked seemed blurry and distorted, like a hologram before a holo-bulb goes out. On shaky legs, she rose.

It appeared to Eva as though she were viewing the brightly lit room around her through a drinking glass, as objects around her bent in space. She was standing on a white circular platform; another platform, the exact same size and shape, was above her—as if she were in some sort of large container that she could not see out of.

Where am I? A rush of memories replayed in her head. . . . Lacus . . . Arius . . . Besteel . . . running . . . jumping.

"Did I die from the fall?" she whispered to herself.

No, she thought. *If you were dead, you wouldn't feel the pain in your arm.*

"But I feel chilly. Aren't you cold when you die?" Eva rubbed the hem of her tunic. The climatefibers were working, but without the added layer of her jackvest, it felt like she was in a freezer. She tapped the patch on her shoulder, activating AnatoScan.

The tunic reported in its cheerful tone: "Heart, lungs, brain activity, and other functions are within healthy margins. However, fluid intake is low, Eva Nine. Please consume fluids immediately. Thank you."

"Of course," she replied. "What is the temperature?"

"Outside temperature is ten degrees Celsius, body temperature thirty-seven degrees. Thank you."

Well, I'm not dead. Time to get out of here.

Eva neared the edge of the platform. She raised her hands in front of her and touched the wall. It was similar to frosted glass, with a clear wetness slicked over it, like oily condensation.

"What the—?" Eva sniffed the wet residue covering her palm. It was the source of the chemical smell, and though it was clear, it was thicker than water.

What am I in? she wondered.

Eva wiped her hand on the clouded wall that contained her. For a few moments she could see beyond, before the liquid ran down to recoat the wiped area. She was, in fact, confined within a cylindrical cell in a round room ringed with identical cells.

More curious than scared, she walked around her confines, systematically rubbing away the dampness that covered the wall. Eva found that she was between two other cells. One held a small jumping creature that bounced aimlessly against the impenetrable walls. In the other cell adjacent to her, Eva recognized the shape and color of a juvenile water bear through the blur of the liquid coating.

Hello, little guy. Can you hear me? she thought to it. *Don't be scared.*

The water bear did not reply.

There was movement in the center of the room. Eva heard muffled voices. She rubbed away the condensation and spied two figures speaking.

A squat creature waddled in, upright on four stub legs, shorter than Eva. His four flabby arms waved about as he spoke in a nasally tone through a tapered proboscis. "Come, come. You must see the new specimens, Zin; we have been receiving them all week. They are spectacular."

Levitating behind the runty creature was the character addressed as Zin. He was similar in appearance to Arius—though he was smaller and adorned in more decorative attire. Like Arius, he had a large mouth that did not move when he spoke. "Apprise me, please. Did he deliver any multiples or duplicates?"

"Let us see." The runt reached inside one of the many pouches on its belt and pulled out a small handheld device. With a stumpy finger he pressed a button on the remote.

A piercing high-pitched ring shot through Eva's

skull. Gritting her teeth, she covered her ears with her hands to block the penetrating sound. Through squinting eyes she saw the liquid on the glass wall evaporate, revealing the room and all occupants in their entirety. Suddenly the piercing sound stopped.

As she exhaled out the pain, Eva discovered that the expansive brightly lit room was devoid of any color. White paneled floors reflected the glare coming in from the latticework ceiling. It seemed to Eva that the entire high-domed roof was one gigantic light. The creature that held the device was also dressed in white—a tight-fitting bodysuit, the material of which reminded Eva of a latex glove. His entire head was covered with hooded goggles, full of numerous thick lenses.

"It looks like we have only one duplicate," he said as he waddled over to the cell holding the young water bear. "It's a juvenile. He brought it in yesterday with some others. I accepted it thinking it would look great with the adults. Do you want to keep it?"

With one of his many arms Zin produced a writing tablet from the folds within his ornate jacket. He passed it along from hand to hand. "Yes, let us add it to the collection. So the sum total this week would be?"

The runt in the bodysuit stood in place, counting

the captives in the cells. "Thirteen ... No—he brought one more in today. Fourteen total," he said.

"So, thirteen unique specimens total, is that correct?" Zin wrote in his tablet.

"Yes," the other replied, pulling another tiny remote from his many pouches. The cell holding the water bear floated to the center of the room.

"Very well," Zin said, tabulating. "The aggregate amount, then, is seven hundred and forty-nine to date. He's got a considerable amount of capturing ahead of him."

"Well, he said he would have had even more, but some got away." The stubby creature put the tiny remote away, replacing it with another. A thin rod rose from the bottom of the water bear's cell. The juvenile paced inside, hooting.

"Her Majesty is satisfied with what he's fetched up to this point; however, if he is hoping to earn the pardon for that deplorable brother of his, he best not allow any more of his game to *get away*." Zin returned the tablet to his jacket and drifted over to the water bear's cell in the center of the room.

Eva sat back for a second.

He? Who are they talking about? she thought. Then the answer hit her.

"I've been captured ... by Besteel," Eva whispered.

That nauseating coil of dread wound its way into her stomach.

"So prepare this one just like the adult?" the runt asked while he continued with his remotes. Zin tucked his many arms behind his back and hovered close to the glass container that held the water bear. Eva could see his distorted reflection looking back at him.

"No, let's do an anatomical reveal," Zin replied without moving his mouth. "If the huntsman delivers additional specimens of these, though, refuse them."

"Whatever you say, Curator." The stubby creature hit a button on his remote. A fine mist sprayed from the rod in the water bear's cell. The animal froze instantly. Eva gasped.

"Paralyzation is complete. It's still alive, if you'd like to examine it." Zin's partner tapped several more buttons. Sinewy graspers now emerged from the floor of the cell, positioning the frozen water bear in an active pose as if it had been caught midleap with its specialized tail.

"Much appreciated. However, I've the utmost confidence that I now have a comprehensive understanding of these primitive indigenous organisms," Zin chirruped.

"Good enough," the runt said, plugging a white

hose into the base of the cell and turning it on. The container filled with a viscous clear liquid. Eva couldn't make out what was going on because Zin was blocking her view. "Just about finished," the runty creature sang. The liquid drained out of the cell with a gurgling sound. "Nice. This little one is going to look splendid with the adults."

"Yes, indeed," Zin said, rubbing several pairs of his stumpy hands together.

"Let me just move him onto a display base, and then I'll continue with the rest." The runt in white brought over another round platform with the aid of another remote. He pressed more buttons, and the glass wall of the water bear's cell dissipated. The mounted specimen was placed on its finished base. "There you go, Curator Zin. All ready for Her Majesty's museum," he announced with pride.

Eva stared at the water bear as it floated, frozen in midleap, rotating slowly over the base. However, the armor, skin, and much of the musculature of the creature was gone—revealing a detailed view of the organs, blood vessels, and nerves within. It reminded her of the holograms she had captured on her Omnipod—but this wasn't a model made of light. It was real. This water bear had been alive, just seconds ago . . . and now . . .

Eva closed her eyes and held her own insides, gagging.

"Impressive work, Taxidermist," Zin said as he circled the mounted water bear. "Observe: You can clearly view the cardiac stomach and the pyloric stomach . . . and here, the ganglion extends the entire length of the body ventrally. Fascinating. It reminds me of the loripeds we examined on Ceres."

"It does indeed," the squat taxidermist replied. "I do hope the queen will like the new additions."

The queen, Eva thought. *Rovee mentioned a queen before.*

Zin pushed the specimen to a wide circular doorway, and the door's many blades retracted like a fan. "Her Majesty delights in all of your exquisite work, sir, as do I."

"Oh, before I forget," the taxidermist said as he followed Zin to the door. "There was the one specimen Besteel brought in today that he wanted you to have a look at."

Eva's heart stopped.

"Oh?" Zin reentered the room.

"Yes, this way." The taxidermist led him toward Eva's cell. She slid back as far as she could, cowering in the bottom. She watched as the two dissimilar faces peered into the cell that held her.

"Says this rare one was tough to catch, and has to do with all of the relics you've been gathering out in the wastelands," the taxidermist said, jabbing a squat thumb toward Eva.

"Really?" Zin circled her cell. "Now that you mention it, the adornments do bear a resemblance to the items we've unearthed from a remote site, and its unique physical appearance differentiates it from other living specimens collected thus far."

"That it does," said the taxidermist, nodding in agreement. "If it indeed has to do with your other work, then Besteel wanted to know if . . . perhaps . . . the queen would be willing to renegotiate his undertaking."

"I cannot answer that directly, but I will forward his inquiry on to Her Majesty," Zin replied as he studied a trembling Eva. "Please delay the preparation of this one until I hear of Queen Ojo's wishes. Her Majesty may prefer to keep it under observation. . . . Very interesting indeed." Zin zipped back toward the door.

The runty taxidermist followed him. "Good enough. I'll be back here shortly. I need some additional mounting bases." He tapped a button on a remote, causing the ringing sound to return. The cells, once more, clouded with condensation.

Hyperventilation

occurring," Eva's tunic announced. "Please—"

"I've got to get out of here!" Eva said through quick breaths as she shut the tunic off. She heard a familiar muffled chirp coming from her tunic pocket. She fumbled in her tunic and pulled out her Omnipod with shaking hands.

"I can't stop thinking about that poor water bear," she said to herself.

I'm going to be on display with my skin removed too if I don't hurry.

Eva brought the Omnipod to her lips and whispered into it, "This is Eva Nine."

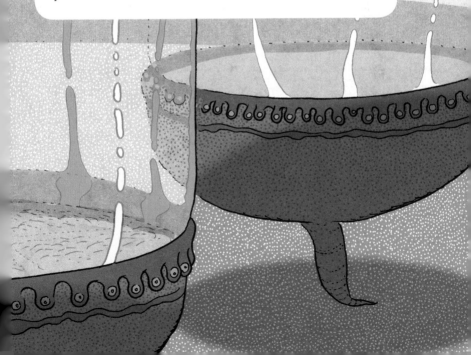

The device whispered back, "Greetings, Eva Nine. You have several unplayed messages, all from Multi-Utility Task Help Robot zero-six. I am instructed to play messages only if you are unaccompanied. May I proceed?"

"Yes, please," Eva responded.

"First message sent approximately eight hours and twenty-three minutes ago," the Omnipod continued.

Eva felt the slightest bit of warm reassurance in her chilly cell as the face of Muthr projected over the device.

"Eva, if you get this message, contact me as soon as possible. Let me know that you are all right," Muthr said with static in her voice. Eva wasn't sure if the static was because the Omnipod had been wet from her dive in the lake, or if it was because the signal was having trouble penetrating where she was being detained.

"Next message, please," she said. Her eyes darted around the room, fearful of the taxidermist's return—but all was still.

"Eva," Muthr's hologram said, "I am trying to understand the language here, but without your vocal transcoder, it has been a bit challenging. Fiscian showed us a map of the lake, and based on the trajectory of Besteel's route, I believe he may have taken you to Solas. I do recall Mr. Kitt saying to Mrs. Haveport that Besteel claimed to be working for the queen, so Besteel may have you contained somewhere on the royal grounds. Try to stay calm and alert, and do not forget your survival skills. We shall be there soon. Contact me immediately so that I may locate your signal."

"Next message," Eva whispered, cradling the Omnipod in both hands.

"Hi, Eva. Please contact me," Muthr said. "I am so worried about you. Please, please. I just need to hear from you."

"End of messages," the Omnipod finished.

The last message didn't sound at all like the robot's usual calm tone. "Can we please contact Muthr?" she asked.

"Attempting voice connection to Multi-Utility Task Help Robot zero-six . . ." The tiny lights began their dance around the Omnipod's central eye.

Eva checked the room as she picked at her fingernail. "Come on. . . . Come on."

"Eva!" Muthr's head floated up over the device. "Eva, is that you?"

"Yes! Yes! It's me!" Eva wiped her eyes with her sleeve. "I'm okay. Besteel's not even here. He put me in a cell. I am trapped in a weird place where they prepare poor captured animals for display for the queen. It's horrible."

There was no reply for a beat, then a vivid circular image of Rovender's head appeared—as if the Omnipod were seeing through Muthr's eyes. "Hello, Eva Nine. I am happy to see you are alive," he said.

"Oh, Rovee!" Eva cried. "You have to get me out of here!"

"Listen carefully, Eva." Rovender's voice was firm. "Otto is transporting us across the lake to Solas, where we will come get you. But we likely won't arrive for at least another hour."

Eva gulped. "I—I don't think I'll be here in another hour." Her mind flickered once more to the skinned water bear. "You have to help me. What do I do?"

"Look around your cell," Rovender replied. "Is there any way that you can escape?"

"I don't know. I don't think so." Eva set the Omnipod down and stood, banging the cell wall with her fist. "I can't even break this!" Frustrated, she slid back down to the bottom of her container. "Can't they just let me go? They have no right to hold me."

"I am not sure why they'd keep you, Eva." Rovender sounded puzzled. "But if asking for your release doesn't work, you are going to have to try another method. Think. Do you see any clues that may aid in your escape?"

Eva leaned over to the glass wall and wiped away the heavy oily condensation. She panned the Omnipod around the white room. "I don't know. I don't think so. Please hurry!"

There was no response. Eva returned her attention to the Omnipod. "Hey, are you guys still there?"

"Sheesa! Look! He's right there!" Eva could see Rovender pointing over Muthr's shoulder. Through the robot's eyes the view turned to a glider swooping down from the sky.

"Besteel! NO!" Eva cried, watching the hologram in horror. The camera's point of view from Muthr scrambled a bit as the huntsman hopped off the glider onto Otto's back, throwing Rovender off into the lake. Pointing his charging boomrod at Muthr, he snarled, "Goody for Besteel. Goody for my brozeel. Twoz of you in one day."

The hologram disappeared. "Connection terminated," the Omnipod announced.

Eva screamed, "No! Try reconnecting! Hurry!"

"Attempting voice reconnection to Multi-Utility Task Help Robot zero-six . . ." The device's lights flickered.

Eva gulped. That cold, jittery feeling snaked

from her stomach to every vein, artery, and capillary within her.

"I am sorry, Eva Nine. I am not receiving a reply. Would you like to leave a message?"

Eva shut her eyes tightly and curled up into a ball.

Muthr needs me. She's just a robot. A robot meant to live in a Sanctuary, and I convinced her to leave. Now, she's . . . she's . . .

That high-pitched ring returned, and the condensation evaporated on her cell walls. The taxidermist reentered the lab, pushing a stack of hovering mounting bases. "Okay. Who is next?" he said, and pressed a button on his remote. A holding cell from the far side of the room floated to the middle of the floor. Inside it, a familiar visage peered around, clicking in cadence calls.

A captive sand-sniper filled up most of its cylindrical chamber. Eva pressed her face to her cell wall as she studied the monstrous crustacean in the white light. Its colorful carapace housed a pair of formidable spiked claws.

It's like the holos I've seen of praying mantises, Eva thought. *An enormous praying mantis.*

It appeared that the captive was only a nymph, much smaller than the giant she had seen the other night with Rovender; however, the creature

was still larger than she was. Eva activated Identi-capture.

"Are you ready to pose for the queen, my little beauty?" the taxidermist purred, pressing more buttons. Inside the sand-sniper's cell a rod rose from the bottom.

A clicking sound was emitted from Eva's cell.

The sand-sniper clicked back in an accelerated tempo.

"What is this?" The taxidermist turned to look at Eva. Inside, she stood with the Omnipod pressed against the glass wall of her cell. The recorded call of the adult sand-sniper she had encountered played at full volume.

A loud crash erupted from the captive sand-sniper's cell. It had cracked the glass with its claws. The runty taxidermist fled backward, stumbling over the hose that pumped the skin-dissolving solvent. He landed flat upon his back, his various remotes spilling out across the tiled floor.

The now free sand-sniper clicked and snapped as it pounced onto the cowering runt. The sand-sniper's bowl-like eyes rotated as they took in its alien surroundings. Eva waved the Omnipod around, and the many-legged monster bolted toward her cell. The taxidermist opened the door and scrabbled out of the laboratory. The door slid shut behind him.

"Come on!" Eva yelled as she backed up in her cell. The sand-sniper circled her chamber, probing the glass wall with its many antennae. She replayed the recorded call once more. "Come and get me!"

The monster reared up, cocking its powerful graspers back. Faster than a blink, the glass walls of Eva's cell shattered and the top collapsed. Eva fell backward from the force of the eruption and landed hard on the floor outside of her cell, the wind knocked out of her. In seconds the sand-sniper closed in, clicking and clacking in confusion at the Omnipod. Eva cowered, covering her face with her hands. As she did so, the sniper swiped at the Omnipod, flinging it from

Eva's hand. The device slid across the polished floor to the far end of the lab, while the call continued to play. The sand-sniper followed it.

Eva let out a piercing scream. Two of her fingers on her right hand were bent backward, and blood ran from a gash in her palm caused from the sand-sniper's blow. She tried to swallow down the throbbing pain and focus. With her left hand she tapped the shoulder patch on her tunic.

"You are hemorrhaging blood in the right hand, Eva Nine," the tunic reported. "What is the nature of your injury?"

"I . . ." Eva lay curled up on the floor, her hand searing with pain. "I've hurt my hand really, really bad. I think my fingers are broken."

"AnatoScan: Emergency Situation activated. Please sync Omnipod using IMA."

With teary eyes Eva looked across the floor at the sand-sniper prodding the Omnipod at the far side of the lab. "That's not going to happen," she groaned.

"Pull right tunic sleeve cuff over laceration wound immediately," the tunic instructed.

Wincing, Eva yanked her cuff over her hand. The deep cut soaked the sleeve in scarlet.

"Procoagulate glue applied to trauma site, followed by SpeedHeal ointment," the tunic said. The climatefiber in the cuff wept a cloudy liquid, and the bleeding in Eva's palm stopped. The bloodied cuff then unwove, separating itself from the sleeve. It constricted tightly over Eva's hand, acting as a bandage over the cut on her palm.

"Administering pain control," the tunic announced. Eva felt a prick in her shoulder, just under the patch. A warm wave of calmness emanated into her body, numbing her hand and her shoulder. She exhaled and refocused.

"Beginning anti-swelling treatment on phalanges. Please pull remaining tunic sleeve over injury and restrict movement." The tunic instructed.

Eva did so, feeling the nip of ice as the climate-fiber surrounding her broken fingers chilled.

"Further medical treatment must be handled in conjunction with the Omnipod. Thank you." The tunic finished.

Still dizzy from the medication, Eva scrambled to her feet. With her good hand she scooped the taxidermist's scattered remotes up from the floor.

"I'm not letting any of you die," she said, pressing the buttons on the remotes rapidly. Cells floated about the room, banging into one another; probes rose up from the floor; the hose began squirting its solvent into the sand-sniper's empty cell; and overhead lights flashed off and on. At last one button caused all cell walls to ripple, like liquid membranes, allowing the captives within to crawl, hop, and flutter free. The sand-sniper now focused its attention on the freed animals, pursuing them around the laboratory. In the fray Eva snuck around the lab's perimeter and grabbed her Omnipod before exiting out the lab's large door, which shut automatically behind her.

She found herself in a dim, lofty, cathedral-style corridor that arced gradually around a bend. Recessed circular doorways were positioned along the length of the hall, and elaborate jellyfish-shaped chandeliers lit the way. The walls of the hall were ribbed with enormous segmented pillars. These pillars were textured in such an organic fashion that it looked as if they were once alive. Eva was but a few doors down from the lab when she heard voices around the bend.

"This way! Hurry, Zin!" the taxidermist said as he rushed toward her. His rattled voice echoed throughout the hall. "We need this specimen contained immediately. It cannot escape into the museum."

Eva slipped into the shadows of a doorway and held her breath. It was like hiding from Muthr during hide-and-seek.

The two zipped right past her. "It was that unusual bipedal creature. It somehow called to the sniper and commanded it," the taxidermist continued.

"Fascinating," Zin replied as they paused at the entrance to the laboratory. "Can you please mist the room before we enter? That should paralyze all within."

Eva risked detection, peering from her hidey-hole.

"I dropped all of my remotes, including the emergency pillar guard controls!" The taxidermist sounded desperate.

"Pillar guards?" Zin floated back to one of the pillars near the entryway. "That's certainly one approach to nullify the danger." He pulled out a dark remote from his jacket and aimed it at one of the pillars. He waved a stubby hand over the trio of lights on the remote.

Eva looked up. From high atop the pillar three glowing slits revealed themselves, and a blatting sound came from within.

"Follow me, please," Zin commanded as he floated to the lab door.

A long square leg stepped forward from the pillar, followed by two more. Eva's eyes went wide as a six-meter-tall automaton emerged, marching out from the pillar base it had been standing on. Rows of small lights inside its armored alien coating flickered in rhythm from its three feet to its three eyes. Segmented arms, ending in endless talons of every size, extended down from its sides. Eva sunk into the recesses of the shadows in the doorway, watching the pillar guard. It stood in the high-roofed corridor in front of the lab door and looked down at Zin.

"Behind this door is a feral carnivore that has escaped," Zin explained as he fluttered around the guard. "I need you to enter and immobilize it immediately. Use any means necessary, understand?"

The pillar guard blatted in response as Zin opened the door. A flying crab creature chirped as it soared out of the lab and down the hall. The door closed behind the pillar guard after it entered.

"This is overkill, don't you think?" the taxidermist asked as he listened to the chaos on the other side of the door. "Those things are supposed to be used only if we are under attack. We probably could have just had a few royal guards handle this."

"Perhaps, but if that large subterranean arthropod is as deadly as Besteel says, then let us not risk any casualties. The pillar guard will handle it efficiently," Zin chirruped.

While their attention was focused on the battle within the laboratory, Eva slipped down the hall.

CHAPTER 28: ARTIFACTS

Eva Nine discovered that the bending corridor was simply a big loop with mysterious rooms radiating off it. With a sigh of relief she found her way out, undetected. As the exit door retracted open, Eva stepped out onto the topmost floor of an enormous multilevel open hall.

The Great Hall's ceiling was similar to the one she'd seen in the laboratory, but executed on a much grander scale. A network of aged support beams was woven into a mesmerizing geometric lattice, supporting the transparent arched roof. Outside, Eva saw colorful banners fluttering in the afternoon breeze—all of them adorned with the symbol of a single eye with a horizontal iris.

Here and there, pedestrians of every shape, size, and color ogled at the rows of exhibit cases that lined the ribbed walls. The architecture was so organic, so magnificent, so otherworldly, that Eva momentarily forgot the peril she was in and strolled about, taking in the grandness of it all.

She gazed down from the balcony to the floor of the museum. Perfectly preserved trees from the Wandering Forest were displayed down the center of the hall, their topmost boughs just short of the floor she was on. Suspended from the ceiling beams were a variety of flying creatures, frozen in midflight. Eva moved down the aisle of displays, looking for a face in the crowd—any face—that was similar to hers in appearance. All that she saw staring back was a myriad of horns, tusks, beaks, and snouts.

She made her way down the impressive grand ramp, pausing at each of the other three floors before she was on the ground level. Weaving in and out of the busy foot traffic, Eva continued her search for another human in the mass. She passed the towering pillar guards standing rigidly as they lined the Great Hall like gigantic supports for the building.

"Please tend to fractured fingers immediately. Thank you," Eva's tunic reminded her.

As she approached an impressive display of Orbonian plant life, Eva slipped between the densely placed trunks of forest trees. Slumping down behind a mounted specimen of a wandering tree, she checked to see if she was well concealed from all passersby. With her unharmed hand she activated the Omnipod.

"This is Eva Nine. Initiate Individual Medical Assistance, please," she whispered. "This is an emergency."

"IMA initiated. What is the nature of your emergency?"

It hurt Eva to admit it. "I've broken my fingers on my right hand." She recalled Rovender's warnings about sand-snipers.

"Please place Omnipod over injury," the device responded.

Eva held the Omnipod over her hand. The central eye became an X-ray, allowing her to look inside her body as she moved the Omnipod around. She could see that the thin bones above the knuckle of her ring finger and pinky were split across the middle.

"Digitus annularis and digitus minimus manus have sustained simple fractures in the proximal region. Accessing HRP utilitunic for splint preparation. Please wait," the Omnipod said.

Eva poked her head out from behind the mounted tree and realized that in the bustle of the Royal Museum no one seemed to be paying any attention to the human girl hiding in a display.

"Remove reinforced rubberized toe cap from within right sneakboot," the Omnipod said as it projected a diagram showing how to remove a U-shaped form nestled in the toe of her shoes.

Eva set down the Omnipod and yanked off her right sneakboot, keeping her wounded hand as still as possible. She pulled out the U-shaped toe cap.

"Okay," she said. "I've got it."

"Place fractured fingers inside toe cap as shown." The Omnipod illustrated its instructions. Eva followed them.

"Remove cuff from left sleeve of utilitunic," the Omnipod said. The climatefiber on the left cuff unwove, leaving the cuff free. "Now wrap tightly around toecap as shown."

Eva did as she was instructed. She winced, gritting her teeth, as she tightened the wrap around the toe cap, which now acted as a splint for her fingers.

"Splinting complete," the Omnipod finished. "Avoid activity that may aggravate injury, and keep dressing clean and dry. Have IMA recheck injury in twenty-four-hour increments. Thank you."

Eva slid her foot back into her sneakboot and tucked the Omnipod back into her pocket. She snuck out of her hiding place and back into the throng of museum visitors.

As she walked the floor of the Great Hall, she discovered that there was an entrance on either end. Eva trotted toward the closest, the back entrance, passing a preserved herd of grazing water bears. She was almost at the back entrance when she spotted Besteel.

While his back was to her, Eva slipped behind an enormous tank full of spiderfish and spied on him. The huntsman turned his head as he talked to another museum patron, and Eva realized that it wasn't Besteel at all but simply another Dorcean. She let out a sigh of relief and headed off in the opposite direction—toward the front entrance— just to be safe.

She hurried as she neared the door. She felt the warmth of the late-day sun beaming in from the decorated high-arch windows over the wide half-circle doorways. She was just about through the entrance when something caught her eye.

Something in one of the exhibits.

The exhibit that attracted her attention was down a corridor to her left. Eva paused at the front door as throngs of pedestrians slipped past her. Mesmerized, she walked slowly toward the exhibit corridor. Hanging at the corridor's entrance was a gold-speckled flying contraption, but it was the illuminated display below it, welcoming visitors into the exhibit, that caught her eye.

A dingy yellow jackvest, with long sleeves covered in worn emblems, was mounted under thick glass. Below it were a soiled, crumpled pair of wooly socks and a single sneakboot. A display full of tarnished clunky versions of the Omnipod stood nearby. All around, glass bubbles floated with captions projected onto their round surfaces. Eva could not read the symbols that they projected, but she remembered something Rovender had said about her WondLa.

I have seen similar objects in the Royal Museum in Solas.

She entered the exhibit, staring at the encrusted items arranged in the glass displays: a collection of corroded spoons, stacks of chipped bowls, sheets of nonworking electra-paper, a cracked holo-bulb, and the unmistakable head of a robot, its silicone facial skin long eroded away.

Eva slumped forward, leaning her forehead on the display's glass.

Well, this proves it for sure, she thought. *Muthr and I weren't alone on this planet.*

"But it looks like we are now," Eva whispered, gazing at the lifeless eyes of the robot head. Its braincase was shattered, the top of it missing.

She felt the hairs on her neck stand on end. Without moving Eva saw the familiar face of the taxidermist reflected in the glass next to her. With a gasp she spun around. The squat creature sneered at Eva. In his nasally voice he said, "No use running. You cannot escape." Behind him a tall helmeted royal guardsman stood on either side. Each held a polished decorated sonic boom-rod.

The hard muzzle of a boomrod shoved Eva in the back as she stumbled into the taxidermist's lab. "Ow, that hurts!" she whined, struggling against her tight arm binds.

"Ah, it speaks!" the taxidermist said, thrilled.

"You must have a v-coder on you, I suppose?" He nodded to the guards. "Search her."

A tall guardsman frisked Eva, placing the found items on a white table: the vocal transcoder, several stolen remotes, a half-eaten SustiBar, and the Omnipod.

This is not good, Eva thought.

"Very good!" The taxidermist examined the Omnipod closely through his thick goggles as he turned it over in his tiny hands. "Guards, I thank you for your assistance. Please inform Curator Zin that we've found the fugitive. I'll have it prepared for the queen shortly."

Thankfully I am still in range of the transcoder and can understand what he is saying.

The royal guardsmen left the room through the shutter door. A still-loose flying crab chortled from its perch on top of an empty cell.

Nice work. The place is pretty trashed, Eva thought.

"You've caused quite a mess in here," the taxidermist said as he pressed a button on his remote. An empty cell floated to the center of the floor. "It will take some time to clean all of it up." The taxidermist retrieved one of his stolen remotes.

Eva looked around; green-yellow goo was spattered all about the previously sterile white laboratory. The sand-sniper was nowhere to be found.

I have to get out of here.

"I can see why Besteel wanted to renegotiate his task after your capture," said the taxidermist. Another button was pressed and the glass walls of the cell rippled like a watery membrane. "You must have given him quite a hunt. And Besteel loves a good hunt, that he does."

Eva glared at the taxidermist's many eyes. "He destroyed my home. He nearly killed me. You have no reason to do this. Please let me go," she said.

"For a dirt-burrower, you sure do chatter a lot." The taxidermist snickered as he shoved Eva into the cell. She slipped right through the membrane, tripping onto the cell floor. She scrambled up to hop out, but the membranous wall solidified, holding Eva inside. A thin rod rose up in the middle of her cell floor.

"Please, don't do this! I've done nothing to you!" Eva pleaded, her vision blurred as tears streamed out. Her body was numb from the pain medication, but she trembled in fear nonetheless.

"You are going to be a fantastic addition to our collection." The taxidermist hooked the hose to the base of Eva's cell and aimed his remote at her.

CHAPTER 29: MARKINGS

What have we here?" Zin floated through the shutter doors to the laboratory. Behind him several royal guardsmen entered, followed by a tall creature draped in resplendent finery.

"Curator Zin, Your Majesty," said the taxidermist as he approached the queen and kissed one of several pendants hanging from her frilled neck. He glanced around the messy lab, nervous, like one of his own captives. "I wasn't expecting your presence. I am . . . honored."

The queen nodded and glided into the room past her guardsmen.

Though she had yet to be frozen by the deadly mist, Eva was paralyzed with dread as she awaited her fate.

A pair of iridescent eyes, each with a dark horizontal iris, regarded the girl. The translucent, pearly face was decorated with painted scroll-like markings. The angular head was wrapped in a dual frilly collar and adorned with a wreath made of colorful fungi and lichens. A large vocal transcoder hovered over her, following the queen's every move.

"This is the creature I apprised you of, Your Majesty," said Zin, hovering alongside her. "It was delivered to us by Besteel, as part of his mandatory task. I believe it may be related to the artifacts we've exhumed from that remote site south of here." Both of them looked fixedly at Eva. Next to the towering Queen Ojo, Zin appeared small, like a tiny bird flitting around.

"If I may add," said the taxidermist, clearing his throat, "this little bug slipped out of here momentarily. It was captured in the Hall of Artifacts near the artifacts you speak of, Curator Zin."

Overcoming her nerves, Eva stood to face the queen. "Are . . . are you Queen Ozo?"

"It is pronounced Oh-ho," the taxidermist scoffed. Queen Ojo looked at Zin.

"Its dialect is strange, Your Majesty," Zin said, intrigued. "Unlike any I have heard before."

"Can . . . can you help me?" Eva swallowed down the iciness that chilled her very core. Her arms, bound in front, were shaking right up to her shoulders.

"Shouldn't she kiss our sacred earth before speaking to Her Majesty?" the taxidermist asked, looking at Zin for affirmation.

The mouth of the queen opened slowly, like the holograms Eva had seen of fish breathing underwater. The voice that burbled out was throaty and erratic, like a pot of thick stew about to boil over. "What are you?" she asked.

Eva glanced quickly at Zin before answering, "I . . . I am Eva. Eva Nine."

"An Eva Nine, Queen Ojo," Zin repeated. "Fascinating."

The queen circled around the captive girl, studying her. "It had others with it?" she asked.

"Not that Besteel mentioned," answered the taxidermist, following the queen.

"Your Majesty," Eva begged. "I'm not sure why I am here on your planet. I grew up peacefully in my underground home that your huntsman, Besteel, destroyed. Since then I have been trying to find my people." Eva addressed the other onlookers in the laboratory, who watched and listened. "Rovee and Muthr . . . oh, and Otto, and me. We were coming here to Solas, hoping to find some clues. So if you just let me go, I'll continue my search. I'll leave right away. I promise."

Eva could see the queen's dark-lined eyes change color as she considered the girl. Ojo turned to the table where Eva's few belongings were arranged. "So there *are* more like you? You are not alone?"

Eva wasn't sure how to answer the question. She shifted, nervous. "Like me?" she said, slumping back in her cell. "No. Not *exactly* like me."

"So you are the only one?" The queen faced her.

"I . . . I don't know." Eva's throat went dry. "I hope not."

Ojo studied her reaction. As her bright eyes pierced Eva, the queen commanded, "Send for our resourceful hunter Besteel. I'd like to have a word with him."

"It appears, for all intents and purposes, that the fool's errand you've sent him on has metamorphosed to be quite a productive undertaking," Zin mused.

"Yes, indeed." Ojo held her eyes on Eva for one more beat and then turned to leave. "Prepare this living fossil, and all of its relics, for display. It will be a highlighted addition to my museum collection."

Eva's heart stopped. Her body shook as she beat on the glass. "No! NO! Please! Just let me go! Please don't do this! PLEASE!"

Queen Ojo swept out of the room, followed by her royal guards. Zin floated close to the cell. "Let us immobilize the specimen first. I wish to thoroughly examine it prior to display preparation."

"As you wish," the taxidermist complied in a cheerful tone.

"No! Please!" Eva sobbed as she slapped her hands against the glass. She slid down to the bottom of the cell next to the rod.

She thought of the first time she'd heard Otto's song . . .

. . . of Rovender handing her voxfruit . . .

. . . of Muthr singing lullabies while giving a her a bath when she was three . . .

. . . of a crumbling picture of a robot holding a little girl with an adult, smiling. Happy. Moving forward out into the beautiful, wonderful world.

"Halt!" Zin's voice piped, as loud and clear as crickets.

He hovered close to the cell wall, examining Eva's left arm.

Her wrist.

The mark on her wrist.

A circle within a circle.

"At what location did you receive this glyph?" Zin asked, his tiny eyes blinking.

Eva withdrew her arm from the cell's wall. "Someone gave it to me. But why should I tell you?"

As Eva wiped away the tears, she could see that Zin was flustered. He buzzed about the lab, talking to himself. The taxidermist also noted this peculiar change in behavior. "Do you want me to continue, Curator?" he asked.

"No!" Zin fluttered back up to the cell. "No. I require a live study of this species Eva Nine. Yes. Please have it delivered promptly to my study. . . . No. Never mind. Release the specimen now, and I shall personally escort it to my study immediately."

"Begging your pardon, sir," the taxidermist said,

his remote aimed at the cell. "But the queen just ordered—"

"Yes, yes," Zin snapped. "I shall take personal responsibility and inform Her Majesty of my amendment to her commands regarding the future of this individual."

"Whatever you say." The taxidermist hit another button on another control. The rod in Eva's cell sank back into the floor, and the walls returned to a jellylike membrane. Eva hopped out.

With red-splotched eyes and a runny nose, she faced Zin and asked, "Now what?"

He grabbed her effects, including the Omnipod. "Now you shall accompany me, Eva Nine."

Before we

continue, I need assurances that you shall be respectful of my study," Zin said, floating down the dimly lit hall. They approached a door identical to the one that had led to the taxidermy lab. "Give your word, Eva Nine: no mischief."

"Yes," Eva said, happy to be out of the horrible lab. "I won't wreck your study. You have my word."

"Very good," Zin replied as he waved a hand over a central eye on the door, causing the door to slide open. "You may enter."

"I'll tell you about the glyph, but before we continue . . ." Eva paused at the doorway, looking him up and down. "Give me your word that you'll help me out of here."

"I will aid in your release by all available means," Zin replied, crossing his arms. "You have my word."

Eva nodded and stepped into Zin's grand chamber. The domed skylighted room was darkened, as twilight stained the world outside in a deep blue. Gigantic tuliplike fixtures ringed the work space, their exteriors crisscrossed with numerous diamond-shaped pull drawers. A low, wide circular table dominated the center of the study, and was covered with preserved plants, animals, artifacts, and various tools. Directly overhead an impressive chandelier hung from the latticework ceiling, reminding Eva of a curled starfish, with each tiny tube foot emitting a glow of candlelight.

"Please, allow me to remove these," Zin said, cutting Eva's binds. "This is *Morrenia laquem*, or straintwine as it is commonly referred to." He placed the cords that had bound her onto his worktable. "It's an indigenous plant species whose stems naturally contract when one pulls against them. Quite an

324

ingenious defense against would-be herbivores."

Eva rubbed her forearms where the straintwine had been wrapped. "Yeah, I'm aware of it." Her memory flickered to Besteel stringing her and Rovender up by the foot.

"Ah, now it should be apparent that I intend you no harm." Zin hovered in front of Eva, looking at the marking on her wrist. "So, elucidate this mysterious glyph for me. Tell me, how did you acquire it?"

"First, you tell me," Eva said, pointing a finger at the floating being, "why do you kill everything you catch and put it on display?"

"I?" Zin was affronted. "*I* don't terminate any life-forms. That is the responsibility of the taxidermist. My position is to pursue knowledge through observation and study. Only then can one truly understand an organism."

"How can you understand anything by killing it?" Eva turned away from him.

"True, it must perish, Eva Nine, but it is a representation, an exponent for its species." Zin's eyes sparkled as he floated around his study under the dark cloudy sky outside. He continued, "There exists a vast wealth of knowledge one can acquire by simply peeling away our outer layers and examining what lies inside. Now, you could surmise that within all living organisms there exists a constant, a blueprint, if you will, that is alike no matter what form or environment the organism thrives in. But you would be erroneous in your theorem. There exists no constant, only variables, and yet all organisms strive toward a common goal."

"And what goal is that?" Eva looked at the collection of plants and animals on Zin's desk.

"To understand that, Eva Nine, is to understand one of the universe's biggest mysteries: Why are we here?" Zin floated next to her, a look of self-satisfaction on his round face.

"But couldn't you just ask? Talk about it?" Eva opened a drawer. It was full of vocal transcoders. She picked one up, speaking to herself, "So much more can be garnered by simply inviting one in."

"Come again?" Zin glided to her.

"It's nothing." She turned to him. "I'm sure that the water bear you killed could have told you much more if only you'd asked."

"Don't be ridiculous," Zin said, closing the drawer. "Those creatures communicate through primitive means, likely for herd socialization, caretaking of offspring, and mating. I've studied numerous homologous life-forms on several similar planets."

"You're wrong. They talk," Eva replied, putting

her hand on her hip. "I have a pet water bear named Otto, and he speaks to me all the time."

"That's complete and utter nonsense." Zin crossed his many arms.

Eva sauntered around the large table. "Well, what about this: If you killed and skinned *me*, you'd never know where or how I got this mark, or who I got it from," she retorted.

Zin dropped down in front of her, his voice hushed. "No more games, Eva Nine. I need to know the whereabouts of the individual that placed this glyph upon you."

"Why?" Eva crossed her arms.

"Why? I am not going to entertain your inquiries. Simply—"

"Tell me why," Eva cut him off. "And tell me where you got the jackvest and Omnipods and the other stuff. . . . Then I'll tell you."

"Jack . . . vest? Omnipods? Are these the given names of the artifacts featured in the museum's collection?" Zin asked.

"Tell me where you got them," Eva said.

"You tell me first," Zin's chirrupy voice was rising.

Eva said nothing.

"If you do not cooperate, Eva Nine," Zin threatened, wagging a stumpy finger at her, "I will be forced to return you to the taxidermist's lab."

Eva swallowed, suppressing a shudder. "Go ahead. Do it."

Zin floated centimeters away from Eva's face. She could see that his ivory skin was covered in a fine white down—more like a peach and less like the mushroom texture of Arius.

She held her breath. Held her ground.

"Agh! Very well." Zin blinked and turned from her, floating toward the door. With a wave of his hand, a mechanism within the door locked. While his back was still turned, Eva flicked off the AnatoScan monitoring system on her tunic and searched for the Omnipod. It was lying with the other possessions on Zin's cluttered worktable. She inched toward them.

"Do you know the meaning of the symbol that has been inscribed upon you?" Zin bobbed near Eva.

She shrugged her shoulders.

"It has many interpretations," Zin explained, floating around her. "The circle within a circle. It may mean 'rebirth' or 'reawakening,' like a yolk incubating within the eggshell."

Eva uncrossed her arms and looked down at the mark.

"It may also be interpreted as 'world within a world' or 'a hidden world.'" Zin stopped in front of her. "That is, if you believe such superstitions. If you do, then only time will reveal its true meaning to you."

Eva watched as Zin took her hand. He ran his small fingers over the mark and said in a solemn tone, "It is also the marking of someone I know. You have encountered my sister Arius. A sister I have not spoken to for a very long time."

Eva listened.

Zin sighed. "You see, I am one of four siblings. I have a brother and two sisters. We arrived on this planet many centuries ago, invited personally by His Majesty, King Ojo, to accompany him on the voyage here to Orbona."

Eva grabbed her SustiBar from the table and unwrapped it. "Is he Queen Ojo's husband?" she asked.

"Queen Ojo's father," Zin answered. "To say that I was enthusiastic about journeying here would be an understatement. I long for discovery and illumination gained from venturing into unfamiliar territory. However, after we arrived, and commenced construction of the city, there were . . . complications."

Eva sat cross-legged on the tabletop next to her belongings. She took a bite of the oatmeal-colored bar. "Complications?" she said. "Like what?"

Zin's chirrupy voice became low. "Mainly with my sister Darius, who abhorred this place. As soon as we landed here, she was continually haunted by visions of its brutal and violent past—a past that she tried to block out. Yet she was bombarded by dark memories in her dreams at night and meditations by day. Eventually she fled, looking for refuge—a meadow, a lake, a mountain that had only a peaceful past . . . a place of tranquillity." Zin drifted low to the floor, like a fallen leaf. "She isolated herself from the rest of us. I never heard from her again."

Eva furrowed her brow. "But I didn't meet Daria."

"Darius, no," Zin corrected her, his voice soft. "You met Arius. Darius died under mysterious circumstances some time ago."

"Oh, no," Eva said, setting her SustiBar down. "I'm sorry."

"My brother and other sister were, understandably, upset." Zin fluttered back up, toward the skylight. "They wanted to find her and depart from Orbona immediately."

Eva watched as he looked out into the night sky. "But you didn't, did you?" she asked.

"I had given my word to the Ojo family to remain here as an adviser. I could not disavow my responsibilities to them, or to myself." Zin gazed outside, unmoving. "My family abandoned me, then dissolved communication with me." There was resentment in his voice. "They simply did not understand the pressures I was dealing with."

"But they are your siblings," Eva said in earnest. "Do you know how lucky you are to *have* a brother and sister?"

"Luck has nothing to do with it, Eva Nine," Zin said, and sniffed. He fluttered back down to her. "But, as you suggested regarding the tardigrade, I need to speak with them. Starting with Arius."

"Why?" Eva leaned forward, curious.

"I am intrigued about the circumstances surrounding my sister's death. But that is neither here nor there as far as you are concerned." It was apparent that Zin was losing his patience. "So now, tell me, where does Arius reside?"

"Are you going to see her?" Eva asked. She wondered what the Halcyonus would think of another like Arius floating into their village.

"I've not exited these secure grounds since we settled here," Zin replied. "But I feel it is time. I need to see my sister."

"She told me my future, you know," Eva said, looking down at the mark in her skin.

"Did she?" Zin chuckled. "Can you recall any of her ramblings?"

Eva closed her eyes, focusing on the words that Arius had recited. "She did say something about being held in a court." Her eyes remained shut as she tried to conjure the rest of the fortune.

"That very well could be Solas." Zin rubbed his chin in thought. "You have certainly been *held* here."

A flash flickered through Eva's brain. "Wait! There was something about a sibling setting me on my way. . . . Maybe that's you!"

Zin turned to Eva. "Maybe. What *way* do you seek, Eva Nine?"

Eva thought of the WondLa. It was a small, brittle insignificant scrap compared to all the objects housed here in the Royal Museum. Still, it was *her* scrap—she'd found it. Someone had left it for her to find.

"I want to know where all the humans are. My people." Eva felt a renewed vigor. "I saw all the stuff in the exhibit. Where did it come from?"

"There exists a remote location—quite a considerable distance from here. I am told one has to cross a vast and dangerous desert to locate this cursed place. The few relics we have were obtained with tremendous effort. Many explorers venture out to this wasteland, but few return. However, those who do, describe the awe-inspiring remains of an ancient civilization, buried in the sand," Zin said, inspecting a corroded fork.

Eva's mind flashed again.

Sand.

She recited, "'In the sands of time, the nymph will find the answer to the question that has plagued thy very soul.'"

Eva stared at Zin for a moment, processing.

"I have to go to this ancient city," Eva said, her mind putting pieces in place.

"And, according to Arius, I am to aid you," Zin replied.

"There I will find my people!" Eva felt giddy.

"I would be careful with your assumptions, Eva Nine." Zin floated up to one of the top drawers and pulled it open. "I would surmise that your 'people,' as you say, were there at some point. However, based on the items we've unearthed, it was likely in the distant past."

"But they could just be living underground, like I was." Eva scooped up the Omnipod, and her other things, and slipped them into her pockets.

"It is in ruins, Eva. I have seen it many times before. Civilizations simply cannot prosper for long before they destroy themselves," said Zin as he rummaged through the drawer.

"But I have to go," Eva said, hopping off the table. "I need to know for sure."

Zin glided back down to her. In one hand he held a crystal, roughly hewn in the shape of a cube, while another hand wrapped colored threads around it, making a binding. As Zin finished, he tied the threads off in a long loop, creating a necklace. He placed it over Eva's neck. "This will reveal to you where it is you long to go. Simply shine light into it," he instructed.

Eva grasped the crystal, squinting at its frosted veneer. "Thank you, Zin," she said, looking up at the being.

"You are welcome." He watched her with tiny sparkling eyes.

"Your sister is in Lacus. She lives in a small hut in the topmost tier on the second tower from the shoreline."

Zin nodded in thanks.

"I hope you find her, and I hope you work things out," Eva said, nodding back. She thought of Muthr.

"Be wary, Eva Nine." Zin folded his many hands together. "For hope is a fair-weather friend at best."

Eva curled

up under a thick blanket inside one of the large drawers in Zin's study. The gnomish being had left to inform Queen Ojo that he would be "observing" Eva in hopes of learning more about her mysterious species.

With the room empty and dim, Eva attempted contact with Muthr. She wasn't sure how Zin would react to her communicating with the robot, so she waited until she was alone. To Eva's delight, there was a message already on the Omnipod.

"Eva, dear," Muthr's head said, floating over the device, "I am unharmed at the moment. Besteel captured me over the water, leaving poor Mr. Kitt and Otto behind. I was then taken to a camp deep in the woods, where the malicious brute kept me tethered to a tree, along with several other animals that he had captured." Static fuzzed through the message as the robot continued, "From there, it seemed like he was in communication with someone, though I could not gather with whom. I did not want to risk contacting you at the camp, for fear that he might learn of your well-being. Currently, however, I am in a net underneath his glider and, from the landmarks I have seen, en route to Solas. I do not know when we shall arrive, nor do I know what fate awaits me. Perhaps you already have discovered it. But I hope that, regardless, I am there with you. Stay strong, my dear."

"End of messages," the Omnipod finished.

"Can you contact Muthr, please?" Eva whispered into the Omnipod.

"Attempting voice connection to Multi-Utility Task Help Robot zero-six . . . ," the device whispered back.

Eva peeked out from her makeshift bed. She was still alone.

"Apologies, Eva Nine," the Omnipod said. "I am experiencing interference from Muthr's current location. I would suggest we try again shortly."

"Is she okay?" Eva stared at the device's glowing central eye.

"Most likely," it replied. "Her last transmission was over open water. There was considerable electrical activity in the atmosphere when she sent her message. It is probably interfering with our attempted connection now."

"Okay," Eva exhaled, letting the stress of the day escape from her body. She looked at her injured hand. Her two broken fingers throbbed with a dull ache above the knuckle, but they were tied up, safe in her makeshift splint. The bandage over her palm was hardened from glue and dried blood. She would have to remove the bandage and clean the wound soon.

Muthr can help me, she thought. *It will be perfect. Besteel brings Muthr here. I convince Zin to free her, and we go to the ancient city, where we'll find humans and live happily ever after.*

Exhausted, Eva pulled the blanket over her head and fell into a deep slumber.

Through the skylighted domed roof sunlight shone down on Eva Nine's face. With a yawn she stretched and crawled out of her drawer bed. She soon realized that the Omnipod was chirping for her attention. Eva scanned the room—Zin was nowhere to be found. "This is Eva Nine," she said. "Proceed."

"Good morning, Eva Nine," the device replied. "I tracked Muthr zero-six's progress throughout the night, allowing you some rest."

"Where is she now?" Eva pulled her sneakboots on.

"In this building, at your prior holding location," the Omnipod reported.

"The taxidermy room!" Eva grabbed the heavy blanket and pulled it over her head, like a hood, and exited Zin's study.

The vacant corridor leading to the taxidermist's lab was a short distance. Even so, Eva kept her head down and walked without hesitation for fear of being discovered. She arrived at the entrance to the lab and listened at the closed door.

"There's someone talking in there for sure," she whispered to herself.

But who? she thought. *If Besteel is in there, I'm done for.*

Eva breathed into the Omnipod, "Can you detect the sounds in this room?"

"Yes," the device replied. "Simply place the Omnipod flat against a wall surface. Then place your ear next to the Omnipod." An animated three-dimensional diagram illustrated the directions.

"Got it," Eva said, looking around the empty corridor. She placed the device flat against the door.

". . . not quite sure what you'd like me to do next," the taxidermist was saying. "I tried the usual euthanasia, but it had no effect. And it doesn't speak in a universal tongue, so I have no idea what it's saying."

"Hmmm." Zin was in the room. "Besteel is meeting with Her Majesty to report the exact circumstances surrounding these two. It is astonishing to me that an ancient race has somehow survived against such catastrophic odds."

"That it is," the taxidermist replied. "The other one is still in your custody? It didn't wreak havoc like it did in here?"

"Not at all." Zin's voice sounded confident. "We discussed some of its primitive society last night, but it was weary, likely from acclimation here. I am hoping to learn more before we prepare her for display."

Eva grimaced.

"Let's prepare these other specimens that have been delivered," Zin ordered.

"As you wish, Curator," the taxidermist replied. "And the organic machine?"

There was zeal in Zin's voice. "It is an amazing find. A crude, yet functioning, relic fabricated from extinct hands. I cannot wait to thoroughly disassemble it to discover how it functions."

He's talking about Muthr!

"It's time we get out of here. All of us," Eva said. She reached into her tunic pocket and pulled out Zin's pillar guard remote.

I'm glad he didn't see me swipe this when I grabbed the Omnipod back, she thought. Aiming the remote at the nearest pillar guard, Eva waved her hand over the three lights. The eyes of the towering guard opened, focusing downward at the girl as it blatted a greeting.

"Follow me," she commanded, "and do as I say." Eva opened the large circular door to the laboratory.

"Eva Nine!" Zin's tiny eyes were wide with a look of surprise. "What's this?" The giant pillar guard stepped in behind her.

"Not again!" the taxidermist moaned, scurrying away. In the center of the room was a cell containing a robot.

"Muthr!" Eva was relieved to see that the robot was unharmed. Eva scanned the room for the hiding taxidermist. She spied his squat body behind a cell full of fluttering insects and called out to him, "Release the robot, or the pillar guard starts destroying."

"Eva Nine," Zin said, approaching Eva. "This is not the best way to handle—"

"Now!" Eva yelled. The taxidermist aimed a remote at Muthr's cell, causing the walls to dissipate. The robot rolled over to Eva. "Come on, let's go!" Eva said, keeping her eyes locked on Zin as she backed out of the room and into the corridor. The pillar guard followed, and the large door slid shut behind them.

"Lock it!" she commanded the pillar guard. The giant jammed one of his clawed hands into the door, causing it to buckle so that it could no longer open.

Eva turned to Muthr. "Are you okay?"

"Yes, dear! Are you?" Muthr embraced her. "I am so happy to see you!" She paused, giving Eva the once-over. "Oh, dear! What happened to your hand?"

"Don't worry, Muthr. I'll be fine," Eva replied, a bit sheepish. "At least this time I remembered IMA."

CHAPTER 32: THE GOLDFISH

We have to hurry. Follow me!" Eva said, jogging down the corridor. "And use this!" She tossed a vocal transcoder to Muthr, swiped from Zin's study. The robot activated it and hurried after Eva, with the pillar guard close behind them. Around the bend, they ran right into a squad of royal guardsmen. Confronted by a loose pillar guard, one of them shouted, "Call for reinforcements!"

Eva pointed at the royal guardsmen, the remote in her hand. "Pillar guard, clear the way!" she commanded.

The giant automaton let out its low blat sound as it stepped over Eva and Muthr swinging its long segmented arms. Guardsmen were thrown against the wall while others retreated down the hall.

In moments Eva and Muthr were at the doorway leading out to the top floor of the museum's Great Hall. Eva glanced behind her. From a safe distance Zin appeared holding another remote, the taxidermist scurrying alongside him.

"You gave your word that you would not destroy this place," Zin said in an alarmed tone.

"You said you would help me escape," Eva said with a sneer. She turned and ran through the door with Muthr. The pillar guard followed.

Out on the top floor of the Great Hall, visitors fled from the rogue pillar guard. Eva looked toward the ramp leading down to the exits. A full squadron of royal guardsmen was ascending with boomrods ready.

"Well, that way is blocked," Eva muttered as she pulled out the Omnipod. "This is Eva Nine. Can you see if there is another way down from here?"

"Greetings, Eva Nine. Radar scanning superficial

structure," the device chirped. "This may take several moments to render. Please hold."

"We don't have time!" Eva saw that the palace guards were almost to the top floor.

"Is there another way down?" Muthr asked as she surveyed the immediate area.

"Not unless we jump," Eva said, peering over the balcony to the floor far below. She looked back up at the pillar guard and commanded, "Carefully carry us and jump down to the floor level, please."

The pillar guard lifted the girl and the robot up, bounded over the balcony, and landed firmly on its three columnar legs. It came down on top of the display of water bears, toppling the gigantic mounted specimens and sending pedestrians scrambling.

The pillar guard set Eva and Muthr down near its feet. Eva could hear the guards on the top floor turn around and head for the ramp.

"Come on!" she yelled, grabbing Muthr's hand and leading her toward the back entrance. They pushed their way through the crowd of onlookers and headed toward their escape from the museum. As they neared the doors, Eva spied royal guard reinforcements coming in from outside, and spun around. "This way!" she shouted, dragging Muthr right between the pillar guard's towering legs. As they dashed to the front entrance, Eva could see that the squadron of guardsmen was now on the ground level and closing in on them.

"I do not know if this is the best solution, Eva," Muthr said over her whining motor as she wheeled along at full speed.

"We're almost out of here!" Eva exclaimed. The giant pillar guard followed.

They were nearly through the front entrance of the museum's Great Hall when Eva stole a glance at the jackvest displayed in the exhibit hall. She hesitated at the entrance—in mere seconds they would be stepping through the doorway.

In minutes they'd be off of the royal grounds.

And, in moments, they'd be hidden—lost among the throngs of the otherworldly citizens of Solas.

Zin dropped down right in front of Eva and Muthr.

"That's far enough, Eva Nine," he said, waving another pillar guard remote. "I've orders from the queen to detain you both for further questioning. Please deactivate the pillar guard and hand me the remote."

Muthr's head spun around, taking in the situation. Royal guardsmen were closing in from every direction. "Excuse me, sir," she said, "but my daughter and I are free to go wherever we—"

"Don't bother. He's just a liar," Eva said, facing Zin. "You lied to me!"

"I did not lie." Zin's voice was firm as he crossed his many arms. "I told you I would try all means necessary. That entailed my requesting your release from Her Majesty—and she denied it. I apologize."

"I apologize too," Eva said, narrowing her eyes at him. Outside, hordes of royal guards were clambering up the steps leading to the museum's front entrance, with their sonic boomrods ready. And she could hear the click of the other guardsmen's heels on the polished floor as they approached from behind. Without turning, she figured they were halfway down the hall.

"Don't do it, Eva," Zin said. "You must surrender."

"Pillar guard," Eva commanded, "get Zin's controller."

Zin's eyes went wide with fright, and he zipped away, dodging a swing from the pillar guard's massive clawed hand. Fluttering through the Great Hall, Zin activated the other pillar guards, commanding them to capture the robot and the girl and disable their rogue pillar guard.

Eva watched the enormous figures carved in the pillars open their glowing eyes and come to life.

As they pulled their gigantic bodies free from their roosts, the pillar guards filled the Great Hall with their blatting calls. They stepped out onto the floor in perfect unison. This caused the remaining museum visitors to panic and scatter in all directions. The royal guardsmen spread out through the confusion, fanning around the giant automatons. The pillar guards marched out into the center of the museum, crushing everything in their paths.

Muthr scanned the chaos. "There is no way out, Eva," she said.

"Come on! This way!" Eva yanked Muthr toward the Hall of Artifacts. The nearest pillar guards gave chase, stepped over them, and turned around to block their path.

Eva and Muthr scooted between the giants' stomping legs. One of the pillar guards reached down to grab Eva, but its huge clawed hand missed and sunk deep into the tiled floor. As she moved to avoid the jagged claws, Eva let go of Muthr's hand. She dashed behind the attacking pillar guard and hid behind the jackvest display.

The giant automaton spun around, trying to locate its quarry, and upset the suspended flying machine. The contraption swayed from the rafters like a hanging toy next to the pillar guard. The cables holding the flying machine snapped one at a time, and it crashed down onto the display next to Eva.

As Eva pulled herself from the rubble, she realized the mounted yellow jackvest was lying next to her on the floor under chunks of glass.

The Omnipod, still hanging from her wrist, spoke in its chirpy voice. "Jacket," it announced, projecting a similar hologram. "A form of hip- or waist-length garment for the upper body. In the nineteenth century it was often referred to as a 'coat.' In the latter part of the twenty-first century climatefiber was invented, which revolutionized the fashion industry, allowing for a variety of new and popular styles, including the sleeveless jackvest. Shall I continue?"

Eva clambered up just in time to see a pillar guard barreling toward her. She shot down the exhibit corridor, but the short hallway simply looped around, reconnecting with the main hall. She spied the fallen flying machine lying on top of the display case.

"Hovercraft, model S-five-thirty-one, also known as the Goldfish," the Omnipod said. "This vehicle, often referred to as a 'floatster,' was popular in the—"

"Does it work?" Eva cried over the commotion. She crawled underneath a case full of shabby

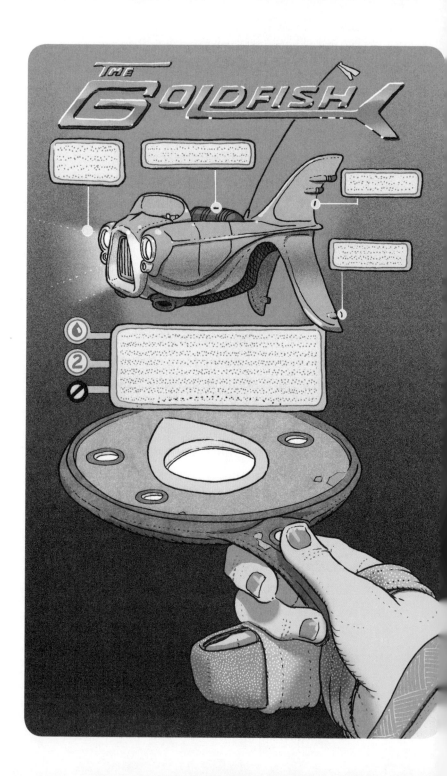

Beeboo toys and dolls, aiming the Omnipod at the hovercraft.

"Sending communication to vehicle and analyzing data. Please wait for a response," the Omnipod replied. A pillar guard picked up a case and threw it across the museum, searching for Eva.

"Hurry!" Eva scrambled to her feet and bolted toward Muthr. A gigantic foot came down onto a display case that stood between them, causing it to erupt in a blast of glass and metal.

As Eva dug her way out of the debris, an immense clawed hand lowered near her, holding a remote in its pincers. She looked up, recognizing that her pillar guard had somehow completed its task.

Eva scanned the havoc in the museum. There was no sign of Zin.

"Destroy the remote," Eva said with a smile. The remote shattered in the pillar guard's massive vice grip.

Without control the other activated pillar guards aimlessly rampaged, destroying everything within their immediate area.

Eva stood, looking up at her guard's three glowing eyes. "You are free," she commanded. "You are no longer under anyone's command. Do you understand? Now go!"

The pillar guard stood, blatted loudly, and walked out of the museum's Great Hall, crashing through the glass of the front entrance.

"Get him!" Eva heard one of the royal guards shout. "The rest of you, get everyone out of here and deactivate the cursed pillar guards!"

Eva dashed into a horde of rushing museum guests, and then sidled behind a tall case that contained a collection of rusted signage. She aimed the Omnipod back at the fallen hovercraft.

A pillar guard rushed toward Eva across the museum, stepping on several royal guards in the process.

"Take down the pillar guards! Take down the pillar guards!" one of the royal guards yelled above the din. The royal guardsmen now opened fire on the giant automatons with their sonic guns.

The pillar guard that was bearing down on Eva received the first blast. One of its legs blew to pieces, and it toppled backward. Debris blew everywhere as the giant crumpled from the fall, filling the entire museum hall with a thick cloud of dust.

"Hovercar S-five-thirty-one is online, though it is at only forty-nine percent functioning ability," the Omnipod stated. "Would you like to access the user's manual?"

"Yes!" Eva dashed through the dust, grabbing Muthr along the way. She yanked the robot toward the hovercraft, thrusting the Omnipod into Muthr's hand. "I need you to access the user's manual now!" Eva shouted.

Eva scrabbled on top of a crushed display and made her way toward the small hovercraft. She climbed onto the craft's dusty body and slipped into the cockpit. True to the hovercraft's nickname, it was indeed shaped like a flying convertible goldfish. Two cracked, dusty leather seats sat high atop the pitted golden chrome body, while an array of fins and stabilizers projected out of the tail.

"Scoot over. I am driving," Muthr said as she climbed into the Goldfish, holding the Omnipod tight in one hand. Eva could see lights blinking in rapid succession on the robot and the Omnipod, even through the dust suspended in the air. With another hand Muthr grabbed the steering yoke of the vehicle. A third hand pried open an access hatch on the dashboard and pulled wires out of the craft. "I have got to give it a little electrical charge first," she said in a calm voice as she plugged a wire into her body.

A squad of royal guardsmen rushed past, ignoring Eva and firing their weapons up at a pillar guard who was plowing through all of the displays straight toward them. "You need to hurry," Eva said as a giant leg crashed through a mounted skeleton.

"A few more seconds. I've only got three functional arms," Muthr said, pressing a button on the dashboard, which caused music to erupt from the blown speakers. She silenced the audio player, and pressed more buttons in rapid succession. "I do not know about this, Eva. This machine hasn't been activated in eons," she said.

The palace guardsmen blasted the pillar guard that was coming at them, disintegrating its head. The headless giant spun around out of control, striking another pillar guard and sending it toppling forward toward the hovercraft.

"You *really* have to get this thing going NOW!" Eva started slapping the dashboard as the shadow of the falling giant enveloped them.

"Got it!" Muthr sang, and the Goldfish made a burbling sound, while a holographic menu flickered onto the windshield. The craft then rose about a meter off of the rubble and began moving, dragging a loose tail fin behind it. The enormous pillar guard fell through the hovercraft's dusty wake. It slammed into the floor at full force, causing the entire museum to shake at its foundation.

Muthr spun the craft around and headed for the back entrance. With deft precision she navigated the vehicle through the throng of royal guardsmen, who were now focused on taking down the remaining pillar guards in the chaos.

Shooting out into the royal gardens, Muthr piloted the malfunctioning Goldfish through the onlookers, trees, and shrubs, leaving a trail of fallen branches and leaves in her path.

"Fuel level low," the craft said in a garbled voice. "Please stop and refuel immediately."

"Are you kidding me?" Eva said, looking back over her shoulder. No one appeared to be following them.

"The vehicle runs on a water-based fuel," Muthr said. She struggled to steer, compensating for the damaged tail rudder, and blasted the craft through a garden of tube-creatures. "Currently it is drawing its power from me. Hopefully, we can get to a secure location to refuel it shortly. Let us just hope it remains intact long enough *to get us* to a secure location."

CHAPTER 33: REUNION

The citizens

parted as a dilapidated hovercraft maneuvered down the bustling streets of Solas. The lanes and sidewalks were packed with all manner of city folk: coachmen driving large feathered beasts of burden through

throngs of foot traffic; little ones flying about on floatscooters alongside the Goldfish, begging for change; and the occasional merchants drifting in hoverjunks overhead selling anything—and everything. Eva Nine thought it was spectacular.

Despite having just escaped an army of towering pillar guards, and having just destroyed the Royal Museum, she wanted to blend in with the locals and explore every nook and cranny of the city . . . but she knew better.

As the Goldfish raced down a winding alley, heading farther and farther from the royal grounds, Eva noticed that the abodes went from large and fantastic to simple gigantic gourds with windows and doorways carved out of them. Eva looked around the quiet neighborhood streets, disregarding the odd stares from the occasional passersby. "Nobody is following us. I think we are safe," she said at last.

"Thank the stars," Muthr replied, and slowed the Goldfish down. It puttered less than a meter off the ground, shaking and rattling like the old machine that it was. "This jalopy is about to drain me of my power reserves. Let us find a water source and refuel it."

"Wait here," Eva said, hopping out. She approached a pedestrian who looked like a hairless rabbit with small arms hopping along on three stilt legs. Eva held up her hand, palm out, as she had seen Rovender do. "Greetings," she said.

The rabbit pedestrian slowed, glancing at Eva with its many round eyes as it passed.

Eva spoke loudly and clearly. "I was wondering if you could tell us where we could get some water, please?"

The pedestrian hurried past her and continued on its way.

"What? Hey, wait!" Eva turned back to look at Muthr.

"It ez only a messenger," a voice came from across the street. "Zay only zuppoz to talks to za recipient." A grotesque, lump-faced, heavyset character strolled over to Eva. Striking cobalt blue wattles hung near its tusked snout in front of large mustard eyes. Its heavy natty jacket was worn and frayed, and it dragged on the ground, concealing most of the creature.

"Namez Caruncle," the creature said, eyeing Eva. "You lookings for ze port?"

"Um, yes," Eva said, "the port would be great." She felt uneasy near the large character. He smelled sour, like he had taken a dip in the same vile drink that Rovender carried around.

"Well, ez jus over zat way." Caruncle gestured with a curled, atrophied arm.

"Okay. Thanks, Carnucle." Eva trotted toward the Goldfish.

"Caruncle," he corrected her. "Zow. You haves flying macheen? Did you builds it? I never seen nothing likes these style. Howz haves you gottens dis?"

Eva climbed in, next to Muthr, who glided the hovercraft around toward the direction Caruncle had indicated. "Thanks again for your directions," Eva repeated.

"And automatonz driver, too?" Caruncle pointed at Muthr. "No ones in Solaz has zeese things essept za queen. Are you a queen? A prinzess?"

"No, just a human." Eva waved as the hovercraft took off. "Bye!"

"Youz stoles it! I knows dis!" Caruncle yelled after them. "Your zeecret is zafe wif me, Justa Human!"

"We are almost ready," Muthr said, pouring water from the lake into the Goldfish's fuel reservoir. They were parked in a run-down dockyard on the outskirts of the city. Eva looked in the distance at a tall spiked, yet graceful, building towering high above all else.

"That must be the palace," she said. She blocked the sun from her eyes with her hands, squinting at the details of the otherworldly architecture.

Muthr rolled up next to her. "It is wonderful," she said.

"The castle?" Eva sighed, thinking of her not-so-wonderful encounter with Queen Ojo. "Yeah, I suppose."

"No, Eva." Muthr brushed Eva's bangs out of her eyes. "It is wonderful to be with you once more."

"I'm glad we're back together too," Eva said, embracing the robot. She could feel the warmth emanate from Muthr's enameled torso right through to her silicone-tipped fingers.

"How is your hand?" Muthr asked. "What happened to it?"

Eva showed her the injury. "I had a run-in with a sand-sniper—a little one, at that. Even *it* was bad news."

"Nice dressing," Muthr observed. "Though, you will likely have a scar. We will clean it up when we get to wherever we are going."

"Where are we going?" Eva asked. "There have been no replies to our distress call from Sanctuary fifty-one."

"Let us recover somewhere and come up with a plan. But not here," Muthr said, pointing at the dilapidated docks. She rolled back toward the Goldfish. "We can still use this, but I do not think our getaway vehicle is going to get us much farther."

"When I spoke with Zin—you know, the short floaty guy," Eva said as she hopped into the vehicle, "he told me there was a place where they've been digging up stuff—like this hovercraft."

"Very well." Muthr nodded. "That may be a good place to look for clues."

"Yeah, it would," Eva replied, "but he said it was really far away. Across a desert. A really dangerous desert."

"I see." Muthr blinked, processing. "Well, perhaps I may be able to repair this hovercraft enough to get us there. But I will need time, and we do not have any provisions for you or supplies for the Goldfish."

Eva sighed. "I know, but I think if we don't leave Solas soon, then—"

A voice drifted into her mind.

You. Me. Find.

Eva's eyes grew big. "It's Otto!"

"Otto?" Muthr scanned the area for the giant water bear. "I do not see him."

"He's not right here," Eva said, closing her eyes and focusing. "But he's not far, either." Concentrating, she pointed. "Go this way. Down the shore and back around town."

With her eyes still shut Eva guided Muthr through the city's small winding alleys. These soon turned into simple footpaths, which led out toward a patchwork of lichen farms and pollen granaries. All trails faded as the land became drier and scrubbier, eventually turning into a great and vast ash-colored wasteland.

"There!" Eva exclaimed, opening her eyes and pointing. Muthr guided the craft in the direction Eva indicated, toward a lone wandering tree. Underneath was the unmistakable shape of a water bear, hooting in the shade. Before Muthr could bring the craft to a stop, Eva hopped out of it and ran toward her armored friend.

Safe. Little one. Back.

"Oh, Otto!" Eva stretched her arms out and hugged his face, feeling the familiar comfort of being near him. She traced her delicate fingers over his bumpy carapace, smiling at him. "Thank you, Otto. Thank you for coming for me," she whispered.

"Eva Nine," a voice came from the other side of the tree's trunk. "My traveling companion. My puzzle solver." A blue lanky creature hopped down from one of the tree's leafy platforms. "It does my spirit good to see you alive and well."

"Rovee!" Eva squealed, and moved to hug her friend tightly. "I'm so glad you're here! I was worried about you." She looked him over. "Your color," Eva said, "it's brighter. You look good. Healthier."

"Thanks," Rovender said, holding Eva.

"You are here to say good-bye, aren't you?" she asked.

"I thought I was leaving," he replied, "but clearly you and Mother need *someone* to keep you out of trouble, right?"

Eva looked at his grinning face and smiled back.

"So I'll tag along for a little longer," Rovender added. "I want to see where your journey takes you—that is, if you don't mind."

"I don't mind at all." Eva beamed.

"Otto, Mr. Kitt," Muthr said as she rolled up. "I am happy you made it."

"You too, Mother Robot." Rovender put a hand on Muthr's shoulder. "So tell me, how did you both manage to escape Besteel?"

Muthr smiled. "Eva rescued me."

Rovender nodded. "She rescued me as well."

Otto hooted in agreement.

Misty-eyed, Eva stood facing them. "You've rescued me, too."

"Oh, before I forget," Rovender said as he walked over to Otto. "Your belongings." He handed Eva back her jackvest and satchel.

She peered inside her satchel and saw that everything was as she'd left it—including the WondLa. She ran her fingers over it and smiled at Rovender. "Thanks," she whispered.

"Of course." Rovender's voice was soft. "Though I assume that while you were detained you had no luck finding clues as to the whereabouts of your clan."

"Actually, I did," Eva said, leaning back against Otto's armored side. "It's across a vast desert. An ancient city lies there."

"The . . . the wastelands?" Rovender's mouth was agape. He pointed to the ash-colored plain that stretched out behind them. "It is here. We are at the edge of it."

Eva stepped forward, walking out from the shade of the wandering tree. An endless barren expanse extended out toward the midday horizon. There was not a tree, or any other living thing, visible as far as she could see.

"Many have traveled into this wasteland," Rovender said, standing next to her. "Many have disappeared. This is dangerous land."

"We will need to find food and water, Eva." Muthr rolled up to Eva's other side. "Enough for you, Mr. Kitt, Otto, and the car."

Rovender stared out at the barren plain. "You can have whatever provisions I've collected."

"We need coordinates," Muthr continued. "I do not believe the Omnipod has the radar range we will require."

"Mother Robot is right," Rovender concurred. "If we don't know where we are going, we are walking to our deaths."

"We know where we are going," Eva said. She pulled out the crystal given to her by Zin that was tied around her neck. "We are going to find the answer to the puzzle."

"A beamguide? Very nice." Rovender hummed, eyeing the cube crystal. "Well, then, I am ready. Let us find your WondLa, Eva Nine."

Otto nuzzled Eva's hand.

"Otto says he's ready too," Eva said, looking over at Muthr.

The robot turned her gaze from the vast sea of sand and faced her. "I am here for you, Eva. Lead the way."

End of
PART III

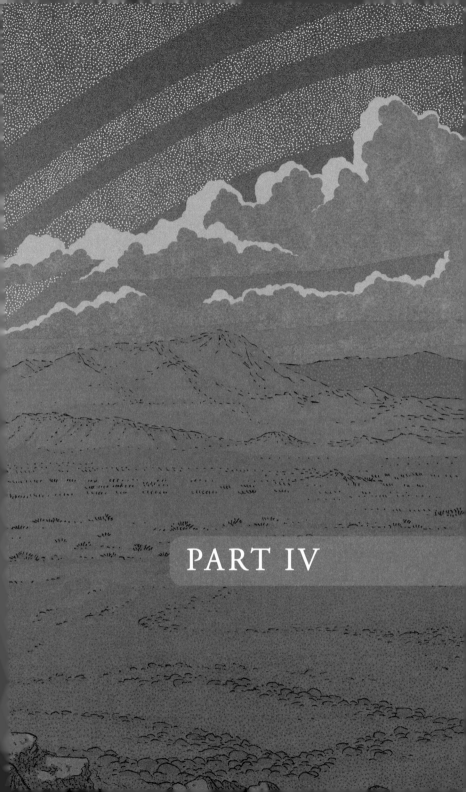

PART IV

CHAPTER 34: GREAT MIGRATION

A hot wind blew dusty gusts over the dark badlands as the procession began. Rovender was saddled on top of Otto, using the beamguide to navigate, while Eva rode along with Muthr in the Goldfish. Eva leaned back with her feet on the dashboard and looked up at the afternoon sky. She watched brilliant patches of blue begin to overtake the gray clouds that blanketed the atmosphere. Even though it was daylight, she saw a distant half-moon peeking down at her through the cloud cover, its face pocked full of craters.

They continued over the crescent dunes for several hours, stopping to refuel near a rocky ridge. Sweaty and nauseous, Eva exited the Goldfish and climbed on top of Otto. She sat next to Rovender as the water bear journeyed onward; their shadows grew long over the dunes.

"Feeling better?" Rovender asked as he watched the endless desert unfurl in front of them. "Your complexion has returned. You look more like yourself."

Eva sipped her Pow-R-drink. "Yeah. Muthr said it was motion sickness." She glanced down at the robot driving alongside Otto. "I think she's happier with me up here on Otto anyway. That hovercraft may look like fun to ride in, but it's a real clunker."

"I am not one to trust a machine," Rovender said, glancing down at it. "They are always limited by the hands that crafted them."

Eva looked down at Muthr navigating the Goldfish. "I just want to find the hands belonging to a person that crafted *anything*."

"Have you ever known another like yourself?" Rovender seemed relaxed on the makeshift saddle he'd created with blankets and bed mats.

"No." Eva's eyes scanned the bleak landscape.

"So then, tell me: Who built your home?" Her companion picked at one of his ivory teeth with his fingernail while he watched clouds drift by. "Who built Mother Robot?"

Eva finished her drink. "I . . . I don't know, really. I've seen stuff in the Sanctuary that said 'Made by the Dynastes Corporation,' but Muthr said she knew nothing about that. All she knew was that I was very special. That I was part of a 'future world vision for humankind.'"

"What does that mean?" Rovender looked at Eva sideways.

Eva shook her head, feeling hot. Feeling stupid. "I don't know."

"Well, perhaps we'll find out soon," Rovender said. He placed a reassuring hand on her shoulder. "It will take a couple of days to get there, if I've measured the distance correctly."

Eva nodded. "Okay."

They rode in silence for some time as the orange sun sank into the west behind them. With the sky now dim, Otto let out a singsong series of low hoots.

"What is it, boy?" Rovender patted the behemoth.

"He senses others like him." Eva stood and

peered out into the fading twilight. "It's his herd."

Somewhere, far in the distance, carried by strange and wondrous currents, a chorus of water bears drifted and danced through the gloaming.

"They sound like they are northeast of us," Rovender said as he pulled out his spyglass. "But I see no sign of them. They must be some ways off."

"Otto is telling them about us . . . about Besteel." Eva looked down; sorrow racked her face. "And he's singing about the loss of his companion."

"That is amazing," Rovender said, running his calloused fingers over Otto's armored plates. "Many times I have seen and heard these tardigrades in my travels. But always I have thought of them as simple beasts. I never knew them to be so interconnected."

"Just like the forest, right?" Eva sat back down.

Rovender looked up at the sky. "Yes, Eva Nine, just like the forest. Just like everything."

There was a loud blurping noise. Eva looked down to see the Goldfish putter out and drop into the fine hot sand.

"Well, that does it," Muthr said with an electronic sigh as she exited the crippled hovercraft. "Despite my adjustments, Eva, I do not know if we can go much farther with this machine. The tail fins are leaking hydraulic fluid, and I am making it worse by driving it farther. Dirt and grit are clotting the steering lines."

"Let us rest here for the night, if we can," Rovender said. He pointed to a cluster of round lichen-plastered boulders that were half-buried in the dunes. "Those rocks up ahead should be a safe place for camp."

He hopped down on his backward-bending legs. "Come, Mother Robot, I'll guide you by foot."

"Careful, Rovee," Eva said. "Otto says his herd has seen what they call tunnel biters—or sand-snipers—out here."

"Have they? Well, I trust their words." Rovender began thumping the sandy ground with his walking stick. "Let me know if you see anything from up there."

Eva stood on top of Otto and scanned the horizon in all directions. "There's no sign of them," she announced. "I think we are safe."

"Good." Rovender stopped. "Eva, Mother Robot, let us drag the hovercraft to the campsite. We may need it after all."

After hauling the Goldfish close to the massive rock formation, Eva and Rovender set up camp atop the largest boulder of the bunch. Nestled below, Muthr remained with the Goldfish as the Omnipod instructed her on how to mend the tail rudder and stabilizer fin. Otto was beside the busy robot, stripping the lichen off of the wind-worn stones and licking up the trapped moisture underneath.

As he sat high up on their mossy perch, Rovender took out his woven sleeping mat and unrolled it. "For once many of the clouds have cleared away," he observed. "We may get to see the Rings of Orbona tonight."

"Rings?" Eva looked up. A chilled desert wind played with her hair, blowing her bangs into her eyes. With the onset of night she was no longer uneasy about being out in such an open space.

"Oh, yes." Rovender unhooked his lanterns from

the overloaded rucksack. "Orbona is encircled by quite an expansive set of rings consisting of asteroid fragments and dust."

"How long have they been here? The rings?" Eva gazed up at the dark clouds wandering across the horizon.

"Shortly after Solas was established, an enormous asteroid was discovered heading on a direct course to Orbona," Rovender explained as he lit his lanterns. "The Ojo family used an immense sonic weapon, much like a boomrod, to disintegrate the asteroid a safe distance from our atmosphere. Over time the fragments began to circle the planet, forming the rings."

"Did you see it?" Eva asked.

"Oh, no," Rovender replied. "This was long before I hatched. But there remain records of it in my clan."

"Where do they live? Your clan?" Eva stared into the glow of Rovender's lantern as he handed it to her. She glanced down at Muthr, who was working on the Goldfish under the pale blue glow of the Omnipod. With the sun long gone, the cool of night pervaded the land. Eva could feel the climate-fibers in her tunic and jackvest warming her.

"The Cæruleans, which is my clan, live quite a

distance from here. They arrived in Orbona several generations before I hatched, during what was called the Great Migration. They traveled many light-years aboard a ship filled with passengers, led by the great king, Ojo." Rovender handed Eva her bedroll and a blanket.

"Where did they come from?" Eva stood, unrolling the mat. "Why did they come here?"

"They came from many different worlds, most with just the belongings on their backs. Our village shaman was but a nymph when she arrived here, carrying only a necklace from her mother and the severed foot of her slain warrior father." Rovender lit another lantern. He found his pouch of seedpods and offered some to Eva.

"But why here?" Eva grabbed the seedpods and popped them into her mouth. As soon as her damp tongue touched the husk, it split open, producing several small seeds, which tasted nutty. Eva spat out the husks, as she'd seen her friend do, and put another handful into her mouth.

"Many traveled from dying war-torn planets." Rovender's voice was distant with recollection. "You see, the Ojo family had the ability to *reawaken* dead planets—bring them out of their hibernating slumber. They picked Orbona for its climate and extreme distance from our past worlds . . . and past lives."

Eva thought of the painting she'd seen on the ceiling in Hostia's home. The eye painted on the nose of the ship was the same as Queen Ojo's eyes.

"Oeeah! Look there!" Rovender pointed up into the sky. "There they are. You can even see the outer gossamer ring."

The dusky clouds moved on, like a colossal herd drifting away from the stars, and revealed a glittering band arcing across the heavens. Eva followed the celestial ring to the horizon, where the dark desert disappeared into the faded light. With the glimmer of the gibbous moon reflected in the ebony sand below, she imagined their camp was floating out in the middle of the universe—and her friends could not be touched by anyone . . . or anything.

"It is beautiful, is it not?" Rovender took a deep breath.

"I feel . . . so . . . tiny." Eva took in the entire starlit expanse. "So . . . insignificant."

"Tiny—perhaps." Rovender kept his eyes fixed on the rings. "Insignificant—never, Eva Nine. No living thing is insignificant."

CHAPTER 35: TURNFINS

A chorus of soft, low hoots summoned the daylight. Though it was still hazy out, most of the stars had faded. With the cloud cover swept away, the distant Rings of Orbona stretched across the violet predawn sky. The chilly breeze that had prickled Eva's face now danced off to hide from the rising sun.

Eva blinked out the sleep as she woke and spied the source of the hooting. Three turnfins had roosted on a rock overlooking the camp. In the morning haze Rovender Kitt threw bits of old fruit at them, which they captured in their beaky maws. One of the bird creatures flapped its wings and warbled at another, trying to steal its prize.

"Turnfins." Rovender grinned as he finished feeding them. "I don't know how they find you, but they just do—no matter how far out from civilization you are." He rolled up his sleeping mat.

"Turnfins," Eva repeated, and stretched her long, skinny arms up into the pink sky. This spooked the birds, causing them to beat their wings, but they remained on their perch. "Too bad there's no water nearby. They could dive in and catch us breakfast."

"Yes, too bad . . ." Rovender chuckled. He gazed up and studied a small flock circling high above them. "Though, you never know. There may be water out here somewhere."

"Good morning!" Muthr called up from below. "Eva, dear, how did you sleep?"

Eva leaned over her rocky perch and waved. "I slept great, thanks," she said. "How's the Goldfish coming along?"

"I worked on it through the night while Otto kept me company. He is quite friendly, this one." Muthr patted Otto on the head. "The craft shall now run considerably better. We are currently at eighty-seven percent functionality," she reported as she turned on the hovercraft.

In the light of the rising sun, Eva could see that the purring Goldfish looked better than it had the day before. It now floated more than a meter above the sand. The tail fins had been reattached in their proper positions, and even the audio player was singing softly.

"That's amazing!" Eva scrambled down to join Muthr.

Otto came up and nuzzled Eva's left hand for a scratch behind the ear.

"Hiya, Otto. Been watching over Muthr while she fixes this thing?"

The water bear hooted a happy reply.

"I had to use one of your Pow-R-drinks to clean and flush the fuel lines, but it should really enhance its overall performance." Muthr handed a SustiBar to Eva. "After breakfast, and after we tend to your hand, I can teach you how to drive it, if you want."

"Whoa, really?" Eva forgot all about her food, and her injury, and crawled into the driver's seat. A series of buttons and a small control yoke, for steering, greeted her. Brightly projected on the clear polished windshield was a display of numbers and indicators, which included hover height, speed, and wind direction. "This is going to be awesome!" Eva said, turning the yoke back and forth. She paused. "But don't you think I'll get sick again?"

"I checked about your nausea with the Omnipod."

Muthr held up the device. "Apparently kinetosis, motion sickness, may be prevented if you are driving. Plus, navigation of a vehicle is always a good skill to acquire."

"Well, then, let's get moving!" Rovender tossed his jingling rucksack down to the soft sand next to the hovercraft. He followed, hopping down to join Eva, and handed the beamguide to her. "Before we set out, let us check our bearings so that we can confirm we are heading in the right direction." Rovender took hold of Eva's hand and angled one side of the square-cut crystal so that the beams of morning sunlight entered it directly.

With the cube acting as a prism, light projected out, spreading like a flat hologram in all directions. Eva immediately realized that what she was viewing was a detailed virtual relief map of Orbona's surface terrain. She recognized the miniature city of Solas, nestled next to Lake Concors. Eva even saw the tiny pillars of Lacus, on the opposite shore, and the Wandering Forest beyond it.

Rovender pointed to a sparkling dot on the map. "This is our current location, here . . . ," he said, then walked through the hologram and pointed to a cluster of knobby spires rising from a depression in the ground. "And here is where, I believe, we want to go."

"This is quite impressive, Mr. Kitt." Muthr's head poked up through the projected holographic landscape like a great desert sphinx. "However, what are those blackened areas?"

"Uncharted lands," Rovender answered as he rubbed his whiskers. "These beamguides work simply by communicating with other beamguides buried in numerous locations. This is as far as Solas's explorers have recorded."

"What's that?" Eva pointed to a small, flat depression in the map. It was located halfway between their current location and their destination at the ancient ruins.

"It looks like a small body of water, perhaps even an oasis." Rovender knelt close to get a better look.

"Well, we could certainly use more water." Muthr rolled over to inspect it. "And it does not seem far off from our projected course."

"No, it doesn't." Rovender stood with his eyes still fixed on the landmark. He peered out into the landscape toward its direction. "I wonder if that's where these turnfins came from."

"Let's find out," Eva said, handing the cube back.

"Okay, Eva Nine." Rovender climbed up onto Otto. "Lead the way."

Rovender sat high atop Otto, enjoying his lunch and feeding turnfins, as the giant water bear trailed behind the Goldfish. Everywhere Eva looked it seemed the turnfins were about, swooping and squawking—like the holograms she'd seen of crying gulls as they followed ocean-bound ships.

Eva navigated the craft up toward the crest of an ashen gray linear dune. "Muthr, what do you think we will find at the ruins?" she asked.

Muthr was silent, save for her clicking eyelids, as she seemed to process Eva's question.

"I do not know, Eva, dear." Muthr looked out at the horizon. Little lights flickered on the back of her head. "To be truthful, we are so beyond the limits of my programming that I have had to continually reprogram myself as we continue our journey."

Eva glided the Goldfish over the crest of the dune, and down the slip face. "I feel like I've had to reprogram myself too. No holography chamber prepared me for this."

Muthr nodded. "I have to wonder what our makers had in mind when they put us on this planet. It can be such a volatile environment."

"You've got that right." Eva chuckled and steered the hovercraft up the next windward slope. "But it is beautiful, too."

"I agree, but honestly, none of our programs were accurate." Muthr let out a static sigh. "I feel like I failed you, Eva."

Eva looked over at Muthr. With her head looking down at her wire-veined hands, the robot appeared to be despondent.

"You didn't fail. And it's going to be okay," Eva said, patting Muthr's hand. "We'll go to this place and see if we can't find some clues, or even other humans. And, if we don't, we'll keep searching . . . right?"

"Right," Muthr repeated. "I just want you to know that I am so very proud of you, Eva. I believe in you. I believe that we are doing the right thing."

"I think so too." Eva smiled as she brought the Goldfish up the windward slope of yet another large dune.

"Up there!" Rovender yelled.

Eva turned to see him standing on top of Otto, goggles in hand. He pointed toward the horizon. "The oasis is over there!"

Eva aimed her gaze in the direction he was pointing. In the far distance flocks of turnfins circled. She steered the hovercraft toward them and pulled the throttle back, sending whorls of grainy sand swirling about in her wake.

E

va watched a cluster of small wandering trees meander around a muddy pool in the middle of the dark sands of the wasteland. Like a mirror reflecting the azure sky, the surface of the pool was as flat as glass, even as the occasional turnfin approached the bank and stole a quick sip. In the dampness surrounding the large waterhole, a variety of colorful lichens and mosses blanketed the desert sand.

"Now, Eva, dear," Muthr cautioned as Eva parked the Goldfish in the shade of a low ridge. "Let me examine the mineral content of the water before you add a purification tablet and consume it."

"Okay." Eva hopped out and threw her jackvest onto the seat. She walked over and joined Rovender.

"One more request, Eva," Muthr said as she opened the access hood on the side of the hover-craft. "If you could bring some water back to refuel the Goldfish, that would be good. I do not want to use up all of your hydration tablets to keep it running."

"No problem," Eva said, and stroked Otto as she passed him. The water bear shuffled over to join Muthr and the Goldfish in the shade.

"Otto does not want a drink?" Rovender glanced back over his shoulder as he walked with Eva.

"He said he was fine," Eva said, padding over the damp sand toward the pool. "His herd is not far off, and he'll be rejoining them soon where there is plenty to eat and drink."

"Oh, I see," Rovender said as he knelt down at the shoreline with several bottles. The large crystalline pool contained numerous rocks and sticks visible on its shallow bottom. All were coated in a fine silt. Eva flopped down and began to pull off her sneakboots and socks.

"Oh, this is going to feel so good," she said with a giggle, and rolled her leggings up. "The sneakboots make my feet so sweaty!"

Rovender dipped his fingertips into the water and washed the grit off his face. The pattern of pores that composed his nose sensed the water. "Something isn't right," he whispered. He splashed more of it onto his face. "Eva Nine," Rovender called. He stood and scanned the area. "Get out of the water, now."

Eva had waded up to her knees. "Why? What is it, Rovee?"

"Just get out as fast as you can. Look!" He pointed to a stand of wandering trees near the pool.

Eva saw a small flock of turnfins watching them from the nearby trees. "What?" she said.

"None of the turnfins are in the water," he said. "Get out!"

Eva waded back toward shore. Behind her rose a monstrous flower bulb from the center of the pool, supported on a thick, hairy stalk. Wide-eyed, Eva stopped, turned, and watched as the bulb opened in the warm sunlight, a prodigious bloom full of speckled, spattered color. It reminded her of a gigantic exotic orchid as it released a cloud of pollen particles into the air surrounding it.

"It's so beautiful," Eva said. Dazzled, she stared at its center. The banded filaments of the flower stretched like tentacles as they unfurled toward her.

Rovender splashed into the water, shouting, "Eva, I don't think . . ." He paused when he reached her, looking at the giant flower. "You are right," he murmured. "It is a lovely, magnificent blossom."

The uncoiling filaments unrolled toward the mesmerized pair, and the powdery anthers neared them. Eva let out a deep sigh as the fuzzy end brushed against her face.

"It's . . . wonderful . . . ," she said, breathless.

"So . . . sublime . . . ," Rovender said, and wheezed.

As she watched from the shore, Muthr called out to them, "Eva! Mr. Kitt! I would recommend you back away immediately from this unknown plant species."

Otto hooted loudly and shifted back and forth in the damp sand on his many legs.

"Stay here, Otto, dear." Muthr wheeled over to the hovercraft and snatched up the Omnipod. "I am not sure what this monstrous bloom is doing, but it appears to have them in some sort of a hypnotic state."

The robot rolled out into the water toward an unmoving Eva. "Eva Nine, can you hear me?" Muthr shouted. "I need you to—oh, my!"

Eva's skin was tinted blue, and her eyes fluttered. She exhaled in a long gagging yawn as the air was sucked from her lungs through her open mouth.

"Oxygen levels in this area are critically low for human respiration," the Omnipod chirped. "Please avoid immediate area at all costs without proper breathing aids, or hypoxia may occur."

Muthr picked Eva up and turned back to shore. As she carried the added weight, the robot's single wheel dug into the sediment below. Otto bounded toward the pool.

"No, Otto! Stay!" Muthr commanded as she sank farther into the pool's muddy bottom. "This plant is bad!" She glanced over at Rovender, who stood motionless while the flower sucked the air from his lungs. She was now up to her waist in water, her single wheel digging her deeper and deeper into the muck.

"Remote ignition of hovercraft S-five-thirty-one, please," Muthr commanded the Omnipod as she kept Eva's unconscious face above water. The disturbed silt revealed a murky bed—not of rocks and sticks but of bones and skulls.

"Ignition of hovercraft commencing," the Omnipod chirped. "Hold for one moment, please."

"I do not have 'one moment'!" Muthr said. "Get me virtual navigation of that vehicle immediately!"

The Goldfish burbled to life, hovering toward Muthr as she guided the craft with her free hand. Water sprayed out in a fine mist as the Goldfish drifted over the surface of the pool.

Otto squawked loudly.

Muthr turned her head in time to see the filaments of the flower coil around Rovender, squeezing the last breaths out of him. With most of her metallic torso now submerged, the robot hoisted Eva's lifeless form into the Goldfish. Muthr navigated the hovercraft toward shore. She grasped tightly on to the tailfin and pulled herself from the mucky grip of the pool's bottom.

With the Goldfish hovering back over land, the mud-caked robot called out to Otto. "Grab her, please!"

The passenger door opened and Otto lifted Eva from the car with his beaky mouth and carried her far from the pool. Muthr climbed into the driver's seat and raced the Goldfish back out over the pool toward Rovender.

He appeared lifeless, constricted in the banded tentacles of the monstrous plant. As soon as Muthr neared him, the bloom belched out more pollen, dusting Muthr's lacquered surface. She grabbed the filamentous tentacles that held Rovender and began twisting and turning them, and ripped them from the flower head.

As she struggled to haul Rovender's unconscious body into the hovercraft, the plant sent more tentacles out toward the Goldfish, wrapping filaments around anything they came in contact with. With tremendous strength it began to pull the hovercraft into the water toward it.

"Omnipod," Muthr commanded the device as she watched the waterline creep over the tail of the craft. "I need to know what will immediately terminate the life of an aquatic plant."

"If it is a freshwater variety," the Omnipod replied, "salt water may affect it, or acid rain, pesticides, lack of sunlight, or other forms of contamination. Shall I continue?"

"How about electricity?" Muthr opened the access hatch on the dashboard.

"It could have quite an immediate effect if—"

"Good!" Muthr yanked out a handful of the Goldfish's internal wiring and submerged them into the water. An electric jolt shot through the pool, causing the monstrous plant to release its grip. It retracted and sank back below the surface.

Muthr brought the sputtering Goldfish back to a waiting Otto on dry land. She exited, carrying a limp Rovender. "Eva, dear, are you well? Please tell me how you are doing?" Muthr asked as she laid Rovender flat on the hood of the hovercraft.

"I'll be okay, I think," Eva said between gasping breaths. She was sitting up in the shade next to Otto. "But I've got a massive headache," she added.

"We have to help Mr. Kitt, Eva, and we need to hurry," Muthr said. She held the Omnipod in one hand while she scanned his body with a red laser. "His physiology is entirely different from yours, so I need you to tell me anything he may have said about how he functions internally."

"He never said anything," Eva said between gasps. "But I did create a file for him on IMA."

Muthr opened up his eyelids, revealing dilated pupils. She probed his mouth with two mechanized fingers. "Eva, dear, I need you over here immediately," she said, her voice calm as she opened a small compartment panel above her wheel casing. While one hand searched for a pulse on Rovender's thick wrists, another pulled out a corrugated tube and placed it into his mouth.

"What—what are you doing?" Eva asked as she stumbled over to Muthr. As her stupor faded, Eva realized the grave situation. The IMA program was rendering a translucent three-dimensional hologram of Rovender over the Omnipod's central eye. Muthr studied the flickering charts on the Omnipod.

"We are attempting to resuscitate Mr. Kitt by blowing controlled bursts of air into his lungs," Muthr said, and tilted his head back. "I will supply the air by using one of my internal cooling fans. To do this, I need you to hold his opercula, or gill covers, shut so that the air will travel down into his lungs. The covers are located underneath his chin, here. Hurry, dear, my hands are full."

Eva looked down. With Rovender's head tilted back, a pair of ruby slits were revealed, just under his jawline. They had been hidden by his beard of barbels. Eva placed her palms firmly over the gill covers to close them. She swallowed down the iciness of dread that began to coil into her stomach.

Please don't die. Please don't die. Please don't die.

Muthr blew puffs of air into Rovender's mouth in two one-second bursts. Eva watched his stomach rise and fall. Rise and fall. Muthr studied the Omnipod and repeated the process.

"Please don't die, Rovee," Eva whispered.

"I am doing all that I can, Eva," Muthr said as she blew the air in again. "He has many organs that are indescribable by the Omnipod. Therefore, I cannot risk cardiopulmonary resuscitation."

"Please, Rovee." Eva tried to keep the chill from overtaking her shaking hands. She kept them firm on the lanky creature's neck. "Please."

She felt a lurch . . .

. . . and a cough . . .

. . . and Rovender Kitt blinked his indigo eyes.

Muthr pulled the tube from his mouth and returned it underneath her metallic shell. In her cheerful movie-star voice, she said, "Mr. Kitt, welcome back. You gave us quite a scare."

CHAPTER 37: SIGNAL

The campsite

that night was the familiar submerged entryway into an underground Sanctuary. With the door long gone, the stairway leading down was packed full of desert sand. Even so, the lone covered entrance provided some shelter against the chilly

windswept desert plain and the preponderance of hunting sand-snipers clicking outside in the night.

"Definitely tomorrow," Rovender said as he looked at the beamguide map. "If we get an early start, we should be there by midday." He tucked the guide in with the other items packed in his large rucksack.

"We have made good progress, despite this afternoon's setback," Muthr said as she looked over at Eva in the lantern light.

Eva was placing all of the contents from her satchel out to dry, as the bag had gotten soaked in the skirmish at the oasis. She glanced outside at Otto, who was sleeping soundly next to the Goldfish.

"I believe we shall have plenty of fuel to get us to our destination as well," Muthr continued. "Once there, we can locate a water source that does not contain such malevolent plant life."

Rovender chuckled, then rubbed his swollen neck. "Yes, let us hope so." He saw the reflection of his lanterns dance and flicker in Muthr's large orbs. "Mother Robot, it is no secret that I am not one who is fond of machines. To be truthful, there have been instances when I have even questioned your upbringing of Eva with such mechanisms as the Omnipod, and even your Sanctuary."

Muthr nodded. "Well, I think we have all seen that

these machines, myself included, do not have all the answers. I do not believe anyone does, Mr. Kitt."

"You are right," Rovender replied. "I am also the first to say when I am wrong about something, and I am wrong in judging the makeup of one such as you. Please accept my sincerest apologies for such small-minded notions."

"There is no need for an apology, Mr. Kitt," Muthr said. "You have taught Eva and me many things about this world that could not be contained in a program or simulation. It is I who should be apologetic for ever doubting you."

"Fair enough," Rovender said with a grin. "Fair enough."

The two sat quietly for a moment, huddled in the abandoned Sanctuary entryway. Eva savored the reconciliation. With her back still turned to them, neither could see her face beaming with pleasure as she traced her fingers over the damp image on the WondLa.

"I think I am really getting the hang of this," Eva said the next morning as she piloted the Goldfish over dark rippled dunes.

"You are doing very well," Muthr replied. "Make sure you adjust the roll a little when we get over this open, flat area ahead. The wind can get quite gusty."

"Why didn't we practice driving hovercraft back home?" Eva said as she focused on the instruments projected on the windshield.

"I am not sure," Muthr said. "We had information on hovercrafts in the Sanctuary's virtual library, but I was not aware of any exercises that would instruct you on how to operate one."

Eva rubbed her finger splint with her free finger as she gripped the yoke, thinking. Her healing palm itched. "I really like exploring a lot. I feel so active, so excited, so *alive* while I am doing it, you know?"

"I do have a sense of understanding what you're saying. You certainly are a most adventurous spirit, Eva." Muthr looked over at her.

"Do you miss being in the Sanctuary?" Eva glanced at Muthr, then back to the landscape in front of her.

"I miss having access to anything and everything when I need it and, by extension, when you need it," the robot replied. "I am designed to be in control of my environment. Out here, it appears the environment is trying to control me."

Eva was quiet for a bit as she thought about this.

Muthr continued, "But I suppose that is the very nature of survival—living and existing despite the odds."

"Yeah," Eva said. *Living despite the odds.*

"Though, I must confess, I do miss our holo-shows. I enjoyed watching them with you."

"Really?" Eva looked over at Muthr, a smile growing on her face. "What shows?"

"I actually enjoyed *Beeboo and Company*," Muthr replied. "Watching some of the episodes with you was quite entertaining."

Eva laughed out loud. "Really? You were entertained?"

"Actually, I was more entertained watching you. Especially when you were younger," Muthr said. "After the show was over, you would pretend that you were one of the characters. How you adored that Beeboo."

"Why didn't you tell me that before?" Eva asked.

"I am not sure. I suppose I was simply so busy making sure you were content," Muthr replied.

"Hey, maybe if we find the other humans, they'll have some of the old episodes," Eva said, smiling. "You and I can watch them again."

"I would like that very much." With her silicone lips Muthr smiled back.

"Ho! Eva!" Rovender called out as he stood atop Otto's back. "Hold up!"

Eva slowed the Goldfish and circled it back over the crescent dunes of black sand and gravel. The hovercraft's metallic flecked paint sparkled through its dusty coating in the late-morning sun as it came to rest alongside the water bear. Rovender slid down and sat on Otto's great head. He placed the crystal beamguide on the flat hood of the Goldfish, and the prism relief map projected out from it.

"Well," Rovender said as he studied the landmarks. "We are almost there. It's just over this large dune up ahead."

"Let us see if we can pick up any clues," Muthr said, and pulled out the Omnipod. She spoke to the device, "This is Muthr zero-six. Initiate LifeScan. Please sweep the area for any other detectable life-forms."

"Initiating LifeScan," the Omnipod replied. Eva watched the familiar radar hologram of the terrain before them. Muthr extended the radar's range, revealing their final destination. There certainly were all sorts of structures present—as well as a lot of glowing life-forms. Large glowing life-forms.

"A first sweep shows that there are approximately two hundred and forty-seven large life-forms aboveground and in the area indicated," the Omnipod reported. "They are elephantine in size and, based on recent images acquired through Identicapture, are likely giant tardigrades."

Otto let out a long, low hoot.

"That's Otto's herd," Eva added. "They've been here waiting for him to rejoin them."

"Really?" Muthr asked.

"He told them where we were going," Eva said, patting Otto; he started purring. "I guess they knew where the ruins were. Apparently there's a lot of food for them there."

"You never cease to astonish me, Otto." Rovender climbed back up to his saddle and shooed away several turnfins that had taken his spot in his absence. "All right, Eva Nine. Lead the way!"

It took some time for the group to scale the windward slope of the largest linear sand dune that they had yet encountered in the boundless wasteland. Loose ebony grains blew about as the hovercraft rose higher and higher at a steep angle toward the summit. Eva parked the Goldfish at the crest and hopped out. Her friends soon joined her, staring in awe at the monumental sight that was now revealed to them.

In a vast valley that stretched across the entire horizon, hundreds—perhaps thousands—of spires, walls, and hunks of architectural rubble, stood half-submerged in the dark drifts of desert sand.

Extraordinary lichens, the largest and most colorful Eva had yet seen, grew from the old remnants of bridges, towers, and other edifices of this lost civilization. Countless turnfins circled and roosted among the ruins, while in the distance a great herd of water bears grazed around the structures.

"Oeeah!" Rovender whistled from high atop Otto's back. He peered into his spyglass. "This is quite a find, Eva Nine. A place unlike any I have ever seen!"

The hot wind tousled Eva's brown-blond bangs. She stared, speechless, as she tried to comprehend the utter enormity of the site. Muthr's motor whined as the robot neared. Eva whispered, "This was once ours, wasn't it? We had colonized Orbona, hadn't we?"

"It certainly seems that way, does it not?" Muthr replied.

They both gazed out at the remains reaching up toward the sky—as if the remains themselves were trying to escape from the sands of time that slowly consumed them.

"The folly of humankind is that it believes it is impervious to decay," Muthr said.

The Omnipod chirped as the lights on it began flashing in a flurry of patterns.

"What is it?" Eva pried her eyes away from the landscape before her. "What's going on?"

"I have never seen the Omnipod act like this," Muthr said, reading the slew of information displayed on the screen. "Let us get closer."

With Eva driving the Goldfish, Muthr navigated the group down the large slope of the dune toward the ruins. As they approached, Eva realized that the corroded spires were gigantic, towering high above them into the afternoon sky. Hordes of turnfins swooped around them and flitted about among the spires. Their chattering had risen to quite a din as the explorers had traveled down the sandy pathways.

Eva felt a tickle in the back of her brain. She glanced back at Otto and Rovender.

"What is it?" Muthr watched Eva.

"It's Otto." Eva closed her eyes for second, trying to get a better read on him. "He's uneasy for some reason. Something is bothering him. . . . It could just be all of these birds."

"And I am sure he is anxious to reunite with his herd," Muthr said.

"You're probably right. I bet he can't hear their song with all of this racket." She focused on driving, still not quite at ease. Eva guided the craft under the remnants of a magnificent steel archway. "So, what's the Omnipod say?"

Muthr continued to read the charts displayed by the device. "Well, according to this, there may actually be some sort of computer system online here."

Eva's eyes went large. "Are you serious?"

"I would say it is improbable, but judging from what we are seeing, it appears to be so," Muthr said as Eva brought the Goldfish around the crumbling remains of a building. She continued, "The signal is weak. It is coming from an underground source."

"A Sanctuary!" Eva's pulse quickened.

"I will not be able to tell for sure until we investigate," Muthr said, studying the location of the signal.

Eva picked at the skin around her thumbnail while she held the steering yoke tightly. As they journeyed past the remnants of a still-standing tower, she looked over at the Omnipod. "Does it . . . Does it detect any others like me? Any humans?"

"At this point, no," Muthr said, her eyes still on the device. "But that does not mean we will not find any sort of clues here." They approached a pair of similarly shaped lichen-encrusted rocks, and Muthr said, "Stop here, Eva! This is the place."

"Rovee!" Eva shouted as she parked the Goldfish. "Over here!"

"We are on our way," Rovender shouted back as he and Otto rounded the path to join them.

"According to this," Muthr said as she exited the vehicle with the Omnipod, "there is a faint signal coming from directly below us. Though the Omnipod is not very accurate at detecting subterranean elements."

Eva stepped out of the Goldfish onto a wide, flat half-submerged rock. "Hey, Rovee, is it okay to walk around? Are there any sand-snipers here?"

"Not here, Eva," Rovender replied, and hopped off of Otto. He stared up at the ancient monuments that surrounded them. "Fortunately for us, they prefer open areas."

"Look!" Eva brushed the sand away from the rock she was standing on. "These are steps."

"Yes," Rovender said. "Steps leading down . . . someplace."

She sprinted across the half-buried step to Otto and put the palm of her hand on his forehead.

Are you okay? she thought to him.

411

Safe. You. Me.

Are we safe?

Noise. Hurt.

It's the sound of the birds, right? she said to him silently. *They are pretty noisy.*

Hurt. Noise.

Eva looked around and noted that there were not many turnfins in this open area. Even though she was desperate to explore, she stayed near Otto. The water bear shuffled over to one of the nondescript rocks jutting up out of the sand and pulled off a large clump of enormous lichen.

"Eva," Muthr said, peeling back one of the wide gray leaves. "Can you ask Otto to remove all of this lichen?"

"Sure." Eva walked over to the stone formation that was jutting up from the top of the steps. The other formation, almost identical in size and shape, was many meters away. They were like large newel posts on the top of a wide stone staircase.

Otto grabbed the lichen with his short, sharp beak and sheared off the growth. As he munched it up with relish, Eva recognized the aged, pitted rock underneath.

It was a sculpture.

A sculpture of a lion.

Both of these

sculptures are of lions," Muthr said, scrolling through endless data on the Omnipod. "I am sure it means something, but it may take us some time to determine what exactly that is."

"It would probably be best to dig down to where these steps lead and take a look around," Rovender observed. "I am sure more clues will present themselves."

"A fine idea, Mr. Kitt," Muthr said, and looked up from the Omnipod. "For the moment I do not detect any large life-forms in the area, and you are positive that no sand-sniper will attack in this vicinity?"

"I am sure." Rovender tapped the stone steps with his walking stick. "Besides, there are not many creatures that I know of that would inhabit an ancient place where spirits likely still remain."

Muthr returned her attention to the display on the Omnipod. "Look here. It seems as if there may actually be a cave, or a chamber, that we could explore. But it is considerably far below the surface. This is going to take some time to excavate."

"I bet Otto could do it," Eva said.

"Really?" Muthr looked at him.

"Let me ask." Eva closed her eyes and stroked Otto's side.

"Yes. He said he'll do it before he rejoins his herd." Eva scratched the giant water bear's chin. "Just show him where you want him to dig."

Eva, Muthr, and Rovender sat under the fragment of a great archway that shadowed them from the late-day sun. In their makeshift camp, they watched Otto tunnel down into the sand. His movements reminded Eva of the recorded holograms she had seen of burrowing badgers. The giant water bear dug into the earth with his front claws, and passed the dirt backward to his back legs, where he would kick it far from the giant hole.

A cascading flume of sand now sprinkled down on Eva from Otto's most recent kick. She stood and shook the sand off her. "If it's okay with you, Muthr, maybe Rovee and I can look around while

Otto digs this tunnel," she said. "Perhaps we can find more clues."

"Only if Mr. Kitt agrees to accompany you, Eva," Muthr replied as she watched Otto dig. "I can keep track of your whereabouts with the Omnipod."

"Of course," Rovender said as he grabbed his walking stick. "We shall not wander too far. Just let us know when you have found the source of the signal, Mother."

"Very well. Be safe." Muthr watched them as they left.

"I will," Eva replied, waving to her. She paused for a moment and looked at Muthr before setting off. The robot stood, balanced on her single wheel outside in the middle of a desert, excavating ruins. Muthr had traveled so far from the hermetic world of the Sanctuary. They both had.

Eva and Rovender hiked out into the colossal remains, sweeping away the sand here, examining crumbling structures there.

"Maybe it was an ancient city of people who worshipped lions," Eva said as they poked around. "Maybe lions were like mythical creatures to them, you know?"

"I do not even know what this *lion* is," Rovender said, flipping over a flat stone with his foot.

"Oh, they were these wild, hairy, giant cats that

were ferocious hunters." Eva made her hands into claws for effect. "They were extinct on my planet, except for in zoos."

"How curious," Rovender said, "that such a wild beast would be contained." He picked up a brick and sniffed it.

Eva was quiet for a moment as they walked along, and she thought about the trapped sand-sniper in the taxidermist's lab. She thought about herself trapped, like a wild beast in a cell . . . trapped in Besteel's camp . . . trapped in her own bedroom. She looked up at the afternoon sun hiding behind the Rings of Orbona and smiled, happy to be free.

"I hope Muthr and Otto can find a way underground," she said.

Rovender knelt down and sifted through a pile of rubble. He added, "Yes, I can only imagine what may lie, untouched, in some ancient vaults. It will be—"

A large congregation of turnfins erupted from their roosts in a deafening clatter, flying in every direction at once.

"What is it?" Eva asked. She could feel her heart rate speed up before her tunic announced it.

Rovender stood still and watched the birds. "Something is not right," he said. "Let's get back to Mother."

They both hurried back to the camp. Otto's song

entered Eva's mind like a windstorm: *Noise. Not. Safe.*

"You're right, Rovee." Eva stopped and closed her eyes. "Otto is worried."

"I am not sure what's going on." Rovender scanned the sky. "What disturbed the flock?"

They both heard the answer. The haunting low sound of a *woom* echoed over the landscape.

Next to Eva and Rovender the remnants of a wall blew apart into shards of rock and dust as a sonic wave shattered it.

"Run!" Rovender pushed Eva behind a tall chunk of wall with ancient bricks still mortared in it. He dashed off behind another edifice.

Eva climbed up the wall using the bricks as footholds. She peered through a window opening and recognized the familiar shape of a glider. She gasped when she saw that the glider was accompanied by others just like it. All of them flew straight toward Eva through the swarm of turnfins.

Besteel had found them.

He had brought reinforcements.

With a shriek Eva let go of her ledge and fell down onto her back just as the top of the wall exploded into rubble. Besteel's glider flashed by overhead at lightning speed.

"He's coming back around!" Rovender yelled as

he rushed over and helped Eva up. Dark crimson blood trickled in rivulets down the side of his head. "We haven't much time. Let's hurry!" He held Eva by the hand as they ran through the ruins.

"Where are we going to hide?" Eva shouted as a frightened flurry of turnfins flew past them.

"I don't know, but he's got royal guardsmen from Solas with him," Rovender answered. "Let's get back to Mother and Otto."

They dashed down through the remains of a narrow alley, which led to a blown-out building. Besteel and the squadron zipped by, blasting one of the alley walls with their weapons and causing it to fall onto the other.

Eva and Rovender scrambled as the stony remains fell downward in a deluge of rock upon them. The pair leaped out of the way as both alley walls came down in an enormous cloud of dust. Eva and Rovender tumbled down crumbling stone steps into the underground basement of a long-forgotten building. As they caught their breath, they descended through the dirt and debris into the darkness below.

"Don't make . . . any . . . loud noises," Rovender whispered in between breaths.

"No . . . kidding," Eva said.

"This vault . . . is full of . . . knifejacks." Rovender

pointed up. "If they're disturbed . . . we're in trouble."

Eva looked up and saw a ceiling packed with tiny, grotesque, sleeping crab-creatures—just like the kind she had seen back in Rovender's old Sanctuary.

They heard a distant boom outside. It sounded like the thunder over Lake Concors.

"They're trying . . . to flush us out," Rovender whispered.

The ground shook. Dust rained down from the ceiling. A few of the knifejacks opened their glowing eyes and squeaked, then settled back down.

"I hope Muthr's okay," Eva breathed.

"Yes. I hope she and Otto"—Rovender flinched at another low boom—"were able to hide."

"Me too," Eva said. She shuddered at the thought of them all mounted on display in the Royal Museum with their skin removed.

"Do you think"—Rovender paused, keeping a wary eye on the horde above them—"that the fellow who gave you the beamguide also gave Besteel one?"

Eva was quiet for a moment as she considered this. Zin didn't seem like the type to turn Eva in. On the other hand, he had lied about helping her escape . . . and she had destroyed the museum. "I'm not sure," she said. "I don't think so." She recalled her meeting with the fortune-teller, Arius. "I think he truly wanted me to find this place."

There was another vibration, this time much closer, that rattled the walls of their hiding place. Eva and Rovender covered their eyes from the downpour of dust and sand. The dust settled and they looked up to a ceiling aglow with hundreds of tiny eyes.

"Time to go!" Rovender yelled, and pushed Eva back up the stairs.

Hundreds of knifejacks flitted past them, pricking and biting along the way. Eva and Rovender fled back up to the surface and ran right into Otto.

"Otto!" Rovender exclaimed.

"Where's Muthr?" Eva asked.

Hiding. Safe. Come.

Eva and Rovender ran behind Otto as he took off on his six legs. He led them past the tunnel that he'd been digging and out into the open plain surrounding the ruins. As he did so, the water bear began to squawk loudly. Over his calls Eva could hear the gliders circling overhead.

"Eva Nine." Rovender looked back behind them at the squadron up in the sky. "I hope Otto has something planned, because we are easy targets out here."

Eva kept running, and shouted over her shoulder. "He does. Trust me!"

"Here they come!" Rovender yelled, and pointed up.

At the head of the squadron, Besteel led the guardsmen toward Eva. She could hear the hum of their charging weapons mixed with the whine of their racing engines.

Otto's herd emerged from their hiding places in the ruins.

Using their snapping tails, a volley of water bears launched themselves up into the air, rocketing toward Besteel and the squadron.

The huntsman skillfully maneuvered his glider through the first wave of leaping giants, but several of the royal guardsmen were hit. Losing control, they spiraled down, topsy-turvy, to the ground below and impacted in brilliant explosions.

Eva and Rovender ducked behind Otto's armored side as the next wave of water bears shot up. Like gigantic armored cannonballs, they blew through the remainder of the royal squadron. To Eva's chagrin, Besteel once more avoided them as he piloted his craft up, higher than the water bears could leap.

"Nice try, fraazas!" he called down to them. "I cannotz wait to hunts zu all down!"

The herd continued to jump up in chase after the huntsman. They came down all around Eva, Rovender, and Otto at incredible speeds, sending sand and dust in all directions.

Rovender took Eva's hand. "We've got to get to safety!" he said, pointing toward a large steel tower away from the fray. "This way! I think we left Mother just beyond there."

The two scrambled in the direction of the tower just as Besteel's glider zoomed overhead.

A sonic sound wave boomed as it hit the base of the tower, causing it to topple down in front of Eva and Rovender. It hit the ground with such force that it blasted dirt and debris everywhere, knocking both of them backward.

Eva pulled herself up, coughing as she wiped the sand out of her eyes. "Rovee? Rovee! Where are you?" she screamed, feeling her way blindly through the rubble. She soon found her friend, lying as still as a doll, crumpled and half-buried in a pile of rocks.

"No!" Eva wailed. Her heart was pounding. Dread snaked in through her rapid breaths and settled in her belly. She patted Rovender's face. "Wake up, Rovee! Wake up!" She shook his shoulders, but he did not move. A whine could be heard somewhere in the distant dust, intensifying in sound.

"Muthr? Otto?" Eva said. Her words sounded barely audible above her ragged breathing. The desert dust clouded her vision and clogged her nose.

She searched around in the murk. She called out again. As she waited for a response, Eva heard that loud whine . . . and a voice.

"My elusive prize. My leettle runner," the deep voice replied. Out of the thick gloom bounded the burly shape of Besteel. He hopped up onto the base of the toppled tower and charged his boomrod. "Sheesu." He clucked, "Youz have made Queen Ojo quite upzet. She commandz de royal guardzmen to brings youz back for queztionings. But, de guardz dey needs a tracker to leads them. Zankfully de turnyfins you feeds made yous eazy to trail through deez wastelands. Sos now Besteel brings youz back alive and, tada—my impozible task iz complete. Brozeel iz free."

Eva stood up. Sand and dust coated her, from her braided hair to her sneakboots. In her ears the whine grew louder and higher in pitch. She yelled at him, "I'm never going back with you. You'll have to kill me first!"

Besteel let out a throaty chuckle. "No killingz. I promised za queen. But you know, accidentz, zay happeen."

The Dorcean huntsman fired his sonic boomrod directly at Eva Nine.

CHAPTER 39: GROUND

Eva threw

her hands over her face as the intense force of the sonic weapon exploded right in front of her. All she could hear was an electronic scream . . . and then silence. With both her ears ringing, Eva opened her gummy sand-crusted eyelids and realized she was lying face-down in the soft warm earth next to a large, twisted

hunk of metal. She spit the dirt out of her mouth and waited for the ironclad grip of Besteel to scoop her up once more and take her away—but it did not happen.

Her eyes focused on the wreckage next to her. The upside-down letters spelled the word "Goldfish."

"What? Oh, no!" Eva was immediately up on hands and knees, scouring the area. Her trembling hands felt something heavy and round, like a log lying silently on a forest floor.

She found the truth.

Muthr lay still on her back, her eyes as dead as night. The robot had intercepted Besteel's shot to save Eva.

"No, no, no," Eva cried. She tried to lift the robot up, but she was too heavy. Eva looked down at Muthr and saw that the top of one of the braincases was missing. She examined the damage to Muthr's inner porcelain skull, which housed a glass globe. Within that globe was an ivory-colored brain, wired full of electrodes.

The globe was cracked.

A thick pink fluid was trickling out onto the sand.

Eva put her hand over the crack and tried to stop the syrupy fluid from running out. The amber light in the robot's eyes fluttered on, then went back out. There was a gentle nudge from behind.

You. Not. Safe.

"Otto," Eva said, "Muthr's hurt really bad."

Come. Not. Safe. Otto nudged her once more.

"No!" Eva's tears burned her eyes. "We have to fix her. Come on. Help me find the Omnipod."

Opening his maw, the water bear spit the Omnipod out onto the ground in front of her. Eva blinked as she picked up the device, astonished that he'd already found it.

Not. Safe. Tunnel biters. Otto grabbed Eva's tunic with his beak and tugged at her.

"What? No, Otto, I have to—"

Besteel's voice called out to her. Eva stood, trying to see through the haze of settling dust and sand. "Leettle one, no more gamez," Besteel yelled over the hum of his charging boomrod. "Come outz, come outz, wherever you are!"

Come. Safe. Me.

Eva tore her eyes from Muthr, lying under the wrecked hovercraft, and climbed up onto Otto's head. He carried her from the crash site to an open area outside of the ruins. Eva climbed up onto his back and discovered that his herd had surrounded Besteel and his glider.

Why haven't they crushed him? she thought. *Do you want me to watch, Otto?*

No. Come. See.

Eva soon saw what Otto meant, as he made

his way to the front of the herd.

A dazed Rovender Kitt was hog-tied and strapped to the back of the hovering glider. Besteel stood, patient and unmoving, with the muzzle of the boomrod aimed at Rovender's head.

"Oho! She comez!" Besteel gloated. "She iz smart one after allz, eh, Cærulean?"

"Don't do as he says, Eva Nine," Rovender shouted. "Save yourself and Muthr. Get out of here!"

"Enough!" Besteel pistol-whipped Rovender with the butt of his boomrod. He shoved the muzzle back into Rovender's face. "You getz down here and on ze glider, leettle prize, or dis one dies. Now!"

Eva slid down Otto's back toward his head.

Tunnel biters. Not. Safe.

Otto, Eva thought, stopping on the water bear's head, *tell the herd to back up.*

The water bear hooted, low and gruff.

"No more stalling," Besteel growled, pointing the boomrod at Otto. "Or I finish whats I started wiz dis cow. Get down here! I do not ask again."

Otto's herd backed up and created an open sandy circle around the huntsman.

"Yez, dats more like it," Besteel said, waving his weapon at the herd. "Now come down here, leettle one."

Eva stood, pulling out the Omnipod.

"No, no, no." Besteel wagged a clawed finger at her. "No trickz wiz your toy. Give zat to me. Come on."

Eva held the Omnipod up high.

Besteel aimed his boomrod at her.

A hot, gusty desert breeze played with Eva's thin beaded braids as she glared at the huntsman.

Besteel squinted at her, his heavy chest heaving with each breath. The humming, charged boom-rod remained aimed at the girl, unwavering.

She glared.

He squinted.

Eva blinked, then slumped her shoulders with a sigh. She threw the Omnipod down. It landed in the sand out in the center of the sandy circle created by Otto's herd.

"Very goot." Besteel approached the clicking device slowly and steadily. With one pair of arms he groped around in the sand for the clacking Omnipod, never taking his eye, or his aim, off Eva. Besteel scooped up the device and held it tightly in his talons. "Now comez down here and we leave. Nize and easy."

Eva crawled back up to the top of Otto's armored back. She turned to the huntsman and folded her arms. As she did so, the herd opened up even more, giving Besteel more space.

Eva stood silently. Watching.

"You leettle shrew! No trickz!" Besteel yelled. "Getz down here NOW!"

Eva held her ground. All that could be heard was clicking.

"So be it." Besteel's voice was cold. "I kill your friend." He turned around toward his glider to shoot Rovender, but found himself face-to-face with an enormous sand-sniper clicking to the cadence of the recorded call playing on the Omnipod.

Before the huntsman could fire his weapon, a pair of spiked forelegs pierced his body. Stunned, Besteel let go of his boomrod and tried to wriggle free.

The boomrod fell next to the giant sand-sniper just as dozens of juveniles surfaced from the sand. They, too, sunk their pincers into the huntsman and clicked in high-pitched chirps.

Besteel was dragged below the dark desert sands of the wasteland by the sand-sniper and her brood, never to surface again.

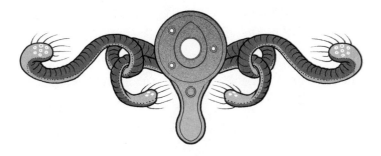

CHAPTER 40: DARKNESS

Rovee! Rovee!

Are you okay?" Eva jumped down from Otto and ran to the huntsman's glider. The herd of water bears broke up, hooting and calling out as they rejoiced in the demise of Besteel—he who had hunted them.

"A bit black-and-blue, but it's nothing a little moss and drink won't fix," Rovender said with a weak grin. He wriggled in his binds. One of his eyes was swollen shut, and dried blood was smeared above it, caked with sand.

"Hold on," Eva said as she rummaged through Besteel's belongings. "There's got to be a knife in one of these bags."

Rovender rolled over. "Here. Try the back pouch on my belt."

Eva found the familiar shape of the small curved knife, the same one she had used to free her friend from the huntsman's camp. Rovender was free in moments.

"I'm so happy you're okay." Eva buried her face in his jacket, staining the shoulder with her tears.

Rovender broke the hug and looked around. "Where is Mother?" he asked.

"Muthr!" Eva put her arm around her friend. "Come on, hurry!"

Together the two limped over to the twisted wreckage of the Goldfish.

As they both knelt down next to Muthr, Eva could see that more of the thick liquid had run out of the braincase, soaking into the sand all around her. Eva gingerly put the palm of her bandaged hand over the crack, as she had done previously, and lifted Muthr's head. A golden glow returned to the robot's eyes.

"Look. This happened before," Eva said. She gazed at Muthr's face and waited for her to speak. "If I hold her back here, she comes back on."

"It is your energy, the electricity within you, Eva Nine, that temporarily revives her," Rovender said. He looked at the fractured braincase. "I am afraid, though, that she may be damaged beyond repair."

Static hissed from the robot's mouth.

"Eva, dear." Muthr's voice sounded far away and dreamy, different from how Eva had heard her speak before. "I get to see you one last time. Is Besteel gone?"

"Yes, he's gone," Eva replied.

Rovender ran his thick fingers over Muthr's face. "He will bother no one ever again, thanks to your resourceful daughter," he said.

"We are free and we're going to make it," Eva said as she tried to stay strong. "You're going to tell us what to do, and me and Rovee are going fix you up. You're gonna be okay."

"Eva . . . ," Muthr said, reaching up to hold Eva's hand tightly. Her grip was cold and metallic.

Muthr paused as an electric current danced over her open braincase, prickling Eva's skin. "Eva, you have to let me go."

"No, no," Eva said. A long tear streamed down her face, like a crystal brook on her grime-smeared cheek. "You will be fine. We will fix you."

Muthr turned her head to gaze into Eva's eyes. "You did fix me, Eva. Do you not see that?"

"No, this is my fault. We should have gone to the other Sanctuary." Eva's voice was barely a hush. "I'm so sorry. None of this would have happened if I had listened to you."

One of Muthr's arms was half-buried in the sand. Now it emerged clutching on to something. With a great grinding effort she handed a worn scrap of panel to Eva.

It was a picture of a girl, and a robot, and an adult. Smiling. Moving forward.

"My WondLa?" Eva took it. "I don't understand."

"Eva . . ." Muthr's voice was soft and slow, like a clock whose batteries were running down. "Did you know that *my* WondLa, my wish, was to experience this wondrous world with *you*, my daughter? My triumph. My joy. All I ever wanted was for *you* to be happy and safe. That is all I ever wanted. . . . And now I know that you will be all these things."

Eva wiped her eyes with her sleeve. "But without you I—"

"Just let me go, Eva," Muthr whispered. "Just let me go."

Eva slid her hand out from under the braincase and laid Muthr's head down.

"You will always be my mother." Eva leaned over and kissed the forehead of the machine. "And I will always love you."

"I love you, Eva. You will grow up to be an amazing woman." Muthr's voice was but a breath. Static on the wind. "I am . . . so proud of you."

With that, Muthr's eyes went dark.

A small fire

crackled brightly against a magnificent lavender-hued sky at the campsite in the ancient ruins. As she sat under a long-forgotten steel archway, Eva Nine stared into the dancing flames and thought of her life before she'd left the confines of her Sanctuary. She thought of Muthr. A hollow pang of loneliness crept over her.

She felt the familiar nudge of a beak on her back and heard the sound of a purr. A warm, knobby tongue began licking her head.

Little one, you are safe.

Eva rose and wiped her face with her sleeve. She

turned, expecting to see Otto, but instead she met with the ancient face of another giant water bear that observed the girl with cataract-clouded eyes. Its carapace was covered in numerous gouges and dents, patched over with rich thick growths of moss and algae. Behind this beast were the many faces of the herd, huddled close to see Eva. All began to hoot in unison.

You are the one, they sang, *the one who risked your life to save one of us—the one who would treat us as your equal.*

Eva blinked as their thoughts flooded in and filled her. They awakened and energized her.

Now you, little one, are one of us. We are one. So shall it be.

A large behemoth stepped forward. Eva smiled as she recognized the benevolent face of Otto. She placed her palm on his pebbly forehead. *You will always be my friend, Otto.*

Herd. Must. Go.

"I understand," Eva said, holding back her tears. "Maybe I'll see you again, someday."

Just. Call.

"Oh, I love you, Otto." Eva wrapped her thin arms around his large neck. "And I will miss you."

Me. Too. Little one.

The herd began moving away from the ancient ruins, across the dark mysterious dunes. As he turned to leave, Otto looked at Eva with his large bulbous eyes.

Go. See. Truth.

The water bear shuffled away to join the rest of his herd. Behind him, the enormous tunnel that he had excavated below the lion sculptures waited in the shadows as twilight flooded the land.

Eva grabbed a lantern and wandered out into the silhouettes of the ruins, toward the giant tunnel. "Rovee?" she whispered.

Sitting up on one of the lion sculptures, alone in the dusky gloam, Rovender Kitt stared out at the skies as the top of the sun sank below the inky landscape. Eva could hear him talking to someone, though it was hard to discern who it was because his back was facing her.

"Hey," she said, approaching him.

"Hello, Eva Nine." He took a swig from his bottle. "How are you?"

"I'm . . . okay . . . I guess. I don't know." She climbed up next to him. "How about you?"

"I am sad for you, and for me," he said, and swallowed more of his drink. "I grieve for Mother."

"I am sad too." Eva pulled her knees up to her

chest and rested her arms on them. She was missing a piece of herself she knew she'd never find again.

"It's funny. We have adapted ourselves to live in a *new world*. A *new land*." He took another gulp. "We have traveled far, overcoming many dangers . . . many obstacles."

Eva was quiet.

"And what happens? What is our reward for such a demanding journey? This?" Rovender let out a sarcastic laugh as he gestured at the towering ruins surrounding them.

Eva's eyes were downcast.

"It's not fair!" Rovender yelled, throwing the bottle. It exploded against a lone standing wall. "You did not deserve this."

Eva put her head down.

"It should . . . It should have been me!" His voice was angry. "It's not right!"

"Don't say that, Rovee." Eva sniffed. Her body felt numb.

"No!" Rovender stood up, shouting, "I should have died! It shouldn't have been Mother. It shouldn't be *any* mother . . . not with little ones." He crumpled back down, his head in his hands. "Not with little ones. They don't deserve this. It should have been me." He sobbed, "It should have been me."

Eva scooted over to Rovender and put her arm around him. They sat quietly as a full blue moon drifted up through the clouded night skies of Orbona.

Eva awoke to the crackling of the campfire in the middle of the night. Balled up under a thick wooly blanket given by Hostia, she peered out into the camp. Rovender sat near her and gazed, as if hypnotized, into the fire. Alongside him, his large rucksack was wide open, its many contents spread about.

One by one he picked up an item and tossed it into the blaze. Eva blinked out the sleep and sat up. "Rovee, what are you doing?"

His voice seemed calm, at ease, as he spoke to the flames. "I am, at last, cleansing my spirit, Eva Nine."

She rubbed her eyes with the back of her hand. "What?"

Rovender picked up the ornate necklace from his rucksack. "These things are nothing more than that—just things," he said, and dropped the necklace into the campfire.

Eva sat in a ball of blanket as she watched the flames consume the necklace.

"They are not memories. . . ." Rovender dropped a handful of belongings into the fire.

"They are not alive. . . ." He scooped up an armload.

"They will never replace the ones we've lost." He stood and emptied the last bit of his old possessions into the growing fire.

Eva got up, still wrapped in the coarse blanket. She grabbed her satchel and walked over to the campfire, turning it upside down. The remaining nutriment pellets, water purification tablets, Pow-R-drinks, and SustiBars tumbled down into the roaring blaze. She sat down next to Rovender and smiled. Her smile wasn't so much one of happiness; it was more one of understanding.

Something else struck her at that moment. Eva crawled over to her sleeping mat and grabbed a small, flat object that was tucked under her balled-up jackvest. She studied the WondLa one final time before she moved to toss the picture into the flames—but a calloused hand caught her wrist.

"Not that." Rovender's tone was serious. "You must honor Otto, myself, and your mother by seeing to it that you find what it is that you have searched for."

"But . . ." Eva blinked in shock. "What does it matter now?"

"*Now* is when it matters most, Eva Nine," Rovender replied as he released his grip. "Honor yourself." She saw the tattered friendship bracelet tied around his wrist.

Eva rose, staring at the fire as it finished eating all the effects of her past life . . . of Rovender's past life. Soon these ashes would be indiscernible from the black desert sands that surrounded them. She dropped the WondLa to the ground and grabbed her jackvest.

"Where are you off to?" Rovender stood. "It's past midnight."

Eva slipped on her jackvest and lit a lantern. "I'm going to finish what I've started."

One of the stone lions was buried under the enormous mound of excavated sand that Otto had dug. As Eva's sneakboots crunched over the fine grains of sand, she looked up at the now cloudless sapphire sky. The celestial Rings of Orbona glowed like wide ribbons stretched across the heavens. She stopped at the entrance to the tunnel leading down. With her lantern raised over her head for a better view, Eva shuddered, realizing it barely illuminated the darkness around her. Another lantern light bobbed up from behind.

"You didn't think I'd let you do this on your own,

did you?" Rovender said, catching up to Eva on his backward-bending legs. "Are you ready?"

"I'm ready." Eva looked at him in the golden flickering light. "I need to know the answer to the puzzle."

He smiled a toothy grin. "I know, Eva Nine. That's one of the things I like about you." As Muthr had done, he reached out his hand, and Eva placed hers in it. They ventured into the giant tunnel.

The enormous shaft went straight down for only a short length, then turned, becoming a more gradual angle down. It wound into the dank, cold ground, eventually leveling out into a subterranean walkway.

"Oeeah! Quite a digger, that Otto is!" Rovender observed the tunnel walls with his lantern, now hooked on the end of his walking stick. "Look at all of this."

Eva knelt down. The earth below her was hard and firm. She brushed the sand away with her hands and discovered numerous little cobbles set in a perfect pattern. She looked up at the earthen walls and roof. "That looks like the Goldfish, doesn't it?"

Rovender added his light to hers. The face of a hovercar peeked out from the sand-packed walls above them. Its empty headlight sockets watched the two as they passed below. They continued down the tunnel path, where Eva recognized numerous items that silently greeted them from their resting places: traffic signs, more hovercars, and even the corroded remains of another robot. Up ahead, a darkened arched portal closed off the end of the tunnel.

Rovender brought his lantern close to the arch. Eva realized it was a pair of large closed doors, encrusted with ancient dirt and grime. Even though one of the doors was still half-buried in the sediment, there was something written on it that was familiar to her.

She wiped the dirt away from the exposed door with the sleeve of her tunic. In perfectly preserved printing, it said:

NEW YORK PUBLIC LIBRARY
RARE PRINTED BOOKS & ARCHIVES VAULT

CHAPTER 42: WONDLA

With great

force Rovender Kitt pushed the time-forgotten door open. A dank, musty smell greeted the explorers as they peered into the pitch-black room. Rovender nodded, then went in. Eva followed and found herself in an expansive round room.

She looked up at the disintegrating architecture before her. A vaulted ceiling, supported by brick and stone, still stood in the windowless open-floored dome. Rising high above Eva, multiple floors ringed the dark vault. Each floor was fully lined with shelving, which in turn was crammed full of tomes from long ago. Brown decrepit books of every shape and size were lying about, some fallen in blocky heaps from their ancient perches, others displayed—like large yellow butterflies and moths—under cracked glass cases. Eva walked into the center of the great library, hearing only her breathing and footfalls in the forlorn silence.

"No one has been here for a long, long time," Rovender said, his voice reverberating throughout the large domed chamber. Grandiose tables with dilapidated chairs stood in rows at the center of the dusty floor. Many parts of the tables had been devoured by insects and had disintegrated to sawdust . . . and yet, other tables stood, firm and strong against the ravages of time. "Do you think Mother figured out what was in here that would help you?" he whispered.

"I don't know," Eva said. She tried not to think of Muthr.

"What are these things that this houses, Eva?" Rovender picked up a crumbling tome. He handed it to her.

"These are books," Eva said as the yellowed bits of paper flaked away in her hands to rest on the floor. "It's what humans used to put all of their writing in long ago."

Rovender blinked in astonishment as he took in the enormous room. "Then, this is a bank. All the ancient knowledge of your kind is housed here. Is that correct?"

"I don't know," Eva said as she put the remnants of the book down on a table. "I've never read one of these before. We didn't have them in the Sanctuary. They're old. They don't contain holos or any other interactive elements."

"So they are of no use?" Rovender picked up the book again. Its cardboard cover separated from the rest of the book; the glue holding it together had disintegrated long ago. He squinted at the cover as he rubbed the dust from it. Its size and shape felt . . . familiar.

"The Omnipod had said it was receiving a signal from this area," Eva said. "The signal had to be from this room." She looked around in the darkness, wishing she had the Omnipod with her now.

She wished she had Muthr.

Eva came to the center of the chamber, where an impressive circular marble-topped desk still stood. She peered over the top of the desk. "Rovee, come here!"

"What is it?" Rovender galloped across the floor, his bouncing lantern sending light dancing throughout the entire vault.

Eva slipped behind the desk and tapped the large glass screen set in the desktop. The surface flickered with static for a few moments, then came online emitting a soft pulsing glow.

"Pffft York Public Li-pffft Rare Printed Books and Archives Vault. How pffft I help you?"

"Oh, my," Eva gasped. With wide eyes of disbelief she stared at the words of a menu through the spiderweb of cracks in the cruddy glass. Placing her hand on the glass, she asked, "This is Eva Nine. Are there any humans in the area?"

"Titles on humanity are pffft floors three pffft four," the desk replied.

"No." Eva leaned closer to the desk and spoke clearly, "Are . . . there . . . any . . . other . . . humans . . . in . . . the . . . area?"

The computer was silent for a moment. Rovender placed a hand on Eva's shoulder. Watching. Waiting.

"Pffft sorry. I don't pffft-stand what you are pffft. Titles on humanity are pffft floors three pffft four," the desk stated again.

Rovender touched the screen. A diagram was displayed of the entire vault, with interactive menus for every floor, shelf, and book. "Eva, this machine may not be like your Omnipod. I believe it knows only the items it maintains."

A despondent Eva slouched. "Well, I guess that's that," she whispered.

"Your answers lie here," Rovender said, gesturing around the library. "This is the history of your clan. They once lived here, and now you shall know of them."

Eva sighed and peered out into the darkness.

"Let me show you," Rovender said, pointing to the desk. "Ask the machine where the books on Orbona are."

Eva did as she was asked.

"Roman pffft-ology is located in the Mythology section. Titles are pffft five," the desk replied.

Eva spoke clearly and concisely. "No. I need information on humans colonizing the planet Orbona."

"Pffft sorry. I don't pffft-stand what you are pffft. Roman pffft-ology is located in the Mythology section. Titles are pffft five," the desk repeated.

"That's odd." Rovender scratched his whiskery beard.

"No. It's not." Eva addressed the desk once more, "Please tell me where I can find books about *this* planet."

"Titles pffft Earth are in the Astron-pffft section, the Geology pffft, and in the Mythology section. Which pffft would you pffft to go?" the desk replied.

"You said Orbona was a sleeping planet, a dead planet, when King Ojo brought everyone here, right?" Eva looked up at Rovender, her face lit by the pulsing glow of the desk's screen.

"Yes, but . . ." Rovender furrowed his narrow brow as he put the final pieces together.

Eva rolled up her left sleeve, showing him the mark she'd received from Arius. "Zin told me what this means. Do you know?"

Rovender shook his head.

"It means," Eva said as she traced the two circles, "a world within a world. A planet within a planet."

"Orbona *was* Earth," Rovender whispered.

"Earth is Orbona." Eva nodded in agreement.

"Oeeah!" Rovender was amazed. "This explains a lot."

Eva sat down on the cold marble floor. She drew her knees up and leaned her head back against the desk. "It doesn't explain what happened to all of humankind, or why I am the only one left here."

"Does it matter?" Rovender sat next to her and leaned his staff against the desk.

"What do you mean?" Eva sniffed.

"Are you alone, Eva Nine?"

"Well, Muthr's gone . . . and Otto had to leave to be with his herd." She wiped her eyes with her sleeve.

"But?"

"But what? I mean, you're here with me," she said, looking over at the lanky creature.

Rovender Kitt put his arms around her. "And I will always be here for you, Eva. I'll take care of you and teach you everything I know."

"You promise?" she snuffled. "You . . . you won't leave?"

"I promise." Rovender held her tightly.

The two got up from the marble floor behind the desk. Eva looked around at the great vault of books.

"Well"—she took a deep breath—"I guess I've got a lot of books I could read . . . and a lot of history to learn. Where should we start?"

"Let's start with this." Rovender pulled out the

charred WondLa from his pocket. He set it down on the desktop and slid it over to Eva.

Before she could pick it up, the desk chimed and stated, "*The **Wond**erful Wizard of Oz* pffft **L**. Frank Baum. Published pffft 1900. Child-pffft Literature, second pffft."

The actual cover, in perfect undamaged condition, was displayed on the screen. Eva slid the WondLa over it, lining it up to view the missing letters and words. She stared at the picture of the little girl, arm in arm with a robot and a man with a wide-brimmed hat, walking about in the wondrous world. They were smiling. They were happy.

Eva tapped an icon in the corner of the screen and the desk displayed a diagram of the library, showing exactly where the book was shelved. Eva left the WondLa lying on the desk and looked over at Rovender.

"Well, Eva Nine," he said, "what are you waiting for?"

Eva awoke the following afternoon in the campsite. She and Rovender had explored the rotting tomes in the large domed vault until exhaustion had finally overtaken them. For lunch they dined on roasted turnfins that Rovender had caught and dressed that morning. Just as he'd said, they were quite delicious.

Later, as the orange sun began to set, a haunting humming sound neared where Eva was sitting. Besteel's glider, now piloted by Rovender, set down next to the camp. Rovender hopped off and held out a hand to Eva. "It is time. Come," he said.

Eva climbed onto the glider. She sat behind Rovender as he navigated the craft higher and higher into the fading sky. They soared over the ruins in the coming twilight until he brought the glider down onto the rooftop of the largest standing structure. With lanterns in hand the two hopped off the aircraft and made their way across the flat roof through roosting turnfins in great growths of lichens and moss.

At the center of the rooftop, lying on her back and surrounded by brilliant flowers, was Multi-Utility Task Help Robot zero-six.

Eva stared down at the closed eyelids and the silicone rubber face. Her busy mind settled and became quiet as dusk soaked everything in the land. Rovender put an arm around her. "I hope it is as you have wished it, Eva Nine," he said, his voice soft.

Eva sniffed. "Now she can always see the real sun—the real moon—forever."

Rovender knelt down in front of Eva. "Your mother contained a good spirit. A loving spirit. A spirit that will not cease to exist."

Eva looked at him, her brows furrowed.

Rovender placed his arm around Eva's shoulders. "You see, she lives within you now, in all of the lessons that she taught you. Lessons you will never forget. Lessons you will always carry with you . . . and will one day pass on."

Eva nodded. From her satchel she pulled out the old tome, *The Wonderful Wizard of Oz*. She bent down and placed the book, pristine and untarnished, in the robot's rubber-tipped hand. Over her heart.

"Thank you," she whispered.

"Your WondLa." Rovender looked down at the book. "You do not want it?"

"It's okay, Rovee," Eva said, and took his hand. "I've found what I was looking for."

So, do you

think this thing will get us there? Back to your village?" Eva and Rovender were back at camp loading their few supplies onto the glider.

"Yes. It may take a couple of days, and we'll need to refuel from time to time, but if the weather is good, then it should be a pleasant trip," Rovender replied as he cinched up his rucksack. Eva noted that his pack was considerably smaller as he pulled it over his narrow shoulders. She could also see that he had changed in color. The washed-out cerulean markings on his skin had become a striking blue, similar to the color in the holograms that she had seen of peacocks. Peacock blue.

"Are you okay with flying?" he asked.

Eva thought of the first time she'd been above-ground and her wish to soar above the world and see it from the safety of the clouds. It had been only a little more than a week before, but it felt like a year ago. "Yeah," she said with a smile. "I think I'll be okay."

"Good." Rovender grinned back.

Look. Up. Stars.

Eva closed her eyes. Far away, she could hear the faint thoughts of Otto singing to her.

"What is it?" Rovender looked at Eva.

Eva opened her pale green eyes. "It's Otto. He wants me to look up at the stars."

Eva and Rovender looked up into the nighttime atmosphere. The waning gibbous moon was glowing brightly in the heavens, far beyond the Rings of Earth. Like a band of diamonds, the asteroid fragments and space dust glittered as they orbited the planet, each fragment sparkling like a brilliant star.

One of those stars, shimmering close to the horizon, dropped.

"Did you see that?" Eva squinted in the fading light, trying to get a better view.

"A meteorite perhaps," Rovender said, and pulled out his spyglass.

The luminous dot fell, down close to the earth, but did not hit the surface; instead it got brighter, more intense . . . and larger.

In the gentle desert breeze of the night, Eva heard a distant whine. It was an electronic-sounding whine . . . almost like the Goldfish. "Do you hear that?" she asked.

"This is no meteorite." Rovender dropped his goggles. He narrowed his eyes at the approaching star.

A large orb-shaped ship descended from the blackness above, causing dust and sand to billow up from the ground. As Eva and Rovender shielded their eyes, they watched the craft touch down on three stout landing pads.

"Is this from Solas? Queen Ojo?" Eva asked.

"Queen Ojo has no large ships." Rovender studied the scratched and chipped painted insignia. "None like this."

The ship was battered, decorated in bright yellow and black checks, and had a round clear cockpit window set in the nose. A pair of large engines poked out from the back, their noisy turbofans whining as they slowed. Numerous tiny boosters lined the craft's entire body. With a hiss a hydraulic ramp opened up from the belly.

Next to Rovender, Eva stood motionless, in awe, waiting for the driver of the craft to emerge.

Loud music blared out from the interior of the ship, then was silenced. A pair of dirty checkered sneakboots appeared at the top of the ramp. As they made their way down the platform, Eva saw that they belonged to a boy.

A human boy.

"Hello," the boy said. He looked a couple of years older than Eva. His skin was tan, and his brown-and-blue-dyed hair was windblown and tousled. "My name is Hailey," he said as he extended his hand out to shake.

Eva and Rovender exchanged glances.

A sideways grin grew on Hailey's freckled face. With a chuckle he said, "Don't be afraid. I've tracked you down from far away. I'm here to bring you back home."

End of
BOOK I

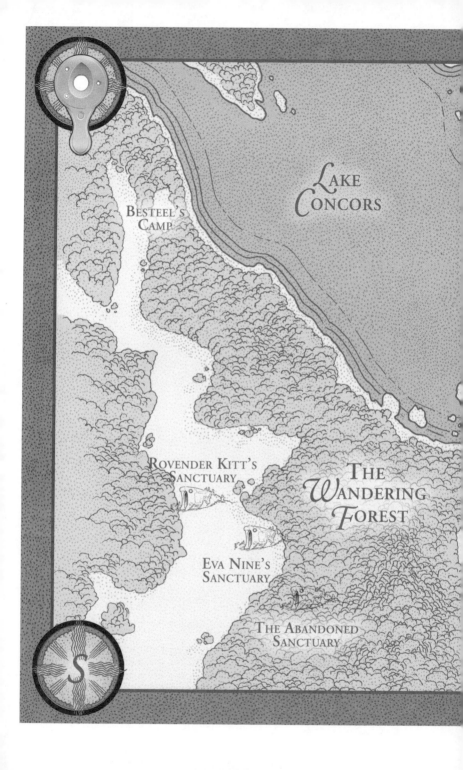

LAKE
CONCORS

BESTEEL'S
CAMP

ROVENDER KITT'S
SANCTUARY

THE
WANDERING
FOREST

EVA NINE'S
SANCTUARY

THE ABANDONED
SANCTUARY

THE ORBONIAN ALPHABET

Acommon alphabet is used by the inhabitants of Orbona. The chart that follows is the key to unlocking their written language. The main alphabet consists of thirty-two characters (as opposed to the English alphabet, which comprises twenty-six), and many of these are derived from symbols of familiar objects, actions, or ideas. They are shown in alphabetical order with the compound letters at the end, although this is not the order Orbonians would use. Orbonians would align similar symbols alongside one another so that their youth could identify different characteristics more easily.

Orbonians write in a vertical manner and from left to right. Compound words are often broken up, with their individual parts written alongside one another as seen here in "the Wastelands":

Capital letters are larger versions of the lower-case letters. Proper nouns use a large version of the letter with the remainder of the word written to the right of it, as can be seen here in the word "Lacus":

There are many shortcut symbols for small words like "of" and "the," both of which are included on the chart. However, the focus here is on the main alphabet so that readers may be able to decipher Orbonian writing in this and future books.

471

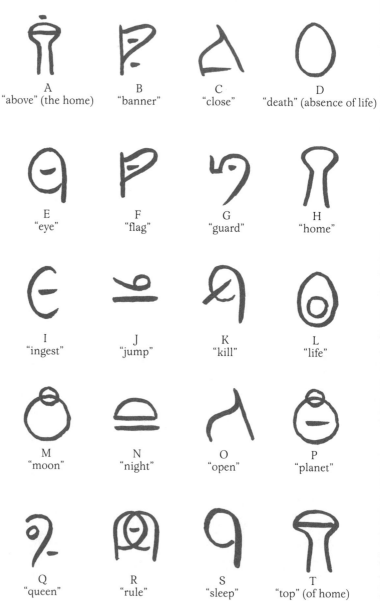

A
"above" (the home)

B
"banner"

C
"close"

D
"death" (absence of life)

E
"eye"

F
"flag"

G
"guard"

H
"home"

I
"ingest"

J
"jump"

K
"kill"

L
"life"

M
"moon"

N
"night"

O
"open"

P
"planet"

Q
"queen"

R
"rule"

S
"sleep"

T
"top" (of home)

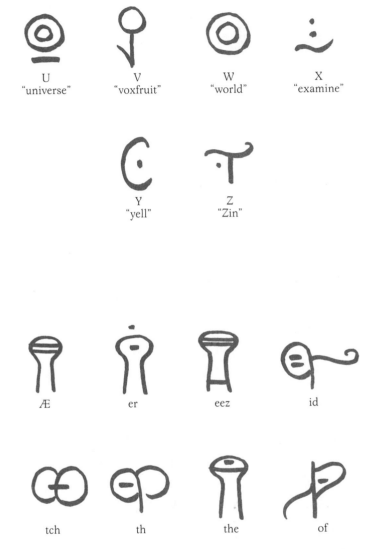

U
"universe"

V
"voxfruit"

W
"world"

X
"examine"

Y
"yell"

Z
"Zin"

Æ

er

eez

id

tch

th

the

of

ACKNOWLEDGMENTS

Every book has a journey of its own—a quest the storyteller must take to find the purpose of his or her tale so that others may fully enjoy what he or she has to say. Despite there being only one name on the cover of this book, there were many friends along the way who helped me craft the story you have just read.

First there was my wonderful manager, Ellen Goldsmith-Vein, and her business partner, Julie Kane-Ritsch, who were enthusiastic about the notion of Eva's story from the start. Along with Rick Richter and Kevin Lewis, *WondLa* secured its home at Simon & Schuster.

The team at Simon & Schuster Books for Young Readers has always been incredibly supportive of me, and I am proud to mark a decade of bookmaking with them with the publication of this story. From my editor, David Gale, and art director, Lizzy Bromley, to my copyeditor, Dorothy Gribbin, I thank you for helping me with the words and pictures. Chrissy Noh also inspired me with her tireless enthusiasm and innovative marketing ideas. To Jon Anderson, Justin Chanda, and Anne Zafian, I am humbled by the passion you and your staff have infused into Eva's world.

As the story came into focus, I had feedback and support from family and peers, who helped me come to understand what this story was truly about. I had many fundamental conversations with my mom about what the point of this story was, and many more coffee chats with my old assistant Will Lisak about what the future of Earth may hold. My mother-in-law, Linda DeFrancis, and my good friends Donato Giancola and Holly Gibson also offered their thoughts and cheered me onward.

I had early supporters—writers whom I greatly admire—like Kate DiCamillo, Guillermo del Toro, and Holly Black, who gave me the encouragement to write this tale. There were two amazing writers who were my go-to readers—Ari Berk and Steve Berman. Your insight and challenges as I worked on the various drafts allowed me to become a better storyteller. I am indebted to you both.

A couple of other dear friends, who happen to be teachers, offered insight into the world of a twelve-year-old girl. Lauren Decker reminded me of what life is like when one is twelve, with one foot planted in childhood while the other steps into adulthood. Kim Pilla offered up several ideas for timeless pastimes, including making friendship bracelets. (Rovender is still wearing his.)

I also had some incredibly experienced bibliophiles come in at the end of the writing and share their vast reading experience with me. Lisa Von Drasek, Joan Kindig, Ed Masessa, and Heidi Stemple pointed out those last little story scuffs and scratches that allowed me to polish it to a brilliant luster.

Illustrating a book that harkens back to the spot-color processes at the turn of the century is no easy task. I received substantial inspiration and understanding of the richness of this style with help from Peter Glassman, who shared original Oz art from his collection and allowed me to pore over his treasured first editions. The creation of the art itself had help in the form of Bryant Paul Johnson and John DesRoches, both of whom aided me in creating the two-color plates. A tremendous thanks goes to John Lind, who was with me from the beginning in creating the art, as he helped with design, illustration, and constant suggestions to help me fully realize my vision. You were right, John, a logo designer would really make the title look outstanding, and Tom Kennedy did a fine job.

As I neared completion, words of excitement were spread through the amazing publicity of Maggie Begley and the team at Media Masters.

Lastly, there are the two most important people in my life who were with me every step on my journey to create this book. A big hug goes to my wife, Angela, and a kiss to my daughter, Sophia. Your love, support, and patience sustained me day in and day out. You are my WondLa.

Never abandon imagination.

TONY DITERLIZZI WOULD LIKE TO THANK
EVERYONE AT SIMON & SCHUSTER WHO
WORKED ON *The Search for WondLa:*

President
JON ANDERSON

Publisher
JUSTIN CHANDA

Deputy Publisher
ANNE ZAFIAN

Editorial
DAVID GALE
NAVAH WOLFE

Design
LIZZY BROMLEY
TOM DALY

Managing Editorial/Copyediting
AMY BARTRAM
DOROTHY GRIBBIN

Production
FELIX GREGORIO
CHAVA WOLIN

Marketing
LAURA ANTONACCI
CHARLIE CORTS
MICHELLE FADLALLA
JOHN MERCUN
MICHELLE MONTAGUE
HOLLY NAGEL
CHRISSY NOH
MATT PANTOLIANO
LUCILLE RETTINO
CATHARINE SOTZING
ELKE VILLA

TONY DITERLIZZI

is the visionary mind that conceived of the Spiderwick Chronicles. He has been creating books with Simon & Schuster for a decade. From fanciful picture books like *The Spider and the Fly* (a Caldecott Honor) to young chapter books like *Kenny and the Dragon*, Tony has always imbued his stories with a rich imagination. His series the Spiderwick Chronicles (with Holly Black) has sold millions of copies worldwide and was adapted into a feature film.

Inspired by stories by the likes of the Brothers Grimm, James M. Barrie, and L. Frank Baum, *The Search for WondLa* is a new fairy tale for the twenty-first century.

THE SPIDERWICK CHRONICLES
by Tony DiTerlizzi and Holly Black

THE SPIDERWICK CHRONICLES

THE FIELD GUIDE

THE SEEING STONE

LUCINDA'S SECRET

THE IRONWOOD TREE

THE WRATH OF MULGARATH

ARTHUR SPIDERWICK'S FIELD GUIDE TO
THE FANTASTICAL WORLD AROUND YOU

CARE AND FEEDING OF SPRITES

BEYOND THE
SPIDERWICK CHRONICLES

THE NIXIE'S SONG

A GIANT PROBLEM

THE WYRM KING